KINGDOM OF BLOOD & SALT

∽ BOOK ONE ∾

CONTENTS

Copyrights	1
Written by Alexis Calder	3
Dedication	7
Acknowledgments	9
Chapter 1	13
Chapter 2	21
Chapter 3	27
Chapter 4	37
Chapter 5	45
Chapter 6	55
Chapter 7	65
Chapter 8	75
Chapter 9	83
Chapter 10	97
Chapter 11	105
Chapter 12	119
Chapter 13	129
Chapter 14	143
Chapter 15	151
Chapter 16	163
Chapter 17	171
Chapter 18	185
Chapter 19	193
Chapter 20	201
Chapter 21	217
Chapter 22	227
Chapter 23	239
Chapter 24	247
Chapter 25	261
Chapter 26	273
Chapter 27	283
Chapter 28	299
Chapter 29	311

A note from the Author	319
Next in Series	321
About the Author	323

KINGDOM OF BLOOD & SALT
THE SERIES

COPYRIGHTS

This is a work of fiction. All names, characters, locations, and incidents are products of the author's imagination, or have been used fictitiously. Any resemblance to actual persons living or dead, locales, or events is entirely coincidental.

No part of this e-book may be reproduced or shared by any electronic or mechanical means, including, but not limited to printing, file sharing, and email, without prior written permission from the authors.

Copyright © 2023 Alexis Calder
All rights reserved.
ISBN: 978-1-960823-00-7

Edited by Faywriter & Court of Spice
Proofreader: BAH
Cover Design by Fay Lane. All Rights Reserved.
Interior Design and Formatting by Stephany Wallace at @S.W. Creative Publishing co. All Rights Reserved.

Reproducing this book without permission from the author or the publisher is an infringement of its copyright.

Published March 30th, 2023

WRITTEN AS ALEXIS CALDER

Shadow Wolves Series
Shadow Mate

Royal Blood Series
Obsession
Hunger

Rejected Fate Series
Darkest Mate
Forbidden Sin
Feral Queen

Moon Cursed Series
Wolf Marked
Wolf Untamed
Wolf Chosen

Royal Mates Series
Shifter Claimed
Shifter Fated
Shifter Rising

Academy of Elites Series
Academy of Elites: Untamed Magic

Academy of Elites: Broken Magic
Academy of Elites: Fated Magic
Academy of Elites: Unbound Magic

Brimstone Academy Series
Brimstone Academy: Semester One
Brimstone Academy: Semester Two

Kingdom of Blood & Salt
Kingdom of Blood & Salt

WRITTEN AS LEXI CALDER:

In Hate With My Boss
Love to Hate You

DESCRIPTION

In the last human kingdom, securing our future requires a sacrifice. I just never imagined it would be my heart...

Surrounded by monsters, Athos is once again facing the Choosing. Every nine years, the Fae King demands human tributes in order to keep the peace.

It's supposed to be a time of celebration; in reality, it's a death sentence for anyone selected.

As the illegitimate daughter of the king, I am powerless to change the rules of the treaty, but that doesn't mean I can't play my part.

The Fae King's ambassador is arrogant, condescending, and inhumanly handsome. He's also taken an interest in me. Which leads to my father's request: keep the ambassador distracted while he's in our kingdom.

I despise the ambassador, and while I will do my duty to occupy him, I don't keep my feelings about the Choosing to myself. The growing friction between us intensifies as threats rise from within Athos itself.

Alliances blur and centuries of lies begin to unravel.

And I'm faced with a choice.

No matter how much I hate him, the ambassador might be the key to preventing war.

But it may mean sacrificing everything….

DEDICATION

For those of us who are disappointed when the villain doesn't get the girl

ACKNOWLEDGMENTS

A million thanks are in order for this book. This was a work of my heart, and I wouldn't have completed it without the support of so many.

First, to my amazing readers, thank you for your support and your patience as I dropped everything else to live in this world for months. I am beyond grateful for all of you. The fact that I get to create imaginary worlds and dream up adventures I can share with others still blows my mind. Thank you for all the journeys you have taken with me.

Thank you to my husband for being the best cheerleader I have. Your support while I ramble about make-believe worlds and swoon over imaginary characters keeps me going. Love you xo.

Stacey, thanks for being my sounding board and first reader of this. All those conversations where you talked me down or gave me a push were completely necessary and so appreciated.

None of my books would be what they are without the amazing team I have behind me. Thank you to my mom for always beta reading and to Faewriter for her excellent feedback. Magan, thank you for the edits and for the pep-talks and support. You're the best!

Finally, one of the best parts about this book is all the visuals that help make it come together. Thank you to Sarah Waites for the incredible map of my world, to Fay Lane for the stunning cover, and Stephanie Wallace for the gorgeous formatting.

I am beyond grateful for all of you and I am so glad I have you all in my corner.

KINGDOM OF
BLOOD AND SALT

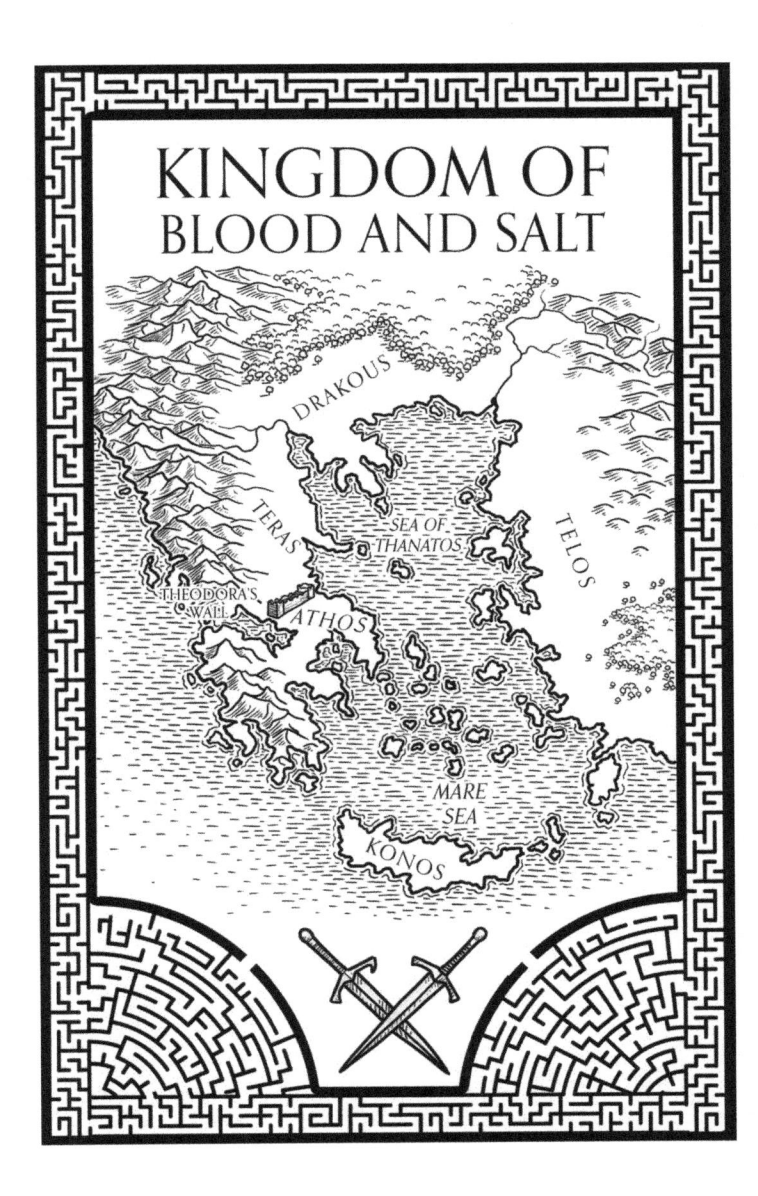

CHAPTER 1

Every muscle ached, and my skin was tight from the coating of dried mud. The only thing I wanted to do was take a bath and hide away from the court until after the tributes were selected. But that wasn't possible. My father would insist I attend every event for the next two weeks while we entertained the Fae King's liaison, even if the queen didn't want me anywhere in sight.

The marble floor was cool under my sore feet and I lingered in the open air corridor, staring out at the whitewashed buildings of the city below. Everything was bathed in the golden light of the setting sun, making it look even more ancient and worn than it was. From my view at the palace, I could see nearly everything my father ruled over.

The cramped, crumbling structures in the city of Athos gave way to rocky cliffs that dropped off to the turquoise waters of the Mera Sea. Closing my eyes, I breathed in the air, catching the hint of brine. This was home, at least for a little while longer. Even if I was the one who had asked to leave, I'd miss this place. And I'd miss my sisters.

My eyes fluttered open, and my throat tightened as I let my gaze travel toward the horizon. Even from here, I could catch a glimpse of the perpetual gray clouds over the island of

Konos. The sight brought me back to my current situation and I frowned, hating the thought of getting dressed up to meet the contingent from Konos tonight.

I tore my eyes away from the shroud of darkness in the middle of the sea and continued forward. At least I'd have my sisters by my side through this farce.

My bare feet left a trail of mud on the marble floors. I winced at the thought of the mess I was leaving behind. It wasn't entirely my fault. My sandals had been lost early in the training session today and David, my training partner, insisted I always train as if our battles were real. Which meant no stopping to dig out your sandals.

I turned the corner and nearly collided with a flurry of turquoise robes. The priest stopped, pressing his hands over his heart. "My dear Ara, you nearly gave me a heart attack."

Istvan, my father's high priest, took in my muddy form then scowled. His thick, dark brows pressed together as he narrowed his beady eyes. He was a small man, shorter than me, and he tried to compensate by looking down his hooked nose at everyone he met. "I was looking for you, girl."

"You found me," I replied flatly.

"The queen demands your presence at once. The delegation from Konos was spotted, and they'll be here within the hour." Istvan straightened, as if proud of himself for playing messenger for his beloved queen.

"You have nothing better to do than deliver messages for the queen?" I inquired.

"It is an honor to be of service to her, as you would do well to remember." His tone was condescending.

I wasn't in the mood to deal with him today. Istvan was someone I wouldn't miss. I also wouldn't miss the queen. "Tell *her highness* that I'll be in shortly."

His eyes flicked up and down, taking me in again. His nose wrinkled. "You will bathe first?"

I shrugged. "Perhaps." I lifted a muddy foot. "I'll at least find some new sandals."

He rolled his eyes. "This palace will be a better place after you leave."

"Be sure you tell my father those thoughts," I said.

He straightened, the mention of my father seeming to remind him of his place. And mine. I might be illegitimate, but I was still the king's daughter. Considering the history of our kingdom, it was possible I could end up on the throne if the fates were cruel. So many of our ancestors had lost children or fathered only bastards, resulting in very mixed bloodlines over the centuries. It wasn't even all that scandalous that I existed. It was less likely for a member of the royal family to stay faithful to their spouse. And who'd blame them with the example the gods set for us?

"Apologies, your highness." He bowed, the motion exaggerated and dripping with contempt.

I held my chin high and walked away from Istvan without a backward glance. He was one of many here who were in the queen's pocket. It didn't matter that my eldest sister was preparing to take the throne or that I'd requested to leave as soon as the Choosing was over. I was a reminder of the one thing the queen would never have: my father's love.

Rumor had it my mother had enticed my father away from the palace and he'd fallen madly in love with her. He'd spent months away, leaving Ophelia and my eldest sister alone. Shortly after he'd returned, I was dropped with the palace guards. Apparently, my mother didn't survive childbirth.

I think Ophelia had always questioned if I was truly my father's offspring. But as I grew, there was no denying the similarities in our appearance. If somehow I was not of his blood, whoever had sired me must have been my father's twin. Even Istvan had declared that I was of royal blood, even if he might regret it now.

It didn't matter that I had no interest in the crown. If Queen Ophelia had her way, she'd have tossed me into the sea and left me to the sirens. What can I say, the feeling was mutual.

My bedroom door was open a crack, not doing anything to mask the gasps and moans from behind it. With a sigh, I pushed open the door silently and lingered in the darkened space as my eyes adjusted.

A guard's uniform lay crumpled on the floor, the first in a trail of abandoned clothing leading to my bed. A male was stretched across the mattress, his fists gripping the crisp white sheets, while a blonde head bobbed up and down between his legs.

Crossing my arms over my chest, I let out an annoyed sigh. "On my bed? Again?"

"Oh, gods!" The guard shoved the woman away, then scrambled to his feet. "Your highness, I'm…"

I held my hand up. "Please, don't finish that sentence." My eyes dropped to take in his impressive length, still at attention. Cheeks heating, I cleared my throat and turned to find my younger sister, Cora, strutting forward. She stood tall and proud, not at all embarrassed by her actions. Sex was a game to her. A way to find a sense of control in her very structured existence.

The guard was young and handsome. Probably newer to the palace, as my father had been adding new recruits daily for the last couple of months. I wondered if he knew he was a way to fill the void for Cora.

The only time I'd ever seen her settle down was when

she'd spent an entire summer with one of the noble's sons. But he'd left last winter on a foolish quest to explore new trade routes across the Sea of Thanatos. I wasn't sure he was still alive and I think Cora was trying to forget he ever existed.

"You want me to send him to you after I'm finished? Or I can find one of his friends," she offered, stopping next to the guard. She traced her fingers down his chest.

The guard's brows lifted, and one side of his lips quirked up in a hopeful smirk. "Not necessary. Go to your own room, Cora." I picked up her discarded peplos and tossed it to her.

She caught the bundle of fabric, then fashioned her expression into an overdramatic pout. "Father stationed guards outside my rooms." She glanced at her partner. "And not the young, handsome kind."

While I was permitted to do as I wished, Cora didn't have the same luxury. She wasn't training to be the next queen, so her lessons weren't as intense as Lagina's, but she was expected to learn enough that she could step in if anything were to happen to Lagina. "Out." I pointed to the door.

Cora huffed. "You're such a bore. You ship off to the wall soon. You might as well enjoy your life before you go. Take a lover. Drink too much. Indulge. Live a little."

"I am living just fine," I said.

"By rolling around in the mud with those soldiers?" She wrinkled her nose. "At least do your rolling around somewhere cleaner. Or do something besides training to fight all the time. I'm sure you could find some volunteers if David isn't up to your standards anymore."

"I like training," I said. "And how I spend my time with David or any other man isn't your concern."

"I'm available," the guard said with a grin.

"You're dangerously close to me calling for help to get Cora out of here," I said.

His eyes widened, and he quickly moved for his discarded clothing.

"You ruin all my fun," Cora said, stomping her foot like the spoiled child I still saw her as. She was eighteen summers, only two years younger than me, but she would forever be ten in my memory.

"Time to go," I said again. "I'm in dire need of a bath." I glared at Cora, then the guard. "Alone."

As soon as the door closed behind my sister and the guard, I could hear their giggling. Her life was so different from mine. There were days I wished I could know that sense of ease, but it wasn't possible for me. I'd been a target since I was born and if I'd shown any interest in court life, politics, or even finding a good husband, I would have been seen as a threat to my sisters. The queen made that clear when I was a child. She only eased off a little once I asked if I could join the army instead of getting married, but she still used any opportunity she could to remind me that I didn't belong fully.

The thing the queen didn't seem to understand was that I would never stand in my sisters' way or do anything to harm them. They were a major factor in why I'd decided to follow in my aunt Katerina's footsteps and volunteer to guard the wall.

As long as our soldiers kept the dragons from breaching our borders, my sisters were safe. I'd gladly give my life so they could have a happier one. Besides, I had no interest in playing the politics game, anyway.

A gentle knock sounded on the door and I turned just as Mila, my maid, walked in. Her face was scrunched up, making her look like she'd just sucked on a lemon. "The queen changed the time."

"I know," I said.

She sighed as she took in my appearance, but didn't comment. She'd been assigned to me five years ago, after a slew of other maids had requested to be reassigned. My sisters each had three maids. I would prefer none, but that wasn't an option. Mila turned out to be a blessing. We got along well and she didn't report everything I did to the queen. I got the sense that she saw right through the public façade that was my stepmother.

"I'll prepare the bath," she said. "I assume you want to choose your own clothing?"

"The purple and gold, I think," I said, referring to one of my most feminine peplos. I'd be expected to look the part tonight when we welcomed the Konos delegation and if I played nice tonight, maybe I could get out of the other formal events. I was tempted to wear a tunic and trousers, just to piss off the queen, but I wasn't trying to upset my father. He would be upset enough as it was. Nobody liked the Choosing.

The warm water was soothing on my aching muscles and the soft scent of citrus and mint from the oils Mila added helped me forget about the upcoming tribute selection for a brief moment.

"Looks like you and David had a good training session," Mila said.

"We had to go to the gardens today. Too many guards milling about the training grounds. I think my father must have hired at least a dozen new guards."

"Not a surprise with the Choosing," she said.

I shifted in the water, sending it sloshing over the side. Mila squealed as she jumped away, trying to stay dry.

"Sorry," I said. "It's that damn Choosing. It just makes me so angry."

"I know." Mila guided me to the back of the tub. "There's nothing we can do to change things, though."

"I'm so tired of hearing that. All these years and nobody could figure out a solution?" I closed my eyes as she poured water over my head and began to soap up my muddy hair.

"Do you remember the last tribute selection?" Mila asked.

"I do. It was the first one I was permitted to attend." My jaw tightened. I hated everything about this event. Especially the fact that it was treated as a celebration when it was nothing more than choosing lambs for slaughter.

"I was eight when they took my eldest sister," she said.

I turned so I could face her. "I never knew that."

She smiled, then forced my head away from her. "I've never told anyone here."

"I'm so sorry." I couldn't imagine losing any of my sisters. It must have broken her heart to say goodbye at the Tribute Ceremony, knowing her sister was being sentenced to her death.

"It's the price we pay for safety, right?" she asked.

"It doesn't mean it's right," I replied.

"We don't have much of a choice," she countered.

"I want to change my dress," I said. "It should be black. There's nothing about today we should celebrate."

CHAPTER 2

My hair was still damp, but Mila had twisted it into an elaborate series of knots on the top of my head. Despite my protests, she'd woven a subtle crown of pearls to indicate my status as a member of the royal family. I always declined the tiaras my father had sent for my use, but every so often, Mila would add some sparkle to my hair.

To be honest, I hadn't protested as much as usual. Not after I found out that she'd lost her sister in the Choosing when she was young. I couldn't imagine if I had to bear that sort of heartache. Losing any of my sisters would probably break me. While it wasn't fair, being royalty afforded us the ability to bypass the selection process. We weren't considered as tributes while every other member of our kingdom aged eighteen to twenty-five was considered fair game.

The whole thing made my stomach clench, and nausea rolled through me. I wished I could stay in my room and avoid the whole thing.

When I was younger, I'd spent countless hours begging my father to put an end to this event. I'd begged him to send ships to Konos, to fight their king and free our people of the ancient treaty. Every time, he'd smiled and patted my head, telling me how much he loved my passion. Every time, he'd explained how dangerous Konos was and that our sacrifice of fourteen souls every nine years was nothing compared to the annihilation we'd face if we tried to resist.

It still didn't make it right. Fourteen of our people, humans from the last remaining human city in the world, would be loaded onto a ship and sent to the Fae capital where they'd become fodder for the monsters who served the king. We didn't know for sure what happened once they arrived, but the rumors were terrifying.

The worst was the story of the labyrinth the Fae King had deep underground. It was said to be impenetrable, pitch black, and housed a monster at its very center. Nobody had ever survived.

Humans were nothing to these creatures. We lived short lives compared to them and we were so fragile. I hated how helpless I felt knowing I was to stand by and smile and allow the whole thing to happen.

The open-air courtyard was teeming with people dressed in their finest peplos dresses, long tunics, and cloaks in rich, brightly colored fabrics. Shades of turquoise, purple, red, and yellow surrounded me. A rainbow of colors casting a festive mood in anticipation of such a horrible tradition to come.

Hundreds of lanterns hung from strings above us and glittered from every surface, giving the appearance of walking through the stars. The scent of roasted meat mingled with pine and the breeze carried a hint of the sea. It looked every inch the celebration we all pretend it was, but I couldn't shake the weight of those who would sail to their doom at the end of these two weeks.

I stepped forward, entering the fray in search of my father. Each footstep felt like wading through knee-deep mud as guests parted for me, their eyes taking in my black gown disapprovingly.

"Someone is looking for attention." The cool, high-pitched voice sent a shiver down my spine.

I forced my expression into one of indifference before turning to face Queen Ophelia. "Good evening, your highness."

"You're late," she said.

"The party was to begin at sundown," I replied.

"I sent Istvan to tell you it changed. You missed greeting our guests in the throne room." She fixed her cool aqua gaze on me, unblinking and devoid of emotion. Like all her daughters, she was stunning. Long golden hair, eyes the color of the sea on a calm day, and curves that would send any man to his knees. It was a complete contrast to my dark hair, making me look like an outsider when I was with my sisters.

"I figured you'd rather I arrive late than arrive covered in mud," I said, maintaining eye contact.

Ophelia narrowed her eyes just a touch, sending a clear message. She was the champion of making you feel small with just an expression. It used to shatter my self-worth when I was a child, but it hadn't worked on me in years.

She sighed dramatically. "Don't make a scene, child. Your poor choice in clothing is already drawing too much attention."

I clenched my jaw, overly aware of the fact that there were dozens of eyes on us, all hoping to see something to fuel the gossip mills. I bit my tongue, choosing to remain quiet this time.

Ophelia turned her back to me, then paused, slowly facing me again. "Remind me to punish that maid of yours. She's clearly not doing her job if she's dressing you in such a fashion for a celebration."

I glared at her. We both knew I chose my dress, and we both knew why. "You won't touch her. You know my maid is my responsibility. I'd hate to have to ask father to remind you."

She tensed, then smiled, her thin lips nearly vanishing. "Well, perhaps I'll simply gift you a better maid. One who knows her place."

I knew her comment was meant for me. "I think she knows her place just fine."

"Go say hello to your father. He won't have time for you once the delegation arrives for their introduction," she commanded before she walked away, a trail of sycophants following in her wake.

If the queen had her way, I'd be sent to a temple where I'd be barred from returning to visit. But I wasn't cut out for a life of servitude to anyone. Not even a god.

Ignoring the stares and whispers, I made my way toward the dais at the end of the courtyard where I knew my father would be sitting on a large, intricately carved throne. At least I had arrived before the Konos delegation. Once the king formally introduced them to the court, I could sneak out and nobody would care.

Something caught the edge of my dress, and I stumbled as the garment slipped dangerously low on my chest. Clutching the fabric at my breasts, I yanked the rest of it out from under a sandal. "Watch where you're going," I hissed, looking up to glare at the culprit.

Dazzling gray eyes that seemed to flicker and glow like the flames in the lanterns around us stared down at me. They pulled me in like the churning of the sea before a storm. "A thousand apologies, madam."

I nearly groaned at the sound of his voice. Rich and deep, with a bit of a masculine rasp to it. The kind of voice you wanted to hear whispering in your ear while doing naughty things.

My heart raced and my chest tightened as I took in every inch of the stranger. Dressed in a black silk tunic and trousers of a fine, shimmery fabric, he stood out like a dark prince against the variety of hues worn by the other guests.

It wasn't just that his clothing mirrored my own; he was unlike anyone I'd ever seen around the palace. He was tall and lean, with dark hair and a closely trimmed black beard. His tanned skin had a golden sun kissed gleam that reminded me of the shimmer of sunlight on the horizon. Everything about him seemed like it was crafted from my dreams.

"You look familiar," he said. "Have we met?"

My lips parted, but sound evaded me. Since when was I speechless?

He smirked. "I don't think we have. I know I'd remember you."

Regaining my voice, I cleared my throat. "I know I have never seen you around here before."

These kinds of events were typically full of familiar faces. Generals, wealthy nobles, and others who were in the good graces of the royal family. A sprinkling of new faces emerged on occasion as new families climbed the social ladder or new soldiers were promoted or rewarded for various endeavors.

"I haven't been in Athos for a while. I just arrived from Drakous."

"You were in dragon territory?" I blinked, staring at him as if he were a ghost. We protected our border with a wall between Athos and Teras, which was an unclaimed, wild land separating us from the dragon's kingdom. I didn't know anyone who had been to Drakous and lived.

"The dragons can be persuaded if you have enough gold," he said with a shrug.

I had a million questions. For the last five years, I'd been training to fight with the intention of serving at Theodora's Wall, protecting my people from the dragons. Aside from my Aunt Katerina, I'd never spoken to anyone who'd met a dragon. And my aunt only had stories of how she'd slayed them in their dragon form. Never of what they were like when they took on the shapes of men.

"What are they like? The dragons?" I asked. "Can you tell they're dragons when they are in their other form? Or would they be able to pass among us unnoticed?" It was a concern I'd long held that everyone else brushed off. They seemed to think there was no way a dragon shifter could hide their true identity among us humans.

"So many questions," he said with a grin.

Music flooded in and the attendees swept past us in a rush to the dance floor. We were surrounded by swaying figures, twirling skirts and the chatter of polite small talk as dancers moved around us.

"Should we join them?" The stranger held out his hand.

I glanced around, noticing that we were in the center of what had become the dance floor. Searching for an excuse, I stiffened when I caught sight of my father on his throne. He smiled at me, then nodded, before lifting his hand in a gesture of encouragement. I wasn't going to get out of this.

Hesitantly, I set my hand in the stranger's. Tingles danced across my palm at the point of contact, but before I could consider the oddness of my reaction, I was swept into the dance.

CHAPTER 3

"This is a beautiful kingdom," he said. "But I must say, I hadn't expected to find someone like you."

His words, while flattering, left me feeling a little uneasy. "What do you mean *someone like me*?"

"Someone who isn't afraid to go against tradition." He glanced down at my dress. "I'm guessing you defy tradition in a lot more ways than just the color of your dress."

"You wouldn't believe it if I told you," I said. "Tell me more about your travels. What else have you seen?"

"Let's not discuss business tonight, *Asteri*," he slid his hand down my back causing a trickle of little sparks to shiver down my spine, "let's simply enjoy the moment."

Decorum made me clamp my lips together. It was considered impolite to discuss business or politics at a celebration. And while I didn't consider the welcoming of a group who would choose which of my people would die to be a celebration, I was expected to follow specific protocols.

Frustrated, I gave a little nod, then tried to focus on the dance. I wondered if he would be in the city for a while. I could learn so much from someone who had seen the dragon kingdom. Not even our own soldiers had traveled that far as any ship flying our colors would be an immediate target for the dragon's fire.

Whatever this man's business was, he must be very good at it. And he must have procured enough of something that my father or the queen wanted to gain an invitation to this event. The downside was that with such a risky position he was practically dead already. Very few merchants lived to see old age.

Sure, his words were shallow flattery, and the nickname should have sent me gagging, but there was something so deeply intriguing about this man that I let him sweep me up dance after dance.

We didn't speak as we moved through the familiar motions. He was a flawless dancer, light on his feet and more graceful than he appeared. As he gripped me closer, I could feel the hard muscles under his tunic. While he appeared lean, it was clear he was strong. Most of the men in our kingdom trained to fight. Serving at the wall was mandatory for certain positions, and most men chose to complete a two-year stint before settling down to marry. I wonder if he'd already served that time. It was impossible to determine his age. He seemed like he wasn't much older than me, but his eyes were ancient.

The music changed, the flowing melody slowing to the easy rhythm of the Tragic Lovers. It was a dance for couples, with intimate choreography and a heartbreaking story. His fingers slid up the bare skin of my arm, sending a ripple of tingles. He rested his hand on the nape of my neck and my breath caught as I looked into his eyes. Several shades of gray seemed to stir in them, like brewing storm clouds.

His other hand gripped my hip, his fingers digging into me hard and possessive, claiming. Almost hard enough to leave a bruise. The pain made something stir low in my belly.

"This dance always feels so familiar," he said.

"I think many can relate to the story."

His brow furrowed. "There's a story?"

"I thought everyone knew the origin," I replied.

"Enlighten me, please," he asked softly.

The ache in my belly deepened at the way he said the word, *please*. I swallowed hard and brushed it away. Perhaps it had been too long since I'd had some relief. His eyes seemed to flash and I swore I caught the slightest sign of a smirk. It was as if he knew exactly how he was making me feel.

"The song is a tribute to the story of the Tragic Lovers," I said, as if that cleared it all up.

I broke his gaze and looked at the dancers around us, couples who were using this as an excuse to press against one another, men's hands sliding scandalously up the slits of their partner's dresses.

His face moved closer to mine, his warm breath in my ear. "Tell me the story."

Heat flared between my thighs and I resisted the urge to moan at the feel of his lips brushing my earlobe.

"It's an old story," I began, my voice breathy. "The tale of two lovers from different clans who were forbidden to be together. They were meant to be, though, their love already forecast in the stars at birth. But their families didn't care what the gods wanted or what the oracles declared. They were kept apart, unaware of the existence of the other.

"Until one day, the man and his army stormed the city where the woman lived. She was captured and rounded up with the other prisoners. When they set eyes on one another, they couldn't resist each other. It was love at first sight, just as the stars predicted. So, he freed her."

"Then what happened?" His breath was hot on my bare shoulder.

I pulled away, suddenly feeling like I was overheating. "They were caught together while he was buried inside her. A high priest caught them and killed them both."

"That seems extreme."

"Their parents knew if they united, it would force the clans together and they couldn't fight anymore," I replied.

"Wouldn't they want to be united?" he asked.

I shrugged. "It's just a story."

"Most stories are rooted in truth," he said.

"Oh? You think there were two human clans who were willing to battle each other instead of uniting to fight the monsters around us?" I was skeptical.

"Maybe the lovers weren't both human," he suggested.

I laughed. "Impossible. Everyone knows the monsters outside our borders would sooner eat us or enslave us than treat us as equals."

"Perhaps," he said.

My brow furrowed. "What exactly did you see when you were in Drakous?"

"I saw a kingdom full of life. Families, children… not all that different than Athos."

"Then why do they attack us?" I asked.

"Perhaps you should ask your father that question," he replied.

I tensed.

The music stopped, and applause surrounded us. My partner released his grip on me and stepped away. He lowered his head in a bow. "Thank you for the dance, your highness."

My eyes widened. He'd known who I was the whole time.

He rose, a wicked grin on his lips. "I do hope we can spend more time together during my visit at the palace."

My body seemed to physically react to the possibility of seeing him again, and I could feel the flush creeping up my neck and into my cheeks. Hoping he couldn't see my reaction under the glow of the lanterns, I nodded, then spun away.

Something about that man had me feeling so very out of control. When I was with a man, it was on my terms. I didn't allow emotions to get involved. That was how you ended up trapped here. I had plans, a path for my life. And it didn't involve getting into a relationship with any man.

I diligently took my tonic, as most women did, to prevent pregnancy. I had only had one partner, but I was cautious. I kept my heart out of it and rarely caved to my desires. There were rules I followed to keep my heart to myself, and it had worked for me so far. But this man felt different. There was something off about him.

And that made him dangerous.

I couldn't allow myself to feel a connection with someone. Especially not with someone who was as good as dead as soon as his luck ran out. Merchants venturing beyond the wall rarely lived past forty.

I grabbed a glass of wine from a passing maid and drank it in three large gulps, much to the horror of the maid.

"Would you like another, Princess?" She held up a new glass of wine.

I accepted it and put my empty one on her tray. "Thank you."

It was time to go and pay my respects to my father. And of course, he was no longer alone. The queen was now sitting next to him. I groaned inwardly. I had hoped I was finished with her for the evening.

I curtseyed low when I reached the dais. "Good evening, Father." I turned to the queen. "Your highness."

She wrinkled her nose. I knew she hated it when I

dropped my father's title and used hers to remind her of my place in this household.

"Ara, my love, you look radiant." My father rose, his white and gold tunic glittered in the lantern light. He walked down the steps until he was standing in front of me. "You seemed to be enjoying yourself on the dance floor."

"I found someone who could actually dance," I replied.

"That he can," he agreed. "I must say, though, I'm pleased to see you stepping up to your place in this household."

I waited, wondering what the newest guilt trip was going to be. He'd been trying to talk me out of joining the army and going to the wall since I announced my intentions. Surely he wouldn't expect me to marry a merchant.

"Entertaining the Konos ambassador will help us to gain favor. I've asked to maintain the reduced number of tributes so we can send more soldiers to the wall. If you can keep him happy, we might have a chance at getting our request met," he said.

It was as if a bucket of cold water had been dumped over me. I sucked in a breath, rapidly processing his words. "The Konos ambassador?" I glanced at Ophelia, then looked back at my father. "But you never announced them. I didn't realize they were here."

"The ambassador asked to bypass the traditional announcement and just allow the party to be enjoyed. You'll see his men mingling with the crowd. I think it will help them to feel more welcome," my father explained.

I looked around the room and noticed the crimson tunics traditionally worn by those from Konos intermingled with the colorful mixture of fabrics worn by those from Athos.

The ambassador had been in black. I never even considered he could have been one of the men from Konos. "I didn't know that's who he was."

My father tilted his head to the side. "I thought that was why you agreed to dance with him. You never dance at these events."

"I thought he was a merchant," I mumbled.

"Well, he seemed to take a liking to you," my father commented.

"Don't worry, I won't be making that mistake again." My insides twisted in revulsion. I'd been attracted to the man who was sent here to select human sacrifices from my people. What was wrong with me?

"No, I need you to keep him happy," he said.

"What?" I shook my head. "Impossible."

"Do you want us to have to start sending a hundred tributes?" he asked. "More innocent Athonians?"

"I thought it was fourteen," I said.

"We got a reprieve the last five Choosings. A break due to the war at the wall. But time's up. The number was originally one hundred." My father's face looked grim. "We can't afford to lose a hundred able-bodied young people. Our city is struggling. There's not enough babies and the dragons are breeching the wall more frequently. We need our healthy young people at the wall, not sent to Konos."

"You never told me any of this," I said. "You told me the wall was secure. And you never told me it was supposed to be a hundred tributes."

"There are many things I don't tell you."

I balled my hands into fists. "Don't ask me to do this."

"I'm afraid I must. Keep him happy, Ara." His tone was stern.

"Father…"

He held up his hand. "Do not argue with me. Ophelia is

right. I've allowed you too much freedom. If you do not do this for me, you will not go to the wall. I will offer your hand in marriage to one of the lords."

"You wouldn't," I whispered. Where was this coming from? My father had always treated me kindly. He'd always allowed me to chase my dreams, and the only thing he asked of me was to protect my sisters.

"I will do anything I must to keep this kingdom from falling," he said.

"It's that dire at the border?" I asked.

His jaw tensed. "I'm finished discussing this with you. You will do your duty to this kingdom."

I lifted my chin. "I understand."

As he walked back to his throne, I caught sight of the queen. She was grinning at me like a cat who'd just eaten her master's prized bird.

I narrowed my eyes, glaring at her. She won this round, but I wasn't going to forget this.

Irritated, I grabbed another glass of wine before scanning the dance floor for the ambassador. How could my father think I'd be okay with playing nice with this man? And how come he'd never told me the truth about the tributes? Sending fourteen people to their deaths was bad enough. A hundred seemed like an impossibly large number. There were so few humans left as it was. And he was right, not as many of us were having babies. It was risky to raise a child here. While we'd been able to prevent any major attacks since we'd signed the alliance with the Fae King, the threat from the dragons was constant. One of these days, they were going to get past our wall and then we were all doomed.

I sipped my wine as a million unwelcome thoughts flooded my mind. I wasn't privy to most of the inner workings of the kingdom and I thought that was fine, but now I had to wonder how much I didn't know.

A blur of black caught my eye, and I turned to see the ambassador dancing with Lady Marlette, the daughter of a high-ranking lord. My grip tightened on the glass in my hand and my jaw clenched as I watched them spin around the dance floor.

Lady Marlette tossed her head back, her auburn curls bouncing as she laughed at something the ambassador said. He leaned closer and whispered in her ear and I could see the flush on her checks from where I stood.

Apparently, he whispered sweet things to all the ladies he danced with. Of course he did. That was his job, after all. Play nice, get people to like him, then choose fourteen people to deliver to his king.

My father's warning rang in my ears as the song ended and I blew out a breath, resigning myself to requesting another dance before dismissing myself for the evening.

I only got two steps forward before Lady Marlette led the ambassador off the dance floor toward the dark and private garden.

Jealously flared like flames in my chest. There was only one thing couples went to the garden for and it wasn't friendly conversation. Shaking the unwelcome feeling from my thoughts, I reminded myself that I wasn't interested in anyone who worked for the Konos King. It didn't matter how attractive he was or how he'd made me feel. He was better off with Lady Marlette. At least now, he wasn't my problem.

"More wine, your highness?" A passing maid offered a tray.

"No, thank you, I think I've had enough." I knocked back the last of the wine in my glass, then handed it to her.

My first Choosing had been elegant parties and lavish

feasts. I had known it was wrong, I had dreaded the final piece of the two weeks of celebration when the tributes were announced, but I wasn't yet mature enough to come to terms with my feelings. Now, I knew how terrible it was. And I hated that there was nothing I could do to stop it.

CHAPTER 4

"Ara, where were you last night?" Sophia, my youngest sister, asked as I walked into the breakfast room.

Cora groaned, lifting her head from the table. "Wherever she was, she was the smart one."

"How about some breakfast, Cora?" I sat down across from her and pushed the basket of honey coated pastries in front of her.

Her face turned green, and she shook her head. "Excuse me." She rose, then rushed out of the room.

"You should have seen her last night," Sophia said. "She out-drank Tomas."

I lifted a surprised brow. "Tomas is back?"

"That's what you got out of that?"

Cora had always been rebellious, but Tomas brought out something else in her. When he was around, she didn't listen to reason. She was someone else entirely. I wasn't sure if it was a good thing that he'd returned.

"You should have stuck around, though," Sophia said. "She could have gotten herself hurt."

Guilt tightened in my gut. Especially for leaving Sophia alone. It was her first time attending the events for the Choosing. I should have made sure she was safe before I'd gone back to my room. "I'm sorry. I should have checked in with you and Cora before I left."

"Even Lagina was looking for you," Sophia added.

"Oh?" Lagina and I were inseparable as children. Often getting into trouble or spending time in places we shouldn't. Since she'd started training as the next ruler of Athos, it was as if she'd become a different person. I didn't even recognize her anymore.

"She said something about a special job that father asked you to do..." Sophia left the words hanging unfinished.

I frowned. Of course he would task her with keeping me in line.

"What was she talking about?"

I shoved an entire honey cake in my mouth.

Sophia wrinkled her nose. "Fine. If you won't tell me, I'll just get it out of her."

Shaking my head, I chewed quickly, regretting shoving the whole cake in my mouth. If Sophia spoke to Lagina, our eldest sister would command Sophia to help. While Lagina and I were close as kids, Sophia was the one I couldn't say no to. She was joy personified and I couldn't help but buckle to anything she asked of me. "I'm to entertain the ambassador."

"Really?" Her forehead wrinkled. "You weren't even at the greeting ceremony. No wonder Gina is looking for you."

"Father asked me last night at the party," I said.

"So, naturally, instead of staying to play nice, you left," she replied.

I shrugged. "What can I say? I don't like being told what to do."

"It's a wonder I have any sense of self-preservation at all with you and Cora as role models."

I laughed. "Lagina more than makes up for what Cora and I are lacking."

"And how exactly do I do that?" Lagina asked as she strolled into the room. Her honey-blonde hair hung loose to her waist, and she was the picture-perfect embodiment of what a princess should be. Wearing a lilac dress that managed to look both demure and seductive at once, she strode to the table with grace. She was flawless. As usual. If she was anyone other than my sister, I might have envied her. Instead, I was nothing but proud of how she handled herself. She was going to make an amazing queen. Even if she had abandoned her playful side for the role.

"Responsibility," Sophia said. "You're the only good role model I have."

Lagina laughed as she took a seat next to me. "Good thing you're too young to remember the trouble that Ara and I used to get into when we were younger."

"We outgrew that the day you turned seventeen," I pointed out. The morning after her party, our father had announced that she was to begin shadowing him in all aspects of his rule. She's been by his side ever since.

Lagina reached for a pistachio tart and set it on her plate before adding some fruit and a honey cake. She filled her glass with water from the pitcher. "That's what gives me hope for you and Cora. I had to snap out of it when I was forced to."

"I don't think that's possible for Cora," Sophia said.

"You'd be surprised," Lagina replied. "Sometimes we must do things we don't want to for the sake of duty to our kingdom."

I groaned, knowing where this was going. "I know, I know."

"You left the party." Lagina said. "He asked about you. Several times."

Heat flared unbidden low in my belly, and I squeezed my

thighs together in protest. I was *not* going to be attracted to the man who chose which of my people would die.

"I think he fancies you," Lagina said with a sing-song tone.

"Do you think he's one of them? Fae like the king?" Sophia asked. "Or maybe he's one of the monsters that needs human blood to survive?"

"I didn't see any fangs," Lagina said with a shrug.

"I doubt he's fae." I couldn't imagine they'd send one of the high fae on this task. From what we'd heard, there were few of them left, even if they were nearly as powerful as the gods. As far as we knew, the delegation was typically made of vampires.

We were to provide blood donors to their rooms if they requested it, though last time, they'd fed from father's prized bull. He'd burned the poor creature alive after they left, saying it was no longer fit for sacrifice to the gods after the monsters had violated it with their fangs.

"Maybe he's human. There's enough of us scattered around the other kingdoms. Perhaps he gained some favor with the fae and serves them." Lagina suggested.

"That makes him even worse," I hissed. "A human helping to send his own kind to slaughter."

"We don't know what happens to the tributes on the island," Sophia pointed out. "Nobody has ever returned to tell us the truth. What if they treat them kindly? Use them as vampire food?"

"Even if they don't drop them in the labyrinth to feed their beast for sport, who would want to live a life as food? Where's the dignity in that?" I asked.

"Father says the tributes live good lives there. They can feed from animals, but they thrive on human blood. We're important to them. They need to keep as many alive as they can so they can survive," Lagina said.

"Maybe that's why they want more of us this time," I said darkly.

Lagina pressed her lips together. Her reaction gave everything away.

"What do you mean?" Sophia asked.

"You knew." I stared at my sister in disbelief. "You knew, and you didn't tell us?"

"She knew what?" Sophia demanded.

I turned to her. "They want a hundred humans. The fourteen was a limited time thing. We're supposed to send a hundred human sacrifices this year."

"I've been assured that each human tribute is well cared for and has no want for anything. I think the stories about the maze are myth. Most of the tributes we send will live a better life there than they would in the slums here," Lagina said.

"Then we should improve our slums," I hissed. "Nobody should have to hope they live a life as a blood donor to escape a worse life here."

"It's not that simple, Ara," Lagina chided.

"Maybe some people want to be tributes," Sophia offered hopefully. "You've heard the stories. They say it's pleasurable when they bite."

"Maybe Ara can find out for us," Lagina suggested.

I stood so fast my chair clattered to the ground. "If he tries anything with me, I'll cut off his balls and Father can clean up the mess himself."

"Ara…" Lagina's tone was pleading. I could tell she knew she'd gone too far, but I was already out the door. It was bad enough hearing her defend Konos. It was worse to hear her expecting me to step into the role of entertaining their leader so brazenly. Her words made it clear what she expected of me. What my father expected of me.

They weren't looking for me to bat my eyelashes. They wanted me to give him everything I had as long as it kept him happy. Was that my role here?

Unlike my sisters, I wasn't going to be married off as a bargaining chip. So this was my fate, I supposed. A tryst that would get my father out of the bargain the ancient kings had made. It was one thing for me to bed a guard. Nobody cared about that. If I did this, if I welcomed someone from Konos into my bed, I was ruined.

The halls were quiet, and a gentle breeze sent my dark hair fluttering around my face. I paused as I usually did, taking in the view of the sea. My expression darkened as soon as I saw that dreaded island. The audacity of my father to expect that I keep the ambassador busy. I supposed if I was to go to the wall as soon as the Choosing was over, it wouldn't matter. None of the soldiers at the wall were permitted to wed, and most of them didn't return to Athos ever again. Casualties were high, and many chose to remain at the wall. It was a mark of honor to serve Athos there. One of the best ways we could help our people.

I closed my eyes and took a deep breath, letting the salty air calm my nerves. What would it matter if I soiled my reputation? Aside from my father and my sisters, I didn't care what anyone thought of me.

Besides, I wanted to help Athos. I'd do my duty as requested, but it would be on my terms. There were plenty of ways to keep a man entertained without getting naked. I turned and nearly collided with the one person I was not ready to see. "Fuck."

The ambassador smirked. "Such an interesting word to hear from a princess."

I scowled. "If you ask the queen, she'll tell you I don't even hold the title legitimately and it should only be bestowed on my sisters."

"I have a feeling the queen would tell me just about anything I wanted to know about you," he said.

"She might, but it would likely be lies."

"Oh?" He looked intrigued.

"Let's clear one thing up right now," I said. "I am not going to fuck you."

He laughed. A full-bodied, shoulder-shaking laugh. I tensed and my chest tightened as embarrassment heated my cheeks. Perhaps I'd read the whole thing wrong? Maybe I wasn't even his type. I knew plenty of men who preferred the carnal company of other men over women. If that was the case, I knew several guards I could introduce him to. Besides, he'd found a partner without much effort last night. He didn't need me for sex.

As he doubled over, the laughter dragging out, my embarrassment turned to anger. I crossed my arms over my chest. "Are you about finished?"

"Oh, Princess," he said between gasps. "You misunderstand my advances."

I opened my mouth to apologize, but he closed the distance between us so quickly I didn't have a chance to get the words out. His voice was low and wrapped around me like silken shadows, "I won't touch you until you're begging me to. And when you do, I'm going to break you down completely before I put you back together."

My breath hitched, and I stared at him unblinking. His shoulder brushed against mine as he walked past me. "I'll see you around, Princess."

I turned slowly and watched him walk away, fighting

against the roaring lust gnawing at my insides. What had just happened?

Shaking him from my thoughts, I continued forward. He was trying to get in my head. It was clear he knew my father had asked me to entertain him. Or maybe this was the queen's doing. I could see her telling him I was available. And easy.

Well, the joke was on them because it was never going to happen. If I had to play nice in public, I would. But there was no way I was going to entertain that man behind closed doors.

CHAPTER 5

Sweat stung my eyes and my muscles burned as I dodged and ducked, avoiding my attacker. The sound of steel against steel rang through the stillness of the morning, the sound like music in my soul. I clenched my teeth, fighting against the reverberations sending shivers down my arms. Launching forward, I struck, but our blades met again, the kiss of the steel met with grunting as I held firm against the impact.

I was slowing down, struggling to continue the fight. Determined to see this through, I charged forward, yelling as I struck. He blocked me, his sword slamming into mine with a power I couldn't match. My blade flew from my grip and clattered to the ground.

My eyes darted to the side, then I lunged, my shoulder hitting the dirt hard as I reached for my fallen weapon. When I rose, I was greeted with cool steel against my cheek. "You lost focus."

Panting, I lifted my chin and stared down my opponent. "You cheated."

"I would never." David lowered his sword, then wiped the sweat from his brow, pushing his dark hair from his face. He grinned, the dimple on his left cheek letting me know the smile was genuine.

David had been sparring with me for years. He was one of the few guards willing to help me train when I first started and he'd continued to help me, even after his promotion to head guard last year.

When Lagina stepped into her role as future queen, it made me consider my future as well. She'd been my constant companion through childhood, but with her gone, I'd felt empty. My options were limited to joining a temple or finding a husband.

I'd rather leap from the cliffs into the sea than take either of those paths. As I was wallowing in the grim outlook for my future, my father's sister, Katerina, had made one of her rare visits. Listening to her stories of fighting at the wall and touching her dragon scale armor had been all the inspiration I needed.

The following day, my father had agreed to let me try for a spot at the wall. Which meant I needed at least some basic skills. The thing I hadn't counted on was how much I'd grow to enjoy the workouts. There was no better stress relief than working up a sweat in the training yards.

Okay, maybe there was another way to work up a sweat that also served as stress relief. But I didn't do that often. And David had become my partner for both of those exploits.

Thankfully, when I'd hunted him down after my run in with the ambassador, he was happy to oblige my need to work out some of my stress.

I blew out a breath and wiped my brow. "Every time I think I've caught up, you still best me."

"I've been doing this a long time," he reminded me. "Besides, I'm here," he tapped his forehead, "mentally. I don't know where you are today."

"I'm here," I said defensively.

He hummed. "You're distracted. Maybe we should find another way for you to blow off some steam?"

His offer was tempting, but my mind took me back to the ambassador every time I considered the thought of sex. "Thanks, but I'm not in the mood."

The worst part was, I was *very* in the mood. The problem was, I wasn't thinking about David.

My friend grabbed my training sword, holding both his and mine with one large hand. It reminded me of just what he could do with those fingers and for a moment, I let myself consider getting naked with him. Maybe that's what I needed to break myself from the unwelcome attraction to the ambassador.

"Want to talk about it?" he asked as he sauntered back toward me.

"There's not much to talk about. I'm just distracted," I said.

"What's going on?"

"It's this stupid Choosing. My father wants me more involved this year and I don't want anything to do with it," I admitted.

"You don't have anything to worry about. It's not like they'll take you to the island," he said.

"I don't want anyone to go," I replied. "The whole thing is archaic and insane. Why do we have to send humans for them to feed on?"

"We'd all be dead without the Fae King's protection," he pointed out.

"I know." The bargain kept us safe from the Vampires and the Fae and who knew what other creatures that lurked in Telos. We were already spread too thin by fighting off the dragons. We'd be wiped out if the other monsters came for us.

"There has to be another way," I complained.

"I heard a rumor," David said with a shrug.

"What kind of rumor?" I asked.

"That the key to taking out the creatures on Konos is the Fae King himself. It's why nobody ever sees him. Why he doesn't come here to speak for himself."

"What do you mean?" I pressed.

"They say if you kill him, all the other fae die with him. And without the fae, the vampires are weak. It's an opening to destroying them all." David's expression was serious. He really believed this.

"If that's true, why hasn't anyone just taken him down?" I rested my hand on my hip and cocked my head to the side. "I mean, he's just one man."

"An immortal, powerful creature with who knows what kind of magic," he said.

"Every creature has to have a weakness. Magic or no, there has to be a way." Even as I said it, I knew it wasn't so easy. The Fae King had been alive for hundreds of years. As far as we knew, it was the same king asking for tributes who made the original deal.

"I don't know, Ara; how do you kill someone who lives forever?" David asked.

"There's a difference between living forever and not being able to die," I said.

"Maybe they've tried," he said. "If the rumors are true, don't you think someone would have tried?"

"Well, if he's impossible to kill, then there's no way to defeat the monsters." It felt too final. Wasn't there anything we could do?

We were both silent for a long while as that depressing thought hung over us like a thick cloud.

"I know you and I aren't exactly close," David said.

I lifted a brow and turned to look at him. "You've seen me naked."

He smirked. "True, but I know my place. I know I'm not special."

I frowned. He was making me feel shallow. I probably was. Ever since I decided I was leaving, I'd decided two things: one, I wasn't going away to live at the wall as a virgin; and two, I wasn't going to get emotionally attached to anyone. But there hadn't been anyone else besides David. I had other options, but I only felt safe with him. How could he not know how special he was? "David, you know I like you. We're friends."

"Please, don't waste the pretty words on me. I was looking for the exact same thing as you every time we've been together." He elbowed me gently.

We were more than that, but how was I supposed to leave here if I let myself consider the possibilities.

He'd be a respectable husband for someone of my status. He was handsome, strong, brave… all the things a woman was supposed to want in a man. Add in that he was the youngest head guard in a century and he was most womens' dream partner.

But I didn't dream of settling down. I needed more. Something that I knew I couldn't get from a life here within the confines of Athos. I'd always felt a pull to somewhere else. To something else.

There was also the fact that if I let him in, he'd get attached. I'd prevent him from finding someone else, and I couldn't do that to him. "You know why I can't get closer."

"I know," he agreed. "I get it. And I'm not asking for

anything deeper between us, but I gotta ask, if there's anything you can do to keep my sisters here…"

I sucked in a breath, and my heart pounded. David had twin sisters that he helped look after. His father had died when they were young, and David sent most of his pay to his mother. "I forgot your sisters are of age."

"They turned eighteen last week. Bad timing. Maybe you can tell the ambassador their birthday is next month?" he asked hopefully. "I know it's a big ask, and I don't even know if you can help them, but my mother would be heartbroken if she had to hand either of them over."

"I'll see what I can do," I assured him.

He pulled me in for a hug and my eyes widened in surprise. I patted him on the back as guilt squeezed my insides. I wasn't sure there was anything I could do and worse, I was supposed to be keeping the man who made those decisions happy.

As David released me, I fought against the rising nausea. Between my father's request and David's, I was going to have to play a little nicer with the ambassador. I wanted to do something to help and while I wasn't sure I could help our whole kingdom, at least maybe I could help David.

"Wait, what about you?" I suddenly realized I had no idea how old he was. I really was a terrible friend.

"Twenty-six as of yesterday." He smiled, but it was a shallow, sad kind of expression. He was saved from the Choosing, but with both his sisters in the running, it didn't hold as much joy as it should.

"Yesterday? I was with you yesterday and you never said a word."

He shrugged. "We've never celebrated each other's birthdays."

I grabbed his hand and pulled him to his feet. "We're changing that. Right now. I'm taking you out."

"Don't you have other things to do?" he asked.

"The ambassador can wait. For now, I'm all yours."

He grabbed me around the waist and pulled me in close. I squealed in surprise, but leaned into him. Maybe some time with David was exactly what I needed.

Someone cleared their throat, and I pulled away from David, startled by the sound. We'd been alone since I arrived, but the other guards must be returning from their duties. It wouldn't be the first time someone had seen us being friendly, but I still wasn't comfortable with it.

Cheeks heating, I spun to find the source of the interruption. My eyes narrowed when I caught sight of Istvan standing outside the training ring. He looked annoyed. That made two of us.

"What are you doing here, Istvan?" I demanded.

"Looking to learn how to wield a weapon as well as you wield those words?" David asked.

The priest scoffed. "As if I'd have a need of such things."

"Then why are you here?" I repeated.

"Your presence is requested at dinner tonight," Istvan announced. "Your maid awaits your return to help you prepare."

I opened my mouth to protest, but David spoke first, "Tomorrow. We'll pick up where we left off."

Istvan's beady eyes bulged a little, and he coughed. I couldn't help but enjoy the look of discomfort on his face. He was the one who was out of place here.

"I don't need five hours to get ready."

"It's fine," David insisted. "I should go check on the new recruits, anyway."

"There are a lot of them lately," I commented.

"Tell me about it. They're green, too. None of them know what they're doing," he said.

"Your highness, the queen was insistent that you prepare for tonight immediately," Istvan cut in.

I sighed. So this was how my next two weeks were going to go. Dressing up so I could be put on display. "Tomorrow?" I confirmed with David, hoping he couldn't see the desperation in my expression. The only way I was going to get through tonight was by reminding myself that I had something to look forward to.

"I'm off after dinner," he said. "You can have me all night if you want."

"I'm going to take you up on that offer," I teased.

"Princess..." Istvan hissed.

David gave me a playful shove, and I reluctantly turned to the priest. "I can walk to my room myself."

"I was instructed to take you there," he said. "Your father might trust those strangers, but I certainly don't."

"You think someone from Konos is going to attack me while I'm in the palace?" I was skeptical. Aside from the fact that it would violate our treaty, if they wanted to harm any of us, there was a good chance they could. If their strength was even half of what the rumors claimed, none of us would stand a chance.

"These are strange times. The Oracle's visions are foggy and my own skills have dwindled. The future is at a precipice; even one action could tip it to a version we've never predicted," he said.

I didn't respond. Istvan was widely accepted to be one of the best soothsayers of the age, but I had my doubts. His predictions were often so open-ended that any outcome could be considered as evidence of his word. The one exception being that he'd correctly predicted the sex of each of the king's children. Four girls. Every time, he'd been correct.

Once we were back inside the palace, I turned to the priest. "I think I can handle it from here."

"I must follow my orders," he said.

"You seem to be getting a lot of orders from the queen lately," I pointed out.

"I serve the queen and the king, as you well know," he replied.

I started walking again, figuring the quicker I got to my room, the faster I got rid of him. When we turned the corner, he rounded on me, blocking my progress. Annoyed, I stepped aside, but he blocked me again.

He was shorter than me and I could easily push him aside, but I knew I'd hear about that forever if I did. With a sigh, I crossed my arms over my chest. "What is it?"

"I don't like that you danced with the ambassador," he said.

"Well, that's something we actually agree on," I said.

He lifted a brow.

"You think I wanted to dance with him?" I asked.

"You often go against convention." He shrugged. "And you seem to find joy in embarrassing your queen."

"If I were trying to embarrass the queen, you'd know." I took a step to the side again, and he blocked me once more. "Move, Istvan."

"You should know that all the members of this delegation are new. There's no record of any of them. We don't know what they are or what they're capable of."

"It almost sounds like you're concerned about me," I said. "But that can't be true, because I know for a fact that you and the queen will celebrate when I'm gone."

"There's something in my visions you should know," he warned.

"The visions you claimed aren't accurate right now?"

"There were crimson sails, and so much blood. And you standing right in the middle of all of it." He shook his head.

"It was a dream, Istvan. We all get those. I'm sure it was nothing," I said.

"It was a vision." He stepped closer to me.

I swallowed and tried to push the heavy sense of foreboding away. Istvan had made his share of nasty remarks to me over the years, but this wasn't the same. He looked concerned.

No, he looked terrified.

I wasn't sure I'd ever seen him wear that kind of expression.

"What exactly would you have me do?" I asked.

"Just be careful around them," he replied.

"I'll be careful," I assured him.

He nodded. "That's all I ask."

We were silent the rest of the way and I don't think I took a full breath until I closed the door behind me.

CHAPTER 6

I hadn't been in the formal dining hall in months. The room was spacious, with a long table that could seat fifty. It was reserved for visiting dignitaries or occasions when my father wanted to appear intimidating. I wasn't sure if tonight was meant for appearances' sake or if he was hoping to look powerful enough to demand the reduced number of tributes.

It was a beautiful space, open on three sides. Graceful columns supported stone arches acting as glassless windows, framing a panoramic view of the sea. When you entered the space, you were hit with the stark contrast of the teal water against the bright white columns. It made for a dramatic sight and each time I entered, I had to pause and stare. No matter how many times I stood here, I always felt small.

No wonder my father liked to hold important events in here.

Servants fussed over the place settings, making everything look just right. I moved aside, making sure I wasn't in the way as they went about their business.

Movement caught my eye, and I turned just as Ophelia and my father entered the room. The queen narrowed her eyes, giving me a look dripping with disdain before fixing her face to the same expression she used to address most of the court.

"Are you actually joining us this evening, Ara?" My father asked with an amused expression.

"I am." I wondered if Ophelia had requested I join or if Istvan had taken matters into his own hands because of his odd vision. Neither would surprise me, but I was taken off guard that my father didn't know.

My father crossed the room and paused in front of me. He kissed the top of my head. "You look beautiful tonight."

"Thank you." I smoothed the fabric of my pale rose-colored peplos. Mila had encouraged a color that would make me look innocent. The fabric was loose and missing the dramatic slit up the side that I'd had in my dress last night. She hadn't pressed, but I got the feeling that she knew what I'd been tasked with. She always seemed to know everything.

Even my hair was sending a message. Mila had woven traditional braids around my head like a crown, then added small white flowers. I looked more innocent than I had in years.

"It's a shame you don't show up to the other events we have. You might have had a chance at landing yourself a respectable husband," Ophelia snapped.

"Leave her," my father warned. "She's made her path known."

I smiled at my father. The queen scowled.

"It looks beautiful in here," Sophia said as she entered. "You did an excellent job choosing the decor, Mother."

I wrinkled my nose. The room would look beautiful with or without the potted ferns and flowers sitting at intervals down the long table, which I knew were the only contributions by Ophelia. Not that she'd even put them there herself.

She'd have directed someone else to set up what she requested.

"Thank you, darling." Ophelia walked away from me to greet her daughters.

Lagina and Cora entered behind Sophia, all of them wearing traditional white peplos just like the queen. My choice to wear pink was now making me stand out.

"How was the training session today?" Cora asked me. "Did David take his shirt off while you fought?"

"Cora," Ophelia snapped.

I repressed a giggle and Cora's cheeks flushed. As soon as Ophelia looked away, Cora's eyes widened as if to say, *well, did he?*

I shook my head, and Cora frowned. "There's always tomorrow, right?"

Ophelia shot a warning glare at her daughter.

"My queen, should we see to our guests?" My father asked, ever the diplomat.

To her credit, Ophelia was an excellent hostess. She might hate nearly everyone, but she could make you feel like you were her best friend while she threw you a party. The next day, she might demand your head on a pike, but in that moment while she had to play the part, you'd fully believe she was on your side. It was a gift. Something that I struggled with my whole life. I was much more authentic, something that wasn't a prized skill for anyone going into politics.

"I hate this," Cora said as she situated herself next to me.

"Hush," Lagina said. "They're on their way."

"I spoke to some of them today. They seem nice," Sophia added.

"They are choosing some of our people to be food," I reminded her.

"Maybe they don't have a choice," Sophia said.

"There's always a choice," I said darkly.

The queen walked into the room, a broad smile on her lips. "Welcome to our humble dining room." She swept her arm wide, showing the view.

Behind her, a dozen men, dressed in the traditional crimson tunics of Konos, filed in behind her. My heart raced as I scanned their faces, looking for *him*. The ambassador wasn't with the rest of the group. My stomach dropped in disappointment, and I realized there was a part of me that wanted to see him.

What was wrong with me? He was my enemy. His king might protect us, but his price was too steep. And if we didn't pay it, they'd kill us all. I couldn't allow myself to have any sort of feelings for him. This was a favor to my father, and a favor to an old friend. I'd do what I had to, but I couldn't get close or emotionally involved.

It was better that he wasn't here.

The delegates moved aside, and a woman entered. It was as if all the air was sucked from the room and everyone held a collective breath. She practically floated across the threshold, her strange gray dress moving and flowing in a phantom breeze. She had long brown hair, the color of damp soil, and pale, almost ghostly skin. She was thin and small, almost childlike, but her expressions and demeanor made her seem ancient.

But it wasn't her clothes or her graceful, ethereal movements that made her so unsettling. It was her eyes. They were milky white, empty and dead. But it wasn't that she was blind; it was the fact that I could tell she wasn't just looking at me. She was looking through me. It was as if she could see to my very soul. I could feel it, the measure of that gaze.

Her lips moved into a smile, showing straight white teeth. "I was hoping we'd get to meet the other princess tonight."

Ophelia huffed out an annoyed breath, then grabbed me so she could shove me in front of the blind woman. "Yes, we were so sad she was unable to welcome you properly. This is Ara, the king's illegitimate daughter."

I hated when Ophelia introduced me, but something warned me not to cross this woman or allow myself to show any weakness. "Welcome to our kingdom."

The blind woman drifted closer, floating with airy elegance. I swallowed down nervous flutters and held my ground. She stopped inches from me. "The pleasure is all ours, Ara of Athos." Her voice had an echo to it, almost as if it was spoken in chorus, as if multiple women were speaking in unison.

I'd never seen anything like her. She reminded me of a priestess, but there was so much power emanating from her. I'd never felt magic before, but I think I might have felt it from her. It was clear she wasn't human. I wondered if she was fae. She was clearly more powerful than any of her male companions.

"I didn't get your name," I said, trying to be hospitable.

"I am Morta," she replied in that strange, plural sounding voice of hers. She smiled at me, keeping those dead eyes locked on me.

I felt like I was trapped, locked in Morta's blank stare. My palms grew sweaty and my pulse raced. Panic began to bloom in my chest.

"Now that the introductions are complete, shall we eat?" Ophelia suggested.

Morta blinked, then turned away from me, letting Ophelia lead her to the table. I blew out a shaky breath, never more grateful for the queen in my life.

The delegates settled around the table, and my sisters took their places between them. Morta was seated at the far end, near my father. The queen was at the other end, facing him. As soon as everyone was seated, I took a seat next to a delegate, as far away as I could from the strange woman. There were a few empty chairs next to me, giving me a buffer between me and the queen.

At least I'd only have to make small talk with one of the delegates, and I could avoid being too close to Ophelia. Istvan took a seat near the queen, leaving one empty chair between us. I was grateful he'd chosen to be closer to her than me.

Servants brought out drinks, then followed with platters of fish and lamb, bowls of rice and vegetables, and gorgeous towers of figs dripping with honey. My stomach growled at the sight, and I breathed in the mingling scents.

"Your kingdom is lovely," the man sitting next to me said.

I looked over at him, doing my best to force a smile. "Thank you."

The man smiled widely, and I caught sight of two gleaming white fangs. "Not so different from my home."

Swallowing down the initial burst of fear, I forced my gaze to his eyes. They were watery blue. A faded, unimpressive color. After everything I'd been told about these creatures, I expected something more. They were said to be beautiful, experts at seduction. But this man wasn't any prize. There were plenty of guards in our armies who were more handsome.

"You don't seem to be afraid of me," he said.

"Should I be?" I asked.

"Most humans are," he said.

"And you enjoy being feared?" I asked.

He smirked. "Fear is power, Princess."

"Respect is power," I countered.

"You are young, but you'll learn," he said.

"Orion, are you trying to scare our new friend?" A familiar deep voice cut in.

I tensed, knowing my good luck was up. I looked to my right just as the ambassador pulled out the chair and sat next to me.

"I thought perhaps you'd fallen into the sea," I said.

"Alas, I'm an excellent swimmer. I was... occupied," he said, his eyes darting toward one of the servants in the corner. She caught his eye, then giggled, her face flushing deep crimson.

My stomach tightened in what felt an awful lot like jealousy. Gritting my teeth, I sent the thought away. First Lady Marlette at the party and now servants? With any luck, he'd be too busy finding women to seduce to have any need for me.

A grim thought struck me. Perhaps this was how he chose tributes. Or maybe he promised his lovers a reprieve. "Already making notes for your selection?"

"That wasn't my intention," he said. "I was simply getting to know your household."

"With a servant, Ryvin?" Orion wrinkled his nose.

"None of the princesses were available," Ryvin said with a shrug.

"Nor will they be," I bit out. "You will not touch me or any of my sisters. That applies to all of you." I glanced at each man next to me, before turning back to Ryvin. I knew he was the highest ranking out of their delegation. "You understand me?"

A hand gripped my thigh and squeezed. "I like your fire," Orion whispered in my ear.

Before I could push him away, Ryvin was out of his seat, his chair clattering to the ground. He yanked Orion from his seat. In a blur of black fabric, Orion was on the ground and

Ryvin's knee was on the man's chest. The ambassador held a dagger to the other man's throat. "She gave you an order."

Gasps and the screeching of chairs over the stone floor surrounded us, but I couldn't tear my eyes away from the men on the ground.

"You take the side of a woman over me?" Orion hissed.

"We are their guests," Ryvin said. "If you touch her again, I will remove your head myself."

My heart thundered in my chest, and I had to clamp my thighs together to tamp down the rising need. I'd grown up around the fiercest warriors in our kingdom, but never once had any of them defended me. Apparently, it was a major turn on.

Blowing out a breath, I gave myself a moment to enjoy the thrill of seeing a man stand up for me before reminding myself of who he was. He was still a monster. Just because he stood up to another monster didn't change anything.

"Is everything alright, ambassador?" My father asked.

Ryvin removed his knee, then tucked his dagger into his boot. He stood, then smoothed out his tunic. "I apologize, your highness. We aren't used to human protocols. Sometimes, I forget myself and a little bit of the beast within breaks free." He glanced at me before he turned back to my father. "Please, forgive me."

A lump rose in my throat. His words were a reminder of what simmered below that handsome exterior. I'd wondered if he was human, and it seemed he was giving me a hint. Or a warning.

"I apologize for my forwardness, your highness," Orion said softly. He was standing next to me, eyes downcast.

Everyone in the room was staring at me, waiting for me to react. I licked my lips reflexively.

"If you'd like me to further punish him, I'm happy to

oblige," Ryvin said so quietly I was certain I was the only one who heard him.

"That's not necessary." I had a feeling if I said the words, Orion's head would be torn from his body. I glanced at the man standing to my left. "A misunderstanding."

Orion bowed. "It won't happen again; I can assure you."

"Well, if that's settled," the queen said. "Shall we get back to our meal?"

Orion settled into his seat, and after a few tense moments of silence, the table erupted into general chatter.

Sophia caught my eye, then silently mouthed the words, *are you okay*? I nodded, then made myself eat, keeping my attention on my food.

"I will keep my men in line," Ryvin said.

"Can you send your men home?" I countered.

"As soon as our job here is done," he said.

"You mean after you kidnap humans so you can take them to their deaths?" I hadn't meant to say it, but the words tumbled out.

"I can assure you; all the tributes are well cared for and live a far more luxurious life than they'd have here," he said.

"If you say so," I mumbled.

"I can offer my personal…"

I stood, not waiting for him to finish. The table quieted and Ophelia glared at me. I ignored her, turning my attention to my father. "I'm afraid the excitement has made me tired. If you'll excuse me, I'll take my leave."

"Of course, darling," my father said.

Ryvin stood. "Please, allow me to escort you safely to your room."

"Oh, that is not necessary," I said.

"I insist," he smiled, flashing straight white teeth. No sign of fangs.

My brow furrowed slightly. What exactly was he if not a vampire? He couldn't possibly be human, could he?

It didn't matter what he was. He was a threat.

"That's very kind, ambassador," my father said. "Of course, Ara is happy to accept."

"Shouldn't I have a chaperone?" I asked, flashing my most demure smile.

Ophelia laughed. No, not laughed. Cackled. "I think that ship has sailed, Ara."

I narrowed my eyes at her and threw her my nastiest glare.

"I promise, I won't bite," Ryvin said.

Ophelia stopped laughing. The whole room went so silent I swore I could hear the waves crashing against the cliffs in the distance. If I wasn't so tense, I might have appreciated the way the color drained from Ophelia's face.

"Shall we, Princess?" Ryvin offered his elbow, and as if driven by something outside myself, I complied, sliding my arm into his. I could feel the eyes of everyone at dinner on us as we exited the dining room.

CHAPTER 7

As soon as we turned the corner, I yanked my arm out of his. "You can go back to dinner. I don't need your help."

"You could've fooled me," he said. "What do you call what happened back there?"

"You're overreacting. An asshole put his hand on my leg, and I didn't get a chance to slap him like I should have before you acted like a wolf and attacked him," I said.

"I did not act like a wolf," he said. "A shifter would have ripped the arm clean from his body for touching something of theirs."

I cocked a brow. He spoke like he'd witnessed that kind of aggression personally. I pushed that thought away and focused instead on the second part of his statement. "I am not yours."

He stepped closer, and I backed away until I made contact with the wall. Gray eyes peered down at me as if trying to see into my soul. His gaze was intense, hungry, wanting. I caught the scent of saltwater and wood; a clean, welcoming smell that I wanted to wrap myself up in. But something else lingered in the air between us. Something charged and electric. Something dangerous.

His tongue flicked out, brushing his lower lip. "I yield. You are not. And you clearly don't need me."

"I told you I don't." My words came out quiet and breathless, and I wasn't sure I believed them.

The corner of his mouth quirked in the faintest hint of a smirk. "Yet, you want me. Your body betrays you, Princess."

"You're wrong."

"I can smell your desire."

"I was with someone else today," I lied.

His expression darkened, and I knew I was catching that same conflicting sense of jealousy that he brought out in me. I smiled. "You thought you were the only one who got to enjoy sex around here?"

He caught my jaw in his grip, and I gasped as he lifted my chin so I was staring up at him. "Careful, Princess, or you might push me to the edge."

"Go find a maid to fuck, asshole," I spat.

Ryvin moved so close that his body pressed against mine and I could feel his hardness. Desire coursed through me. I hated this man. I hated his kingdom and everything he stood for. But my body didn't seem to care who he was. "Release me."

"Tell me you don't want me."

"I don't want you." My breathing was shallow, and heat was building to uncomfortable levels between my thighs.

"Liar."

"Go fuck yourself." I turned my head and his thumb brushed against my lower lip as I pulled away from his grip. He traced it over my lip, then pressed the tip into my mouth. I let him, hating myself as I fought the urge to pull his whole thumb into my mouth and suck it like it was something else.

My eyes darted down instinctively toward the bulge in his pants.

He removed his hand from my face, then slid it to my neck before digging his fingers into my hair. "I knew you'd be begging for me."

"I'm not begging for you."

"Not yet." He released me and stepped back so quickly that the absence left me feeling cold and confused. Then I saw the movement out of the corner of my eye and a pair of guards turned the corner.

Ryvin adjusted his tunic, and I sucked in a breath, my heart racing. We'd been seconds away from being seen together.

What was wrong with me? Why had I let him do that to me? I could have pushed him away, and he knew it. He hadn't used force; he hadn't hurt me. I'd allowed that to happen.

"Your highness? Is everything okay?" One of the guards asked, pausing in front of me.

"Fine, thank you." I took a few steps past the ambassador. "I'm sure they're missing you at dinner. You should return."

"As you wish, *Asteri*."

"No. You don't get to call me a cute nickname," I said without breaking my steps.

"Ara, then?" he asked.

"How about *your highness*."

He inclined his head. "Very well, *your highness*. I require an escort to visit the city tomorrow," he called.

I sighed, finally turning around. "Speak with my father. I'm sure he'll be happy to arrange it for you."

"I already did." He grinned. "I'll see you after breakfast."

Now I knew why my father so easily let me leave dinner. I knew I should be trying to get on this man's good side, but the thought made me nauseous. "Why not choose someone who wants to impress you?"

"Where's the fun in that?"

I rolled my eyes. This man was infuriating. "I will do as my father requires, but don't expect me to be nice about it."

"I'd be disappointed if you were," he said.

"Your highness," another male voice cut in. I gritted my teeth at the sound of Istvan's voice.

I wasn't sure which was worse, the ambassador or the high priest. Using the distraction to end my conversation with Ryvin, I turned to face Istvan. "Did the queen have another message for me?"

"No, I came of my own accord." The priest's eyes flicked to the ambassador, then returned to me. "I thought perhaps you could use an escort to your room."

"I was escorting the princess," Ryvin said.

I was used to wandering the palace unnoticed. Normal decorum hadn't been wasted on me and I'd taken full advantage. There was no way I was about to start demanding special treatment now. I wasn't the crown princess or even in line for the throne at all. There was no need to elevate my status.

"I'm sure they're missing both of you at dinner," I said. "Why don't you escort yourselves back to the dining room and this guard will escort me."

I didn't wait for responses before walking toward the bewildered guard. "Shall we?"

He fell into step next to me and I picked up the pace, not looking back to see if the other men were following me.

He was a newer guard, younger than me, but he seemed familiar. I wondered if I'd seen him spar or working around the palace. I didn't know all the guards, there were so many who worked here, but he seemed a better option than allowing either of the other men to continue on toward my room.

Once we'd turned down the hall and began our ascent up

the stairs toward my room, I glanced back. Thankfully, nobody was following us. My shoulders relaxed, releasing some of the tension I'd been holding.

"Thank you for standing up to him," the guard said.

"Istvan?"

"The ambassador," he said. "So many seem to forget that he still represents an enemy."

Guilt swirled. I had stood up to him, but how far would I have allowed things to go if the guards hadn't shown up? I was quiet the rest of the walk to my room, internally cursing myself for feeling anything for him.

When we reached the door, I thanked the guard.

He nodded, then glanced down the hall, as if checking to see if we were alone.

I tensed, wondering if I'd read him wrong. My fingers twitched as I prepared to reach for the dagger strapped to my thigh.

"If they take me, I'll fight them," he said. "I'll try to get to the king and end it all. Protection be dammed."

My fingers relaxed. "You'd have my full support."

"I know," he said. "I can tell from the way you fight. You never use cheap shots, but you find your opponent's weaknesses. You value honor. And gaining protection by sacrificing our own isn't honorable. It's a coward's way out." He shook his head. "I'm sorry, this isn't my place."

"I didn't realize you'd been watching me so closely," I said.

His eyes widened. "I swear, it's nothing but respectful."

I held up my hand. "It's fine. But I wonder, what else did you notice?"

His cheeks turned pink.

"It's okay, tell me. Most guards won't give me details. Just flattery. At least to my face," I said.

"Well, your need to play by the rules of engagement are going to get you killed in a real battle," he said.

"You've seen real battles?" I countered.

"Not yet, but I've seen enough brawls in the streets to know that rules don't exist when emotions are high."

"What would you suggest I do?" I asked.

"Use your disadvantages to your advantage," he suggested.

I lifted a brow.

"Not meaning any offense, your highness," he said.

"Go on," I encouraged.

"Your size, and the fact that you're a woman. It means your opponents are going to underestimate you," he said. "You need to use that. Get small, outmaneuver them, play up your charms if you have to. If you're ever fighting to the death, nobody is going to critique your methods when you're the last one standing."

I smiled. "You're going to spar with me tomorrow."

"Oh, no, I couldn't do that," he said.

"Sure, you can," I said. "I'm meeting David in the afternoon when the other guards head in from training. Nobody will see you."

"I'm not worried about that," he said.

"What are you worried about?"

"That you'll take my head off."

"Why would I do that?" My eyes widened, and I suddenly realized why he was so nervous around me. And where I'd seen him before. Laughter bubbled out, unbidden. "I'm sorry, you look different with your clothes on."

His face went even redder. "I meant no disrespect. I really like your sister."

"You don't have to do that," I said. "She's not expecting a

proposal and I don't care who she beds. As long as it's not in my room."

"I swear I had no idea it was your room," he said.

"Well, now you know," I said, taking a step toward my door. "What's your name?"

"Belan," he replied.

"Well, Belan, I hope to see you tomorrow."

He nodded. "I'll be there."

"Thank you for the feedback," I said. "Sleep well."

He bowed, keeping his head down while I entered my room.

Mila was sitting on a chair near the window, and she rose when she saw me. "Back so soon?"

"You know how I feel about those kinds of events," I said.

"I thought you'd last a little longer after your father's request." She walked over to me and guided me to a stool so she could begin to unravel my hair.

"I have to show him the city tomorrow," I said.

"So he can start to choose," she replied darkly.

My stomach twisted into knots. The delegation never shared exactly how they selected the tributes. Everyone of age was required to come to the palace on the choosing day, but the selection went so quickly that I had to wonder if they already knew who they would take. "I suppose."

"Someone needs to do something about this," she said. "We can't go through this every nine years."

I didn't respond. I hated the Choosing, but with the dragons at our borders, how would we also defend against the vampires and fae? We couldn't afford a war from all sides. I wanted to see an end to it, but I wasn't sure how I could make that happen.

Mila ran her fingers through my long, dark locks, loosening the last of the braids. "Would you like a bath this evening?"

"I think I'd rather go right to sleep," I said.

She pulled a few remaining flowers from my hair. "Your nightgown is on the bed."

I nodded. "Thank you, Mila."

"Of course," she said. "Can I get you anything else tonight?"

"No, I'll see you in the morning."

She curtseyed, then left me alone in my room. I walked to the window and stared out at the dark landscape. Closing my eyes, I felt the breeze on my face and listened for the sound of the distant waves. A pang of sadness formed a pit in my gut. I'd always felt a deep connection to the sea, but I'd be leaving it behind when I traveled to the wall. If I was honest with myself, I'd miss that more than anything else. Even my sisters.

I pulled the drapes across the window, then removed my sandals and dress, letting it fall to the ground in a puddle around my feet. While I went through the motions of readying for sleep, the events of the evening swirled in my memory. Belan's words about taking down the Fae King seemed to meld with David's story about the king being the key to destroying the monsters. If he was right, would it be enough? Would taking out the king end the Choosing? Was it possible to kill him?

By the time I was in my bed, my thoughts had shifted to the ambassador himself. When I closed my eyes, I could see that cocky smile and the swirling gray depths of his eyes.

How was I expected to look at him tomorrow, knowing what he planned to do? What would happen if he and his men were to vanish? What if they simply didn't return to Konos? Would the king send another delegation? Would he attack our kingdom? Or would he and the other monsters starve to death before they could act?

As I slipped into sleep, I imagined myself shoving my blade through the ambassador's chest, blood oozing out, his gray eyes going pale as death took him.

CHAPTER 8

The carriage was surrounded by black-clad guards I didn't recognize. Gone were the formal tunics from last night. Instead, the ambassador's entourage was dressed for battle.

Black leather armor studded with silver that caught the sunlight, making it look like stars against an inky sky. Their helmets covered most of their face, hiding their identities far more than our own guards.

My chest tightened as I realized there were none of our men around the waiting carriage. The only men in the familiar blue and gold were stationed along the stairs and at the front door to the palace. These were their usual places and none of them seemed like they were going to abandon their posts to accompany me.

Surely, my father wasn't going to allow me to ride into the city with only the protection of the Konos guards. Even with my years of training, he'd never allowed me to venture into the city with less than two guards. Typically, I wouldn't be concerned. Our people had never given me reason to fear for my safety. But these men weren't our people.

How many of them were bloodsucking monsters? Without examining their teeth, I couldn't know for sure. The legends said that once, their kind couldn't stand the sunlight. It was why their island was shrouded in eternal clouds. But after centuries of drinking human blood, they'd overcome that deficiency. Perhaps that was what they really needed our blood for.

"Good morning, your highness," Ryvin called as he descended the stairs leading to the long stone driveway. My father was walking behind him, a pleased smile fixed on his face.

I inclined my head slightly. "Good morning, ambassador. Your highness."

"I am looking forward to seeing more of your beautiful city," Ryvin said.

"You have an excellent guide," my father said. "Ara used to spend every moment she could in the city. I'm sure she knows some very lively places to visit."

I pressed my lips together. When I was a teenager, I'd spent far too much time in gaming halls, theaters, and taverns. Often, with Lagina by my side. Though, our visits grew more infrequent as she took on more royal duties until one day, she stopped visiting the city with me altogether. A pang of sorrow made my chest tighten. There were days I missed the closeness we used to have. Our lives had taken such different turns as we walked our separate paths.

"I look forward to seeing some of your favorite places," Ryvin said.

"I'm not sure the places I used to visit are even still there, but I'll see what we can do," I offered. "We can leave as soon as my guards arrive. I have an appointment this afternoon, so I can't be gone all day."

"Your appointment with David can wait," my father said.

I bristled, annoyed that he knew that was what I had planned.

"David?" Ryvin arched his brows.

I didn't respond. What I did with my time wasn't any of his business.

"Don't worry, Princess, I'll have you back in time," Ryvin said. "Shall we?"

"My guards?" I pressed.

"You're well protected," my father said, gesturing to the Konos guards surrounding the carriage.

"You can't be serious," I said.

"How many times have you snuck out without any guard at all?" My father inquired, amused.

"That was a long time ago. And I wasn't in a carriage that announced exactly who I was." I gestured to the black carriage. It was so different from anything you'd see on the streets of Athos that it would instantly give us away as outsiders. And there was only one outsider that ever visited our kingdom.

"My guards are well-trained," Ryvin said. "Besides, your father has assured me that we have nothing to fear from your people. Unless there's something you know that he doesn't?"

I frowned, not liking the implication he was making. "Fine. Let's get this over with." As I walked toward the carriage, I brushed my arm over my thigh, feeling the dagger under my dress.

I'd have preferred trousers on this expedition, but Mila had insisted I wear a dress. Probably to keep up appearances for my father. I wondered if I could get out of entertaining the ambassador after this. The next few days were booked with festivities and he'd be occupied. He might not even notice me missing. Especially if he found himself some more maids to bed. Which was exactly what he should do. And I shouldn't care at all. Not even a little.

One of the guards opened the door and offered his hand. I ignored his waiting palm and hoisted myself up to the carriage using the handles on the side. I had to stay angry. To remind myself of what these people were and who they represented. It was far better than the alternative after what happened in the hallway last night.

Ryvin climbed in after me, sitting on the bench seat next to me. I shifted closer to the side, putting as much distance as I could between us. I swore I saw the flicker of a smile on his lips at my movement. Annoyed, I faced the window, staring out at my home.

We were on the large driveway in front of the palace. Out my window I could see the gardens that stretched until the cliffs that dropped off into the sea. The sky was a clear, endless blue, devoid of clouds. The sun shone bright and warm. If not for the company, I'd have looked forward to a day visiting the city.

"Where should we visit first?" Ryvin asked.

I glanced at my companion. "You're the one who wanted to go to town."

"You're supposed to be my guide," he said.

I twisted my lips to the side as I considered his words. "What is it that you're looking for, ambassador?"

"Please, call me Ryvin," he said.

"No, thank you," I replied.

"Alright, your highness."

"Let's get to the point. You're not here to take in the beauty of my city or get to know our people. You're here to select a meal for your king," I spat.

He arched a brow. "Is that what you think of me? I told you, they will be treated well until their time comes."

"Until their time comes? And how long is this time you've granted them among monsters?" I asked.

"That is for the fates to determine, and is not up to me or anyone else," he replied.

"You take them from their home, from everything they've ever known. From family and friends and you expect me to believe they'll enjoy being blood donors for your people?" I spat.

"Is that your concern? The fact that they'll be fed on? I promise, the experience is pleasurable."

I narrowed my eyes. Was that his play? Was he food for the creatures? Did he enjoy it when they dug their fangs into him? A sudden image flooded my mind of a handsome male with his fangs piercing Ryvin's neck. I could imagine Ryvin's head back, gasping in pleasure as he ran his fingers through the other male's hair.

A strange rush of desire coursed through me at the mental picture, replaced just as quickly by jealousy. Either emotion was enough on its own to have me questioning my sanity, but both were too much. I needed to get away from this man. He was muddling my thoughts.

"I really don't need the details," I said, waving a dismissive hand in the air. "I want honesty. What is your purpose for this visit? Let's not waste either of our time. Tell me so I can take you someplace that fits your goals."

"Very well," he said, his tone clipped and cold. "Take me somewhere where the people might welcome escape. Might embrace a chance at a fresh start."

I frowned, knowing what he was asking. "You're even worse than I suspected."

"Why is that?"

"Because you're asking me to take you to the slums. To prey on those who have little," I said.

"That's not what I said. I asked you to take me to those who might welcome escape," he repeated.

I considered his words, then realized I was the one who had jumped to conclusions. He was right, of course; I'd met plenty of unhappy people who had more wealth than they knew what to do with.

There was only one place we could go. The place I'd visited to escape my life as a teen. It had been my refuge while I struggled with Lagina's transition to her role as future queen and my sense of languish as I tried to find my place. I hadn't visited since deciding to join the army. "The Black Opal."

"Is that a tavern?" he asked.

"Sort of," I said, then proceeded to tell him the location.

He nodded, then peered outside the carriage to inform the driver of our destination, then he closed the door behind us, locking me in with him.

The carriage lurched, and I tumbled sideways into Ryvin's waiting arms. His reflexes were so quick, I hadn't even seen him move. His large hands gripped my bare forearms. "You alright?"

Quickly, I righted myself and moved away from his touch, but it wasn't before that familiar sizzle danced across my skin. I hated that I reacted to him so strongly. Visions of him pressed against me last night made my face heat. "I'm fine."

This was not going to happen. I was not going to do anything physical with this man. Blowing out a slow breath, I pictured the tumbling ocean waves, the wind rustling the trees, anything to get my mind off how hard his cock had been against my belly last night.

The carriage made its way down the long driveway and I stared at the tall, elegant Cyprus trees that bordered each side.

A few of the trees were browning in places, something I'd never seen before. Welcoming the distraction, I studied them, noting all the trees that looked sick. It was odd. I'd have to mention it to my father. His grandfather had planted the trees, and they were a point of pride to the royal family.

I wondered how long they'd been in this shape and realized I hadn't left the palace in months. Perhaps this little excursion wasn't the worst thing I could do. It would be nice to see beyond the palace grounds. Though I had to admit, I wish it was with different company. What would the regulars at the Opal say when they saw me?

It had been years since I'd been there. Were the same people still sitting at the bar? Was it the same guards at the base of the stairs leading up to the private rooms? I wondered if the games of chance had changed or if the dancers were different women.

In the last few years, while I'd been so focused on my goals, I'd done very little to entertain myself aside from the occasional tumble with David.

If teenage me met current me, she wouldn't recognize herself. Maybe that was a good thing.

"Tell me about this place? You're not leading me to some sort of trap, are you?" he asked.

I smirked. "Now you're making me feel bad. I should have thought of setting up a trap."

"Well, at least I know you're not trying to kill me."

"Not right now," I said.

He chuckled. "Angry at yourself for last night, I see?"

"I don't know what you're talking about." Ignoring it was the best possible solution. I only wished I had the luxury of blaming it on too much wine.

"You're wearing a dagger on your thigh," he said.

"I'm sure you have weapons on you," I countered.

"No need for weapons. As I said, I have no intentions of hurting you or any of your people."

"Then explain the guards in combat armor," I pointed out. "We could have ridden in on horses. You chose to have them with us, drawing attention and looking threatening."

"You'd be surprised, but we're not very popular in Athos," he said.

"I wonder why," I deadpanned.

He opened his mouth to speak but I cut him off, "Don't bother. I'm not going to believe that you're a good guy no matter what you say."

He shrugged. "I would never call myself the good guy."

I let that thought linger between us, turning my attention back out the window.

"So this place we're going?"

I sighed. "The Black Opal. It's basically a den of vices. Drinking, gambling, fucking, anything you want, you can find it there."

"Sounds intriguing. And also the last place I'd expect to see a princess," he said.

I shrugged. "We all have our secrets, ambassador."

"That we do," he agreed.

CHAPTER 9

The carriage attracted plenty of attention as we entered the outskirts of the city. We rode past small, hastily built shops with rickety wood walls and thatched roofs. Crates of fruit were stacked outside them and inside I saw a variety of goods for sale. Fabric, yarn, blankets, rugs, even a few items that looked like dolls or other simple toys.

There were more of these shops than I recalled, and a lump rose in my throat at the sight of families huddled around them, desperately flagging us down in the hopes of a sale.

The worst part was that the shops gave way to what I suspected were homes. So many of them. My brow furrowed. How had things gotten this bad? There were at least a hundred simple, unstable looking buildings hastily thrown together out here. Laundry hung from lines strung between homes and shoeless, dirty children raced through the makeshift streets.

"This is the life you want for your people?" Ryvin asked.

I didn't turn to look at him, and I didn't respond. This was no life. These people were struggling. They'd have no running water out here and those children were miles from the closest royal funded school. Had this always been here and I'd ignored it or not noticed?

I shook my head. I'd have noticed. This was new. Sometime in the last year, things had gotten so much worse than they ever had been. I'd seen a few shacks last time I'd been through, but nothing like this. I would have to ask Lagina about this. There were things going on in the kingdom that I wasn't privy to, but I didn't know things had gotten this bad.

The carriage rolled on, leaving the slum behind to enter the city proper. The dilapidated buildings were replaced by whitewashed structures that had stood for decades or longer. Sturdy buildings with faded blue roofs. Small cracks in the aging stucco were hastily patched, causing a glaring streak of white like a lightning bolt where they'd painted over the crack against the faded, dingy white of the original paint.

The shops here had glass windows and actual doors. The people walking around wore sandals and traditional peplos dresses or long tunics. Some of them stopped to look at the carriage as it passed, but many were too engaged in their own activities to notice us. The carriage shook as the dirt road transitioned to stone, making our ride bumpier as we continued forward.

The deeper we went into the city, the more elaborate and beautiful the buildings were. The paint was brighter, the cracks in the stucco were covered and painted over, making them nearly invisible. The roofs were brilliantly blue, blending in with the sky above.

None of the people on the walkways so much as looked up from their conversations as we passed. We were no longer the only carriage on the street and they weren't surprised by our presence.

It wasn't long before we pulled up in front of The Black Opal, the building located in a prime position in the heart of the city. The main floor was obstructed by a large white wall, leaving only the second floor and the massive roof visible.

It was the only building in town that had forgone the traditional blue roof, choosing instead to paint theirs black. The rest of the building was immaculately painted bright white, creating a stark contrast with the dark roof.

An archway sprawled across a stone walkway, lined on either side with meticulously groomed flowers. It made the place seem innocent and classy, like it was leading to a temple rather than a house of ill repute.

Four guards stood outside the archway, ready to stop anyone who was deemed below their standards. Visitors must pass through them to access the courtyard beyond before even stepping foot into the building itself.

There were rules at the Opal, and they were taken seriously. You must have coin to spend, you must not speak to anyone who wears a veil to cover their face, and you must not share anything you see outside their walls. That included information about who you saw. Anyone who violated the rules was banned for life.

That was the draw for me when I was younger. Having a place I could go where nobody would use my title or judge what I was doing was far too appealing. I'd come here a few times after Lagina stopped visiting the city with me, the guards were only too happy to oblige my desire to attend. To this day, I was certain they'd never violated the rules or told my father we'd come here. Once inside, they'd attend to their needs while I did whatever I wished. It was the only place I could be just a normal girl instead of a member of the royal family.

"You'd rather I take the wealthy, connected citizens than save those from the slums?" Ryvin asked.

I turned to look at him. "You asked for people who were seeking escape. That's what this place is, escape."

"But would they want to flee forever or do they just come here for a few hours?" he asked.

"Does it matter?" I snapped. "Do you even care about the lives you're disrupting by taking anyone?"

His expression hardened and those gray eyes of his seemed to swirl and darken as if he had a thunderstorm brewing inside him. "I know exactly what I'm doing, Ara. I know exactly who and what I am, and I never pretended to be anything else. The question is, who are you? When tasked with sharing your city, you chose to bring me here. What does that say about you?"

My jaw tensed, and I glared at him. "Don't you dare try to pin this on me. I am not the one taking people away from their families."

"Yet, you'd like to ask me to spare certain people, would you not?"

My brow furrowed slightly before I realized I'd given myself away.

He smirked. "I thought so. You'd allow strangers to go in the place of your friends. You and your sisters are safe. And you'd give up any one of the strangers in that establishment if it meant it stayed that way. Perhaps you and me aren't so different after all."

"I'm nothing like you," I hissed. "If I had a choice, I'd send no-one at all."

"But that's not an option. Someone must go," he said. "And I don't see you stepping up to volunteer." He opened the door of the carriage and stepped out before turning to offer me his hand. "Shall we?"

I ground my teeth together, furious at him. He was wrong. He was the one with the power here. I wasn't choosing people for their death; he was the one doing that. "I can exit without your assistance."

He dropped his hand. "Of course, your highness."

The title felt like a slur coming from him. Fuming, I leaped out of the carriage and walked away from him, eager to get lost in the bowels of the Opal. He could find his own way from here.

Chin high, I walked to the guards, and they eyed me suspiciously as I approached. I paused, just long enough to throw my most pretentious glare their way. It was a look I'd studied from Queen Ophelia. The guards practically withered, lowering their heads in acknowledgement of my position. It was the only acknowledgement I'd get here, as it was supposed to be anonymous.

"Go ahead, lady," one of them said, his tone respectful.

At least I'd picked up something I could use from the queen. I kept my chin high as I passed them, unconcerned about my charge. If they barred Ryvin from entering, that was his problem.

I took a deep breath as I walked through the courtyard, breathing in the scent of flowers and damp earth. Unlike most of the courtyards in homes, this one wasn't just stone and space. To my right were rows of bright pink peonies surrounding a statue of Dionysus. Water flowed from his raised cup into a small pool around him.

On my left was a bed of aster flowers in every color of the rainbow. A smaller statue was tucked into the flowers, making it more difficult to see. The winged form of Astraeus was entwined with his wife, Eros. The lovers were locked together in an embrace as if they were the only two people in the universe. The dawn and the dusk, together as one.

I shuddered as I recalled the nickname Ryvin had used on me. I was no star, and I was not worthy of a name like Asteri.

As much as I hated to admit it, Ryvin was right. I did nothing to help the people in my kingdom. What good was traveling to the wall to defend them from dragon attacks when they were starving here?

Footsteps shook me from my thoughts, and I glanced back to see the ambassador entering the courtyard. Today was not my lucky day. The guards seemed to think he was worthy of coming inside. But I knew this place, and he didn't. It was easy enough to get lost.

"Ara," Ryvin called. "Aren't you going to show me around?"

"And be accused of condemning my own people? No, thanks. I think you can manage on your own from here." I walked forward and slipped through the beaded curtain that covered the open doorway.

The scent of herbs and incense and food hit me all at once. People lounging on couches imbibing in hookah while others sipped drinks from gold cups. Topless servants, both men and women, wandered the space, offering food from gold plates. Couples or groups engaged in carnal activities on plush violet couches, while others were content to eat and talk.

I quickly crossed through the lounge, making my way to the back of the building. Passing through another beaded doorway, I entered the gaming hall. Tables were full of patrons throwing coins into piles as they enjoyed various games of chance. It was loud in here, the conversations and laughter a constant hum inside the smaller room.

I continued, entering yet another room where seats were set in small circles, each one surrounding a nude dancer who performed for the small group. The spectators didn't speak here, making the music and the dancers the primary focus.

Cutting between the groups of seating, I took the door on

the right, finally reaching my destination. A rush of humidity and heat greeted me when I opened the closed door. Damp stone stairs led down, and I followed, to the belly of the Opal.

This was where I'd spent my time when I visited. The Opal was built atop an ancient spring and they'd constructed several pools and bathing spaces. The water was heated from the earth, making the lower levels warm no matter the weather outdoors.

The pools were less popular than the upstairs entertainment, and like the rest of the place, there were strict rules. Two pools were open for basically anything you were after, while the other two were dedicated to solitude. There was no talking, and no touching allowed. Because most visitors came to indulge in other activities, these quiet pools were usually abandoned. Meaning, I could have some time to soak up the warm water and escape reality.

I walked past the largest pool, looking away from the people who were enjoying each other's company, toward an arched doorway leading to a smaller, quiet pool.

As usual, it was empty. An attendant greeted me, a stack of towels in her hands. I pulled a few coins from my purse. "Any way I can get the back pool to myself?"

She nodded, accepting the coins before leading me through a closed door to the smallest pool. It was much larger than a bathtub, but probably not big enough to fit more than four or so comfortably. This was my favorite space in the Opal. Sure, I'd indulged in other activities on occasion, but the quiet space and warm water were so soothing.

Ryvin could do whatever it was he wanted to do, and I could sit in here. I knew my father had asked me to get close to him, but I couldn't bring myself to do it. I'd already gotten too close last night.

The attendant returned and quietly set down two plush

towels on a bench near the water. "Can I bring you anything else?"

"I'm fine, thank you," I said.

She inclined her head, then left the room, and I breathed in the scent of sulfur and damp rock. Why had I stayed away from here for so long? This was just what I needed. Some time to think before I faced Ryvin again.

I set my clothes next to the towels on the bench, then padded over to the pool. Carefully, I dipped a toe in, testing the water. It was hot and tendrils of steam rose from the green-gray water, inviting me to climb inside.

Using the stone steps, I descended into the warmth and felt my whole body relax as I sank deeper. Dipping down, I leaned against the side, letting the water lap around my neck.

How had I gotten myself into this mess? I told my father and David I would help, but how was I supposed to show kindness to this man? If he even was a man. I never saw fangs, but that didn't mean anything. He'd told me repeatedly that he was dangerous, a monster. I knew I should stay away, but I had promised my father.

And I wasn't sure I wanted to stay away. That was the part that scared me the most.

I pushed the thought from my head and reminded myself I had to find a way to make this work. My father expected me to show him around and he was holding my future hostage if I didn't do as he wished.

It wasn't like I could sneak off and join the soldiers at the wall. All it would take was one message from my father and I'd be shipped back to the palace.

Plus, there was the state of Athos to consider. I'd never been privy to the goings on of the kingdom. Lagina attended the meetings with our father, preparing to ascend the throne on a moment's notice should our father be incapable. But she'd never said a word. I thought things were the same as they had been. There had always been strife; always been those who were struggling, but I thought there were systems in place to help. If there were, why were the slums expanding?

Guilt made my chest tight. How had I been so blind to the challenges my own people were facing? I'd been so cloistered in the palace, so well-protected and cut-off that I didn't even know what was really happening in my kingdom. I wanted to go to the wall to help my people, but the people in the city were suffering more than I knew. There had to be a way I could make a difference.

David's face came to my mind. His pleading expression as he asked me to try to help his sisters. My own family was safe from the Choosing, but no others were excluded. It was another way we were failing our people, as Ryvin had pointed out. I wasn't volunteering to sail to Konos, but there had to be other ways I could help. It wasn't enough, I knew that, but perhaps I could help David's sisters. I owed him at least that much. Aside from my sisters, he was my only friend in the palace.

A sound caught my attention, and I turned, expecting to see the servant. Instead, I caught Ryvin just as he threw his tunic next to mine.

"What are you doing?" I quickly spun around and pressed my chest to the wall, hiding as much of me as I could.

He pulled down his trousers without turning to face me, and my eyes widened as I stared at the most perfect ass I'd ever seen. He turned, hands on his hips, completely naked in front of me.

I drank him like a woman dying of thirst. His broad chest and muscular shoulders demonstrated dedication to keeping himself in top form. His stomach was firm and I could see the muscles leading me right to that vee at his hips. I tried to resist, but my eyes darted lower, taking all of him in.

And there was plenty to take.

I squeezed my eyes shut and turned away from him, covering my breasts. "This space is occupied. Try one of the other pools. I think you'll appreciate the company more."

"I think I'd rather be in here with you," he said.

"I paid for the room," I said.

"I pay better," he countered.

I heard the splash of the water indicating that he'd joined me. Furious, I opened my eyes. "You need to go."

"You're welcome to leave, Princess," he teased.

I gritted my teeth. He knew if I left, he'd get a view of everything. The water wasn't clear enough to show all the details, so I had more coverage in here than I would making my way to my clothes.

"I don't suppose you'd turn away while I left?" I asked.

"Why should I? You didn't look away from me." He leaned against the edge, resting his elbows outside the water as if he owned the small pool we occupied.

My cheeks heated and the memory of him standing there like the statue of a god flared to life. Add in the way he'd pressed against me last night and I could feel the growing need.

"Why do you insist on torturing me?" I asked. "You know I don't like you, yet you ask for my company and follow me."

"Don't tell me you've forgotten last night so quickly, Asteri," he said.

"Don't call me that. And I didn't ask for that," I replied.

"You didn't ask me to stop, and you certainly didn't seem to mind my advances."

"There's plenty of willing and ready women upstairs. Find one of them," I snapped.

"Maybe that's why I stay. I can't recall the last time a woman resisted me."

I scoffed. "You certainly think highly of yourself. I imagine you get enough indifference when you're home. The women here know who you are. They figure if they bed you, you won't take them away. Or they can beg a favor."

"That's probably true. But I am very desired back home." He shrugged.

"Then go home. Fuck those monsters you serve and leave us alone."

"I will. But you misunderstand my position. I don't serve them; they serve me," he said.

My brow furrowed as I took in his words. Part of me wanted to pry, but I shut down the questions. It didn't matter what his rank was or how he was perceived where he lived. He was temporary here.

"There are few places I can go where I'm not recognized and treated differently," he admitted. "Based on the fact that you seem to know your way around this place, a place where names are not permitted and titles are ignored, I get the sense that you know what that is like. You're one of the people who use this place as an escape, are you not?"

"You know nothing about me," I said.

"I know you wish to leave your kingdom, to serve at the wall," he said. "You're wasting your time. The dragons could destroy your kingdom in an instant if they wished to do so. Your wall is nothing more than a security blanket. Like something a child keeps to maintain the illusion of safety."

"My future is none of your business," I said. "And you know nothing about our war. Your king isn't involved."

"Our treaty never included the dragons. Our kingdom protects your people from the fae, the wolves, and the vampires."

"Except for the Choosing," I said bitterly.

"We're going in circles, Ara," he said.

Goosebumps shivered down my arms at the sound of my name on his lips. My nostrils flared in frustration. I wanted to hate him. I *did* hate him, but my body continued to react to him.

"Isn't there another way?" I asked, making my voice sweeter. Perhaps I could change tactics, gain his favor as my father hoped. Maybe I could put an end to this whole archaic thing. "Why humans? Why us?"

"This is the only way," he said.

My shoulders slumped. "You won't take a hundred, will you?"

"The reprieve has passed. I am to take one-hundred this year," he said.

"Why?" I asked. "If you could live with fourteen, why increase?"

"Now you wish me to take the fourteen?" he said with a smirk.

"I don't want you to take any of them!"

He moved closer, and I shoved away, keeping space between us. I shot him a warning glare. He grinned, his expression more predator than man.

"Perhaps you could help to change my mind. What could you offer me to save your people?" he asked.

"To save them all?" I knew I'd do just about anything if there was a chance of ending this forever. But was that because I truly cared or because there was a part of me that wanted him to keep advancing on me? Part of me that wanted him to come closer. To pin me down and hold me in place while he got to know every inch of my body intimately. I could almost picture his lips closing around my nipple, those gray eyes looking up at me with admiration and lust.

I pushed the thought aside, internally screaming at my traitorous body. What was wrong with me?

"Who am I kidding? You're just a spoiled princess," he said, then he climbed out of the water. "I can't imagine ever seeing you sacrifice anything for anyone but yourself."

"You don't know me." I squeezed my hands into fists, my fingernails biting into my palms. He was wrong. I was going to join the army; I was willing to sacrifice everything for my people.

"Even if I wanted to make a bargain with you, there are things beyond my power. The tributes must go; and they will go, with or without me to ferry them to the island." He grabbed a towel and wrapped it around his waist. "You can't see it, but I'm the only thing preventing your people from losing everything. Without me, without the tributes you send, Athos wouldn't even exist."

His words held the weight of a warning and though I had no reason to trust him, I believed him. As much as I might want to see him and his men leave this place, the arrangement of the tributes was the only thing holding the tenuous peace between our kingdoms. To be free of the Choosing, we'd have to do something far more drastic.

"You should get dressed, Princess. I wouldn't want you to miss your time with David." Wrapped in a towel, he grabbed his clothes and left the room.

CHAPTER 10

Ryvin was waiting for me the second I stepped through the door. "Let's go."

"You got everything you needed?" I asked.

"I did," he said.

My stomach twisted. I wanted to know if that meant that he'd chosen the people he'd take back to Konos. Had he found all of them here? That no talking about what happens in the Opal rule wasn't going to survive the gossip. I'd brought the Konos ambassador here. Even if people didn't use my title, they knew who I was. If he pulled all of them from here, it would show that the crown supported, and maybe even helped choose the tributes.

Wasn't that what I'd done? I'd brought him here, specifically.

Maybe I wasn't any better than him.

He was moving so quickly, I had to push myself to keep up, but I didn't mind. I wanted out of here before I had to fully come to terms with what I'd done.

Two of his men were waiting in the courtyard, and they turned and walked toward the exit as soon as they saw us. My pulse kicked up. Something was wrong. This wasn't a normal reaction.

"What's happening?" I asked.

"Just get in the carriage." Something about his tone sent shivers down my spine. Part of me wanted to argue, or refuse to comply, but it was as if I could sense the need for a quick escape.

My ego might have had something to do with it too. The thought of staying behind at the Opal with those I just condemned was too much. I was a coward.

Out of the corner of my eye, I caught sight of a massive group of people racing toward us. They were carrying weapons and tools. Screaming and cursing, they moved forward as one group.

Ryvin's guards moved to intercept them, and the reality of what was happening hit me. We were under attack. My people had finally had enough, and they were going to eliminate the delegation from Konos.

I froze in place, divided between my own safety and my desire to watch Ryvin and his men go down.

"Move, Ara," Ryvin commanded.

"No," I sat. "Go fight them. It's what you deserve."

"We don't have time for this." He grabbed me and lifted me off the ground, throwing me over his shoulder with ease. Startled, I kicked and screamed, trying to wiggle free. His grip was too tight, and I ended up tossed into the carriage like a child. Ryvin climbed in after me and slammed the door.

I rose to my feet, but the carriage lurched, sending me down. Regaining my balance, I stood again. "Let me out of here."

Ryvin captured me, pinning my arms to my side. He glared down at me as I struggled against him. "Are you insane? Do you want to die? You think they're only angry with me? You think they won't go after the royal family that created and allowed this arrangement?"

My jaw tensed, and I met his glare with one of my own. "This is all your fault."

"I own what I am, Princess," he said. "How long has your family masqueraded as the savior while sending their own people away?"

"We can't fight the monsters," I said. "We're not strong enough."

"Your ancestors never even tried." He loosened his grip, and I stepped back, putting a little space between us. The carriage hit a bump, and I fell, landing in the seat. We were speeding down the road, lurching and bouncing as we raced over the uneven stones.

"What are you talking about?" I demanded, trying to stand. The carriage jostled and again, I was knocked off balance. Ryvin caught me and guided me back to the seat before sitting down next to me.

"My people couldn't fight. Whatever you were told, it was wrong. We were nearly dead. The deal with *your* king was our only option." I knew the history. I knew we'd been on the brink of extinction.

"Athos built a wall keeping everyone, including other humans, out. *Your* king was out for himself and sought an alliance without battle. He suggested the terms; we accepted," he explained. "Even if I was dead, the tributes would be sent. Your father would complete the bargain without question. He always does. It benefits him just as much as it benefits my kingdom. Perhaps you should ask him to share his truth one of these days. Then you can make your own decisions."

I stared at him, my mind drawing a blank. Mouth dry, I struggled to find the right words. I had learned the history from my father. He'd taught me himself. He hated the Choosing, but told me it was necessary. "No. No, that's wrong. The monsters appeared and started to turn humans or kill them. We fled here, as refugees. We didn't have a choice."

"Believe what you want to believe, Princess, but there are no heroes in either of our stories," he said darkly.

Suddenly, the carriage halted, swaying so much I worried it would tip. Ryvin grabbed me, pulling me to his chest. I sucked in a breath, my distress washing away in his strong arms. The movement subsided and Ryvin released me. "Are you hurt?"

I shook my head, fear slowly seeping back into my bones as I sat in eerie silence. We'd stopped, but there was no indication of why. No guards shouting, no animal noises, no wind. Nothing.

A blood-curdling scream punctuated the stillness, followed by a growl. Something large slammed into the side of the carriage, sending me forward into Ryvin's arms. Once again, I felt oddly safe. It was wrong. So very, very wrong. But I lingered there in his embrace, listening to the unmistakable sounds of battle erupting around us.

"Wait here," he said, shoving me from his hold.

He lifted the cushion of the seat and grabbed a sword from a stash of weapons. I raised an impressed eyebrow.

"I can fight, you know," I said.

"I know. But I don't trust that you'd fight to defend me and my men," he said with a growl.

I couldn't argue that. I'd wanted to see him defeated, welcomed it, even. If it put an end to the Choosing, I'd kill him myself.

He exited, then slammed the door behind him, leaving me alone with my confused and swirling thoughts. Had our ancestors truly just agreed to sending tributes without a fight? Did people find out? Was that why they were attacking us now after so many decades of ignoring the realities of the Choosing?

The carriage shuddered and my whole body tensed. It didn't matter what he'd said. There was a battle going on beyond these walls and I had to make a choice.

I could stay here and wait for someone to find me, or I could join the fray. The Konos guards were massively outnumbered, and there was a possibility the angry mob would find me here alone. What happened when they did? Would they harm me for being with them?

What would happen if the entire Konos delegation was destroyed? Would it stop the Choosing? Would it help my people?

It wouldn't.

As much as I considered ending the ambassador's life myself, I knew there'd be repercussions on a massive scale if the Konos delegation didn't return.

Like the Fae King himself coming after Athos.

I knew if Ryvin died, it would be worse for the people in my kingdom.

Fuck. This was so bad. I couldn't sit in here and do nothing. The glint of steel caught my eye, and I grabbed a sword from the stash. It was heavier than what I trained with, but it was sharp and ready for battle.

I didn't want to fight my own people, but I wasn't stupid enough to pretend I didn't know what they'd do to me when they found me here.

If I had a choice between defending myself and putting up a fight or sitting here and waiting for the worst to happen, I knew what I had to do. One extra sword might help. If I could even take out one of our foes, it might be enough to help tip the scales.

The carriage shook again as something hit the side. I

caught myself before falling, then tightened my grip on my sword. Whatever I was about to walk into was going to be dangerous and I'd never seen actual battle. I sucked in a breath and reminded myself that this was what I'd been training for. I wanted to fight dragons. If I couldn't make a stand against a group of regular citizens, how could I handle anything worse?

Then I shoved open the door.

A massive wolf lunged past me, teeth bared, growling as it charged a man on my left. I leapt from the carriage, then spun just in time to see the wolf take the man down. The wolf's jaws bit into the man's throat. His cries turned to gurgling sounds as the creature yanked the flesh from his neck. Blood spurted from the wound, covering the man and the wolf in bright crimson.

The beast turned and looked toward me and I swore I saw him narrow his eyes, as if taking me in, before he turned and ran toward a large group engaged in combat. Another wolf stalked up to me, then stopped in front of me. He sniffed me. The blood on his muzzle was still shiny and wet. I tensed. What was going on here?

The creature seemed unbothered by me and took a few steps away, but stood watching me. I knew the beast wasn't a normal wolf. He had to be a shifter. Which meant at least some of the men from Konos could change their shape. A shiver ran through me.

I knew the wolf shifters were aligned with the fae, but I never expected to see one up close. I also always thought there'd be something to give them away. Aside from the fangs on Orion, all the others could pass as human. What if they were all shifters?

Someone yelled, and I returned my thoughts to the

moment at hand. I couldn't afford to be distracted. Refocusing, I looked around quickly, taking stock of my options.

The battle seemed to be ahead of me, away from the carriage. Ryvin and a few of his black-clad guards were fighting their way through the onslaught. They were greatly outnumbered, but based on the fallen bodies of humans, without any guards next to them, it was clear they were holding their own. Maybe they didn't need me after all.

I whispered a prayer to Ares, then inched toward the fray, watching for an opening. This was nothing like my one-on-one training. Ryvin was surrounded by threats on all sides, fighting multiple attackers at once.

I was so not prepared for this. Belan was right, real battles didn't follow the rules of engagement. Perhaps I should return to the carriage. They were far less at a disadvantage than I anticipated.

Someone broke free of the crowd and charged toward me, letting out a cry as he raced forward, sword raised above his head. My eyes widened. No time to go back. This was happening. I gripped the hilt and prepared to fight him, but the wolf was faster.

The creature moved in front of me, cutting off my attacker. In a blur of gray fur and flashing teeth, my opponent was down, his arm completely torn from his body, still grasping the sword.

I frowned. "I could have taken him."

The wolf almost looked skeptical.

More fighters closed in around Ryvin and my chest tightened, fear gripping me from the inside. I'd imagined him dying, but now that I was faced with it, I wasn't sure what I wanted. It felt wrong. And I hated that it wasn't because I was concerned about Athos.

I was worried about him. But I wasn't about to admit that

to anyone. Shoving the sensation deep down, I kept my thoughts on Athos. If the Konos delegation was killed, we'd be punished. That was the only reason I was helping.

At least that's what I kept telling myself.

I moved forward, but the wolf cut me off, letting out a warning growl. I sidestepped him, and he followed, staying in front of me, blocking my path no matter where I moved.

"Stop that," I called. "I can help. Don't you see? Ryvin is in danger." Even as I said the words, I could feel the truth of it. More of the mob was turning on him, abandoning the other guards to fight one-on-one, while the remainder teamed up against the ambassador.

He was a strong fighter, but the attackers kept coming. He couldn't hold them off forever. Where had all these men come from? How were they so organized?

The wolf growled again, baring its teeth.

I shook my head. This was crazy. I was being guarded by a wolf while watching my people attack my enemy. I should be cheering for them, encouraging them, helping them. But anxiety twisted in my stomach, desperate to help Ryvin. Not my people. The ambassador I swore I hated.

"The princess!" Someone shouted, and I looked up just as a whole contingent of the attackers broke off and raced for me.

CHAPTER 11

The wolf lunged forward, taking down the first man who approached, before moving to another target. He took down several men effortlessly before a few circled him, then several broke off and came for me.

I gripped my sword even tighter, praying that my sweaty palms didn't cause me to lose my weapon. Getting into a defensive position, I prepared for impact. I was surprised how quickly my body reacted to my attacker, my sword practically moving of its own accord as I struck to defend myself. Lunging away from a second sword, I desperately tried to fend off the men who now encircled me.

They pulled back, staring at me with amusement. I gritted my teeth and tightened my grip on my weapon. "Stay back. I have no quarrel with you." A bead of sweat slid down my back and my body felt like it was vibrating in anticipation.

"Well, well, what do we have here?" a red-headed man with a long red beard said. "It's our lucky day, boys. We get to take out the Konos monsters, and we get a piece of the royal bastards who send us to our deaths."

"I'm not your enemy," I said.

"Tell that to my cousin who was sent in the last Choosing." Red spit on the ground. "Or to Lou over there who never met his mama cause they took her from him when he was still in swaddling clothes."

Lou, a short man with a huge stomach, bared his rotting teeth at me. "You sit pretty in that palace while the rest of us suffer."

"No. It's not like that." But it was like that. I'd seen it with my own eyes. These men had every right to be angry. What had I ever sacrificed?

They moved closer, and I took a step back. I didn't want to fight my own people. "Stop this violence. It's not going to get you what you're after. It won't change the treaty we have with the Fae."

"What do you know of the treaty, highness? You and your family enjoy all the luxuries from across the sea and, in exchange, it only costs you a few of your people. Do you even know the names of those you've sent to their doom?" he hissed.

"There are other ways to change things," I pleaded. "Come back to the palace with me. We can talk to my father. Figure something out."

"Maybe we shouldn't kill her so quickly," the third man said. He had a scar that went from his forehead to his jaw, just missing his right eye. "I've always wondered what royal pussy tastes like."

"I'm not going to leave anything of her for you to taste." The first man charged forward, and I moved fast, defending myself as I'd been taught. My body reacted on instinct, my blade finding its target, before I even realized what I'd done. My muscles screamed as I shoved my sword deeper through flesh and muscle. Blood sprayed, warm and wet, coating my bare arms and making the handle slippery. I choked up on the blade as realization of what I'd done raced through me like cold water in my veins.

Time seemed to slow down and sound receded as my eyes met my attacker's. Fear flashed, followed by anger so intense I could feel it to my bones.

I'd killed a man.

One of my own people.

Panic seized, making my breaths come out in rapid succession. The sounds around me faded, the world tunneling so all I saw was my blade lodged into flesh.

"Fight, Ara!" Someone screamed, the sound of my name breaking my trance. Sound blared to life, the battle around me encompassing me like a jolt, reminding me of what was at stake.

Yanking the sword free, I shoved the body toward another attacker. The dead man slammed into him, knocking the other man to the ground. He made a surprised grunting sound, but I was already turning toward the other threats.

I didn't want to kill anyone, but I wasn't about to die like this. I shut it all down. All the emotions, all the connections, all the feelings. These weren't my people. These men were threats.

"After I kill you, I'm going to gouge out your eyes and tear out your tongue so you have to wander the afterlife blind and dumb." The scarred man charged.

Anger seethed like molten lava beneath my skin. These men weren't going to let me live. There was no talking my way out of this. Fear was gone. Replaced only by the overwhelming need to fight back. To prevent these men from doing terrible things to me.

Baring my teeth, I moved in to attack, not bothering to respond. The scarred man's eyes widened in surprise as he fumbled to quickly defend himself. My blade struck his, hard and true, and his sword flew from his grip. He'd underestimated me, just as Belan had told me he would.

I didn't hesitate, and as if driven by the anger brewing inside, I shoved my sword through his stomach quickly, then pulled it out. He fell to his knees before dropping backward with a sickening thud. He'd take some time to die, but I knew the blow was fatal.

I wheeled around to face the other man, who had tossed the body of his fallen friend aside. Panting and hair sticking to the sweat on my brow, I glared at him. "It's not too late to walk away. I don't want to kill any of you."

"You bitch." Red snarled, then lifted a pair of daggers. He charged forward, and I ducked down, making myself small. As soon as he was above me, I pointed my blade up and exploded to my feet, aiming for his neck.

One of his daggers sliced across my arm, but my blade was already lodged in his throat. He made a stifled gurgling sound, his daggers dropping to the ground. He flailed wildly, as if trying to remove my weapon, but his movements were stunted and unbalanced. I yanked on my weapon, but it stuck where it was buried in his throat. I had to use my foot for leverage, sending him backward while I recovered my sword. He landed on his back, his head lolling to the side as blood poured from the wound on his neck. He convulsed once, then stopped moving.

My arm was sticky and wet with my own blood, but I couldn't even feel the pain. My heart was racing, but my vision seemed to tunnel in on the final man. He was huge, and I was surprised that he had held back while I fought the others.

I was lucky they hadn't all come for me at the same time, lucky they had underestimated me. Or maybe they'd been trying to capture me alive rather than kill me.

Shoulders heaving as I took rapid breaths, I stared him down. "This is your only chance to run."

I wasn't sure what was driving me or why the anger had evolved into a satisfied sort of rush that was almost enjoying the bloodshed. I shoved the thought away, not wanting to allow myself to continue those dark thoughts. This was survival, nothing more. I was here because I didn't have a choice. The man grunted, then pointed his sword at me. "I'm going to kill you, and then I'm going to defile your corpse."

"Go ahead and try," the words came out much more confident than I felt, but I wasn't about to let myself feel fear. Whatever had possessed me and was driving me was keeping me alive.

The sword was growing heavier, and I felt a little lightheaded. I knew the blood pouring down my arm was the culprit. I was going to start wearing down quickly, so if I was going to take this huge man out, it needed to be now. I wouldn't get another chance.

He charged me and I lifted my sword to defend myself and the familiar pang of steel meeting steel echoed through the air. My arms vibrated in response and I gritted my teeth as I shoved him back. He was strong and fighting him wasn't going to be as easy as the others. I managed to deflect and defend strike after strike, but I got the sense he was toying with me. He wasn't fooled by my dress or my title. We fought, much the same way I sparred against David. The movements and patterns familiar. As if we were working through choreography. Practicing instead of truly fighting.

He was wearing me out, and I was getting tired, moving slower with each impact.

I managed to get close, and drew my sword along his stomach, breaking skin but not causing enough damage to slow him down. He bellowed in pain but rounded on me, returning my attack with one of his own. His blade jabbed into my side and I howled, pulling back before he could shove his weapon in deeper. On instinct, I pressed my hand to my wound, hissing in pain. Blood poured from my side, my hand coated in scarlet. I'd avoided a death blow, but it was likely just prolonging the inevitable. I knew what a wound like this meant. I was on borrowed time. But there was no way I wasn't going to take this asshole out with me.

Grinning, he charged forward, and I lifted my sword to defend myself, but my grip weakened and it fell from my fingers, clattering against the stone road.

Gasping and wincing, I pressed my palm against the gushing wound and swallowed hard as I faced down death. I had tried, and I think David would be proud of how I had fought, but I wasn't prepared for this. Training with a sparring partner seemed ridiculous now that I'd faced a true fight. I'd been practically playing make-believe all these years.

As the hulking man stalked toward me, my mind raced with thoughts of my sisters and my life. They would be devastated to hear I'd met such a violent end. I was more concerned about the fact that I wouldn't be there to comfort them than I was that I was facing my own death.

My chest felt heavy, guilt squeezing my final breaths from my lungs. I'd let them all down. Especially Sophia. She had a sense of optimism about the world that would be crushed by this. I felt hollow and angry. This wasn't an honorable death. Belan was right, nobody critiqued the winners.

I thought I had more time. More time to explore the world, see beyond Athos. Do something important. Though I never admitted it aloud, I always felt like there was more out there for me. Now it seemed foolish. I wasn't special.

An image of Ryvin flashed in my mind. He was standing outside of the bath, smirking at me, a glint of mischief in his silver eyes. His muscles rippled and moved as he wrapped the towel around his waist. Longing surged, followed by deep and painful regret. I sucked in a breath of surprise. I hadn't expected to have him cross my final thoughts.

My attacker slowed, possibly mistaking my confusion as a reaction to him. He paused, then his head turned, reacting to something I hadn't noticed.

A blur of gray raced past me and a wolf leapt into the air, digging its claws into my attacker's chest. The man shoved his sword into the beast's side, then threw him aside as if he was a puppy. The wolf landed hard on the ground and let out a whimper. I screamed, horrified that the poor animal had been hurt trying to save me.

The creature tried to stand but collapsed to the ground, unable to rise. My attacker turned from me, lumbering toward the injured wolf. There was no time to waste.

Using every ounce of strength I had, I reached for my weapon, struggling to hold it upright. Carefully, I shuffled forward, closing in on the man. I stopped behind him, then using all my strength, I shoved my sword into his back.

It wasn't an honorable kill, but it was effective. The man fell to the ground, my blade still in his back. He spasmed a few times, locking hate-filled eyes on me until the movement stopped, and his eyes went glassy.

Blood seeped out in a puddle around him, and I knew he was gone. My shoulders sunk in relief as I let out a long breath. With my injuries and the searing pain, I wasn't sure I had much time left, but I could at least prevent my sisters from hearing that my body had been defiled.

Each breath was a struggle, and every movement sent stabbing pain to my side, but I had to get to the wolf, the creature who had saved my life. Stumbling forward, I made it to his side before dropping to my knees next to him.

"Thank you," I managed. Words were difficult, my

breathing strained. I stroked his coarse fur and felt the rise and fall of his breath.

"Are you alright?" It was a wolf, I knew it couldn't respond to me, but I had to do something. "How can I help you?"

The creature turned gentle, all too human eyes on me as it sucked in rattling breaths. Its paw moved to cover my hand, and I grasped it between my hands as if it were a human that I was trying to comfort.

"I'm here. I won't leave." Instinctively, I knew the wolf was on its last breaths. It had sacrificed its life to protect me and I could do nothing to return the favor except offer minimal comfort.

I stroked the fur around the creature's neck and kept my gaze on its gold eyes, offering a smile and soothing words. It wasn't long before the wolf's eyes closed and the breathing ceased.

Tears were streaming down my cheeks and rage burned red hot in my chest. This wolf wasn't one of my people. Yet it had died defending me from those I had sworn to protect.

This battle wasn't my enemies attacking, this was my own people. Wincing, I forced myself to stand, ignoring the injuries that were probably going to send me to the same place as the wolf in a matter of minutes. If I had anything left in me, I could help. I had to try. The problem was, I wasn't sure which side I was supposed to fight for.

My people had attacked me, but I still viewed Ryvin and his men as my enemies. Taking careful steps forward, I picked up a discarded dagger, knowing I wasn't capable of wielding anything larger right now. I moved on, taking in the scene around me.

The street was littered with bodies, mostly those of citizens of Athos, but I didn't feel sadness when I looked at them. They chose to do this. They chose to attack us. They wanted to harm, not just the ambassador and his delegation, but me as well. Their efforts wouldn't change anything. In fact, they might even start a war with the fae, which would make things so much worse for all of us.

Ryvin's men each had one opponent, and the ambassador himself was facing off against three. As I watched, one of his attackers fell and he turned to face the other two. They moved so quickly I couldn't get a good view of them. Or perhaps that was the fog of my injuries kicking in.

I hesitated, part of me still wanting to see him die. It might not solve the problem of the Choosing, but he was a monster, he told me as much himself. Yet, he wasn't the one who'd tried to kill me. And there was still that part of me that was drawn to him, even if I hated myself for it.

Pressing my palm to my wound, I winced as the confusing thoughts swirled in my tangled mind. My emotions were all over the place. Every time I tried to imagine Ryvin going down, fear gripped my chest, squeezing like a vise. Maybe it was my injuries, but it was almost like I was worried about him.

One by one, the black clad guards took down the citizens until the only fight remaining was Ryvin and his two opponents. I was nearing the fight, almost close enough that I could do something if I got a clear shot. If I had any energy left, that was.

Ryvin pushed his sword through the chest of one of his opponents, then pulled it out with ease, as if it had been shoved into air and not through bone and muscle. He spun to his remaining attacker, but stopped suddenly when he saw me.

Our eyes met, and it was like time stood still. I drank in the sight of him, blood splattered across his face and clothing, but none of it appeared to be his. Relief rushed in and that strange warm sensation I got all too often when I saw him filled my lower belly.

"Lookout!" I screamed, noticing too late that his opponent was on top of him.

Ryvin tore his gaze from me and returned to fight, but his sword was already knocked from his grip.

That's when I recognized the man who now held his blade to Ryvin's throat. "You traitor," I hissed.

"You weren't meant to get hurt, Ara. I told them to spare you," David said, his tone genuine. "Stay back. I'll take you home. Get you fixed up. Everything will go back to normal."

"I told you I wouldn't let him take your sisters," I said.

"You think that's what this is about?" David yelled, moving the blade tighter to Ryvin's throat. "This has to stop. I know you agree with me."

"I do, but this is the wrong way. If you kill him, it's going to make their king angry. He'll demand more. Or worse, he'll attack us. Please, David, don't do this," I pleaded.

"Let him go," One of the nearby guards said. There were four of them standing around piles of bodies. How many more of those deceased people were familiar faces? How many of my father's guards had been willing to sacrifice their lives and mine for a chance at taking down this delegation? Didn't they realize it would solve nothing?

"You take a step closer and I'll kill him," David warned.

"You're going to kill him anyway," one of the guards said. He'd lost his helmet during the fight and I recognized Orion, the man from dinner. A shiver ran down my spine as I recalled those fangs.

David had no chance.

Even if he killed Ryvin, the guard would take him out.

"David, there's no way out of this," I warned.

He narrowed his eyes. "I should have known you were lying to me. All this time, I thought you were different. But you're just another spoiled royal."

His words felt like a knife in my heart. I thought we were friends. I thought he knew me. "How could you say that?"

"Then do it," David said. "I see that blade in your hand. I know you've killed today. What's one more body? You should be the one to take him out. And then we can finish these others together."

I took another look at the destruction around us. Dozens of dead Athonians. None of the dead wore the black armor of Konos. "You'll never beat them."

"We can try," he said.

I stepped closer, all my focus on David. He was sweaty and pale, his breathing shallow. I couldn't see the wound, but I knew he was injured. Even if I wanted to fight against the other men, we'd never stand a chance. I was already on borrowed time and it was possible David was also at Death's door.

"You knew I'd be here," I said.

"I did," he confirmed.

"You told them where I might go." I realized my friendship with David was what had cost me. He knew exactly where I'd go if I went into the city.

"I got lucky," he said.

"No, you didn't. You know me better than anyone." As I said the words, the pain in my heart swelled. As much as I'd tried to keep my distance with him over the years, I'd let him in more than I realized. How many conversations had we had in the dark as he held me? How much had I told him? He knew everything about me. Possibly more than my sisters. "You were willing to let me die."

"I told them not to hurt you," he repeated. "But you know better than most, that sacrifices are necessary."

He was willing to let me die for this. For a false sense of hope that wouldn't change a thing. How could he be willing to risk so much? All these people, his life, and mine. "You're the one who told me the only way we could end this was if we killed the Fae King. What does this solve?"

I was nearly to David, and I could feel the stares of the others. Ryvin, especially, even if I wasn't looking at him.

David watched me carefully, a strange shine in his eyes. I'd never seen him like this, and it was a little unnerving. "They take from us, Ara. Now it's our turn to take something from them. Maybe they'll think twice about how they use us."

As I got closer, David shifted his hold on Ryvin, and I caught sight of his chest and stomach. His clothes were torn, and he was losing blood rapidly. I'd been right to guess he was injured, and from the looks of it, it was a miracle he was still standing.

"Let him go, David. We both need a healer," I said. "Come back with me. I'll get you a position on the wall. We'll leave this place. Together. Me and you. As it should be."

He shook his head. "Don't patronize me, Ara. I know what I mean to you."

"You don't, though," I said. "Because I never tell you. But I'm telling you now, David. We belong together. You don't want to go to the wall? We'll go somewhere else."

"It's too late for any of that," he said. "Kill him, Ara. Or I'll do it, so help me."

"Do it, Ara," Ryvin said. "End this and get back to the palace. You've lost too much blood already."

My heart thundered in my chest, and my limbs felt heavy.

Knees weak, I pushed forward, knowing what I had to do. It was wrong. So wrong. But I knew it was my best option. Even as my heart felt like it would tear in two, I moved closer, hating myself more with each breath.

David nodded, and I approached, stopping right in front of Ryvin. "I'm sorry," I said as I held up my dagger. Tears stung my eyes, and I blinked them away, trying to clear my vision. There was no going back after this.

I drove my dagger into David's throat.

CHAPTER 12

David crumbled to the ground and my throat tightened at the look of betrayal that flashed across his expression before he sucked in his last breath.

I turned away, squeezing my burning eyes tightly to try to hold back the tears. David's words about sacrifice were true. I knew in my bones that if I had ended Ryvin's life, the retribution against our people would be more than I was willing to accept. I also knew David's wounds were fatal.

Falling to my knees, I let the grief swell up inside me, making me shake as I continued to fight against the tears. When I opened my eyes, the world was blurry and faded. Cold seeped in, and the pain from my injuries slowed.

That was the other piece of my calculations. It wasn't just David who was finished on this plane; it was me as well. I'd lost too much blood, and I had seen enough soldiers brought in with wounds like mine to know the truth of what I was facing.

"Ara, you stupid woman," Ryvin hissed. "What have you done?"

I blinked, trying to focus on his face, and realized he must be holding me, but I couldn't feel him. "Don't hurt David's sisters," I managed, my voice gravelly and unrecognizable.

My eyes drifted closed, and I tasted the familiar copper tang of blood in my mouth. Then everything went black.

Muffled conversation sounded nearby and I couldn't figure out why my sisters were in my bedroom. Then, I realized it wasn't just my sister's voice, there were male voices as well. I tried to open my eyes, but they wouldn't budge. My head throbbed, my chest felt like it was on fire. I turned away from the sound and let darkness claim me again.

A hand brushed across my forehead, the touch soothing and warm. I leaned into it instinctively, yearning for comfort.

"Ara, stay with me," a male voice whispered.

"Is she awake?" another voice asked.

The hand moved from me, and I whimpered, desperate for that contact.

"Ara? Please, gods, please let her wake up," Sophia's sweet voice seemed to call to me, helping me stir from the depths.

My eyelids fluttered, the initial light too much. I groaned, then squeezed my eyes closed again before easing them open. I stared up at Sophia's tear-streaked face.

She jumped to standing and squealed in delight. I winced against the sound and let out a hiss of annoyance.

"Sorry," she said, leaning down to me. "Ara. Can you hear me?"

"I can hear you," I croaked. My throat stung and everything hurt. My head ached, my chest felt tight and stiff. As I moved, I felt the sting of the cut on my arm and the soreness of all my bruises.

The memory of the attack and the fight flooded in and I tried to sit up too quickly, causing my head to spin.

"Take it easy," Sophia said, guiding me up and adjusting pillows behind me so I could sit. "You've been through a lot."

"I should be dead," I said, my voice still rough.

"You nearly were," she said. "The ambassador saved you."

I frowned, recalling the sacrifice I'd made to save him. My chest ached more than I thought possible. What had I done?

"David." His name was like a curse on my lips. I'd killed my friend. Killed David to save Ryvin.

Grief settled in around me like a thick, dark cloud. I'd killed him in cold blood. Then there were the others I'd killed. Citizens of Athos. My own people.

Sophia stroked my hair. "Yes, David is dead. The ambassador told us how he died to protect you. How lucky were we that he was in the city at the same time? I can't imagine what would have happened without him."

My brow furrowed. "What? That's not..."

"Hush," Sophia kissed my brow, "you've been through a lot. Wait here. I'll call the healer."

I stared after her, my head spinning as I tried to recall the events of the fight. That wasn't what happened, was it? Was it possible I was remembering things wrong?

My room was the same. It looked just as it had the last time I'd been here. White curtains blew in the breeze. My desk and vanity were where they belonged. My bed looked the same. The arched doorway leading to my bathing chamber was the same.

"Oh, thank Apollo," Mila said as she swept into the room, a bundle of linens in her arms. She dropped them on my desk, then walked over to me. "How are you feeling? Is there anything I can get you?"

"I'm not sure yet," I admitted. "How long have I been here?"

"Three days," she said, clicking her tongue as if I was a misbehaving child. "I was starting to worry you wouldn't wake."

"Even I know she's too stubborn for that," a male voice cut in.

I looked over to see Ryvin standing in my doorway. My eyes took him in, searching him for injuries. He was in a dark gray tunic and black trousers today, looking as handsome as ever. He was unshaven, and his dark hair was mussed, as if he hadn't bothered to look in a mirror for days. To his credit, it made him look even more attractive.

"The ambassador carried you back to the palace," Mila explained. "If not for him, you'd be dead."

I swallowed, recalling the injury I'd sustained. "I thought I was going to die."

"Not on my watch," Ryvin said.

Mila pressed her lips together into a line. I could imagine how conflicted she was feeling because I felt the same way. My emotions were a tangled mess. Relief that I was alive, guilt about those who were lost, and absolute confusion about why Ryvin would have bothered to save me in the first place. I should say thank you, but I couldn't bring myself to form the words. "And your men?" I asked instead, showing concern the only way I could at the moment.

"We only lost one," he said.

I nodded, recalling the wolf I'd comforted as he took his last breaths. Was that the man Ryvin was referring to? I had so many questions but I wasn't about to ask them in front of Mila.

"I'm glad you're awake," Ryvin said. "I'll check on you later."

The healer bustled in, shoving past Ryvin. "Out. Everyone out."

Mila threw him a nasty look but complied, and soon I was alone with Mythiuss, my father's best healer. The ancient man had taken care of our family since my grandfather was king. The fact that he was still around was a testament to his abilities.

He took the chair near my bed that had been occupied by Sophia, then peered at me through tiny eyes surrounded by wrinkles. His skin was paper thin and covered in dark spots. Tiny wisps of white hair sprouted from his head and coarser white hair grew in his ears, nose, and across two bushy white eyebrows.

He checked my arm, gently brushing rough fingers over my injury. I winced, preparing for pain, but found none. Confused, I looked at the place where I'd been cut. My brow furrowed. It was a pink, nearly healed scar. There was some lingering tenderness, but it wasn't as bad as it should be. Maybe I'd thought it was worse in the moment?

"I need to check your ribs," he said.

I nodded, then slowly pulled the simple white nightgown someone had dressed me in above my waist so my ribs were exposed. White bandages were wrapped around my midsection, bright red blood stained through the material.

Slowly, Mythiuss uncovered the wound, layer by layer, until all the material was gone. His furrowed brow made me suck in a breath. He'd patched up enough of my injuries for me to recognize the concern in his expression. I braced myself to peer at the festering injury, expecting to see signs of infection.

He set the bloody bandages on the side of the bed, and I blinked at the wound. The puncture from the sword looked like it had been healing for weeks. The injury was already scabbed over, the skin repairing itself. Purple and yellow bruises covered my stomach and chest, likely the cause of the painful breathing. I'd only been asleep three days. It shouldn't be scabbed over yet.

"You should be dead," he said.

I swallowed hard. I'd thought the same thing during the fight. "I guess it wasn't as bad as it seemed."

"Based on the bloody mess you were when you arrived, I prepared your father for your death. It was deep, Ara. I didn't think you'd wake." He shook his head.

"I guess I was lucky," I said, not believing it myself.

"Perhaps," he said. "Whatever the cause, I do believe the gods have something in mind for you. Otherwise, they would have taken you."

He rose, then glanced toward the door. "Those injuries shouldn't be healed. Not like this, anyway. It would have been a miracle for you to survive. To be this far along so quickly is not natural."

"Maybe you underestimate your own skills," I replied.

"No." He shook his head. "This is something else. I recommend you don't mention the injuries to anyone. Nobody should know how truly bad it was. I'll inform your father that I misdiagnosed. That the blood was deceiving."

"You don't misdiagnose," I pointed out.

"No, I don't." He picked up the soiled bandages. "For your sake, keep this to yourself. The only people who know the truth are you, me, and the ambassador."

I tensed. "What are you saying?"

"Ask him what happened. I certainly have no explanation for it," he said.

"How is she?" Sophia asked, peering into my room, a tray with food and tea in her hands.

"You don't need to be serving me," I said.

"I want to help," she replied.

"She's better," Mythiuss said. "The injuries weren't as grave as we initially thought."

"Oh, thank the gods," Sophia breathed.

"I'll leave you two," Mythiuss said. "If you feel any severe pain or any wounds re-open, please call for me."

I nodded. "Thank you."

Sophia set the tray on my desk. "I sent Mila for your favorite tea. She got the flowers from the farmer at the market you like in town." She walked toward me, a steaming mug in her hands.

I accepted the cup. "Tell me what happened when I got back here."

Her brow furrowed. "You don't remember?"

I shook my head, then leaned down and breathed in the scent of chamomile. It eased some of the tension I was feeling. Carefully, I took a small sip, the warmth a welcome balm on my sore throat.

"It was horrible," she said. "The ambassador and several of his men arrived on horseback. They left the carriage behind so they could ride faster. You were so pale…"

"How did I get hurt?" I recalled the fight, but after what Ryvin said about David, I wasn't sure if I remembered the situation incorrectly or if he'd spun a different tale.

Sophia's brow furrowed. "You were attacked. Perhaps it's a blessing if you don't remember the details."

"Please, tell me," I encouraged.

She let out a long breath, then settled in on the bottom of my bed. "I didn't get the full story. But from what I've gathered, your carriage was ambushed by a group of radicals somewhere near the Black Opal. Thankfully, David and some of the other guards were off duty nearby and they stepped in to help."

"David helped?" I asked.

Sophia set her hand on my leg. "I'm so sorry, Ara. He didn't make it. None of our guards did."

"I see," I said. "And the ambassador?"

"He said he only had minor injuries." Sophia got off my bed and walked back to my desk to pick up the tray. She returned to my bed and set it near my feet. "You should eat. You've been asleep for three days. You have to be hungry."

I wasn't feeling hungry, but I knew my body would need the food to help heal. Though it seemed I'd healed without food. My stomach twisted uncomfortably as I considered what the healer was alluding to before he left.

"I'm tired, Sophia. I'll eat then I'd like to sleep," I said.

Sophia kissed my forehead. "I'll check on you in the morning."

"Thank you for your help," I said.

She nodded before she tiptoed out of my room, closing the door behind her.

I waited a few moments to ensure that nobody else was going to enter, then I climbed out of my bed and pulled off my nightgown.

The skin on my chest, ribs, and stomach was tinted in varying shades of blues, purples, and greens. I lightly ran my fingers over the bruises, hissing at the pain. Then I touched the healing sword injury. The wound should have been fatal, but it was a thick red scab that appeared weeks old. My fingers traced over the mark. The skin was still sensitive, and it was going to leave a scar, but I was alive. It didn't make sense. I studied my arm, noting that the cut there was also mostly healed.

How had that happened?

It shouldn't be, unless something else, something outside our typical healing protocols was used.

I swallowed hard against a lump in my throat.

This wasn't healing, this was magic.

And everyone knew if you received magic in any form, you were cursed.

My heart raced as I padded over to the bathroom and peered into the mirror. My face showed signs of the fight. A black eye was healing under my right eye, the bruises green and yellow, as if they'd been healing for over a week already. A thin line down my cheek looked like another new scar. I didn't even remember getting that mark.

Other than that, I looked like myself. I looked the same.

If magic had been used to heal me, I wasn't sure I even wanted to know. I was alive. And right now, that should be enough.

But people were dead, and my enemy had saved my life.

I couldn't wrap my head around it, but I knew that everything had changed. There was no going back to the way things were before that attack.

I just wasn't sure what that meant yet. Shivering, I pulled my nightgown back on and crawled between the covers. I wasn't ready to face the changes I could feel in my bones.

CHAPTER 13

I woke with a scream, the battle replaying in my nightmares. The faces of the dead, a parade of visions, flooding my mind on repeat. I'd done that. I'd killed people. And not just people, *my* people. The people I was going to give up my life for when I went to serve on the wall.

My door opened, and a lantern illuminated a figure peering in. It took a moment for my eyes to adjust before I could tell it was my sister, Cora. She was looking at me as if I was broken. "Are you alright?"

I hated how she looked at me. Cora rarely took anything seriously and seeing her look at me this way was too much. I didn't like that I came across as fragile or different than I had been before I left in that cursed carriage. "Just a nightmare," I assured her.

Sophia walked past Cora, entering my dark room. "Are you in pain?" Both of my sisters' brows were furrowed in concern, something I wasn't used to from them.

I pushed my sweat-soaked hair away from my forehead. "I'm fine. Just a bad dream."

"You sure?" Cora asked. "You need anything?"

"Both of you, stop. I'm the one who is supposed to watch after you. I'm okay, really," I insisted.

"Sometimes you need to let other people care for you, Ara," Sophia said, sounding so much wiser than her seventeen years.

"It's nothing," I repeated. "I'm fine. I'll call for you if I need you."

"Alright," Cora lowered the lantern. "We'll check on you in the morning."

"Goodnight." I smiled at them, even though I didn't feel like smiling at anyone. Not while the ghosts of the men I killed were still floating in my head.

"Get some rest," Sophia said. My sisters backed out of my room, then closed the door, sealing me into the darkness.

My pulse quickened almost instantly as guilt and fear made my chest tight. Tossing the blankets aside, I padded over to my bathroom. There was no way I was going back to sleep tonight.

Quickly, I splashed water on my face and worked to calm myself down. I'd tried not to focus too much on the attack, but blocking it from my thoughts hadn't eased the guilt.

Those men had waited for our carriage and had attacked all of us. Not just the delegates from Konos. They were after me as well.

How many of them had been soldiers I'd trained with? Or those who'd watched me fight? I never stopped to look at the fallen men, but I knew David had assistance from other guards.

Did that mean we had guards in the palace who were intent on taking the delegation down?

On taking me or my family down?

Was the attack strictly about bringing down the Konos men or was the intention to end my life as well?

I sat down at my desk as I recalled the last time I'd met with David for training. We had plans for the next day. The day I'd killed him. We weren't supposed to meet like that. We were supposed to meet at the training grounds to practice.

Had he been planning his attack even then?

My shoulders slumped as a voice in my head reminded me that I'd never be able to ask him those questions. He was dead. And it was my fault.

The only person who might have answers for me was Ryvin. I lifted my nightgown, taking in the injury on my midsection. Scowling, I dropped the fabric. Ryvin had a lot of questions to answer for me.

Ryvin's black-clad guards were stationed at the entrance to the hallway leading to the visitors' quarters. I glared at them as I approached, daring them to stop me. I was prepared with excuses, but they stepped aside without a word, letting me pass.

There were six rooms in this wing, each of them likely housing members of the delegation. My resolve chipped a little as I paused in front of the door to the grandest room, the one sure to house the most important member of the delegation.

I had so many questions for him, but what if I didn't like the answers? What if he refused to tell me anything?

What if he slept nude?

Little sparks seemed to dance across my skin, making me feel more alive than I had in years. I hated how intrigued I was by him. Hesitating at the door, I considered leaving. Could I trust myself around him?

Of course I could. I would face him because I deserved the answers.

Besides, I'd already seen him undressed.

And I wasn't knocking because I enjoyed the way he looked without his clothes.

Which I did.

But that wasn't the point.

Shaking the thoughts of Ryvin's muscular form from my head, I knocked before I could lose my nerve.

Rustling sounds from the other side of the door informed me that someone was awake. And possibly putting clothes on. I told myself I wasn't disappointed by that.

The door opened a crack and suddenly worried he was going to close it on me, I shoved my way in. "We need to talk."

The room was dark and cold. A breeze told me the curtains were open and goosebumps skittered over my arms.

"I was wondering when you'd come to your senses," a deep voice said, the tone dangerous and thick.

"You're not Ryvin." I stepped away from Orion, aiming for the open door.

In a blur, he blocked my progress. "You came here for him? What an interesting turn of events." His smile was pure predator. "That's okay, I won't tell him." The door slammed.

Flames roared to life in the fireplace, completely on their own. The air tasted sweet and bitter at once, a strange elixir that coated my senses in something both familiar and foreign. I ignored it, instead focusing on keeping myself from showing how terrified I was to be staring at Orion.

My heart kicked against my ribs, pounding in rapid succession I was sure he could hear. I clenched my jaw tight and held my chin high, determined not to let him see any weakness. I need to stay calm, maintain composure, hide my fear.

His lips were parted, showing his fangs. Those blue eyes were a few shades darker than the last time I'd seen him, taking on a hue that was almost violet. He looked hungry, his expression reminding me of how David had looked at me when I removed my clothes. Like he was going to eat me alive.

The difference was that David didn't have fangs.

"Sorry to wake you," I said, turning toward the door. "I seem to have gotten the room wrong."

"I don't think you did." He took a step to the side, blocking the door. "I saw how you fought. The way you ignored your own pain, how you handled your weapon, the way you grew stronger as the bloodlust set in. You're in exactly the right place, little dove."

"I don't know what you think you saw, but I didn't enjoy that fight. And I certainly am not your *little dove*," I snapped. "Now, if you'll kindly step aside, I bid you goodnight."

He moved so fast, I didn't have time to react. I was thrown to the bed, Orion quickly straddling me. He growled, those fangs extending more, glinting in the orange glow of the firelight.

"Get off me!" I shouted, pushing up to sitting and shifting my hips to throw him.

He grabbed my arms and shoved me back. Wrists pressed against the soft bed, I fought against him, kicking and flailing, but it was like fighting against a full-grown bear. He was impossibly strong, a monster honed to fight and win.

"Let me go!" I hollered, continuing to struggle against him.

"I don't think I will. You disrespected me in front of my commander." He leaned down and inhaled deeply. "Oh, fuck, you smell good."

My nose wrinkled. "Stop smelling me and let me go, asshole!"

He switched his grip, so one large hand was gripping both

my wrists. I struggled harder, but even with one hand, I couldn't get him to budge. Grunting and cursing, I struggled to break free. I was not going to let this man get what he wanted from me.

His free hand caressed my throat and shivers of fear skittered down my spine. Was he going to kill me? Or feed from me? Or fuck me?

Maybe he'd do all of them. I stopped moving, suddenly paralyzed by fear as worst-case scenarios played in my mind. He was going to harm me one way or another, and I was helpless against him.

After all the time I'd spent learning to fight, I was useless against these monsters. I'd struggled against humans as well.

All this time, I thought I was strong. That I could take care of myself, but now I wasn't sure.

"Please, don't do this," I whispered.

"Mmm, I love it when they beg," he said.

His hand moved from my throat to my breasts as he roughly kneaded each one over the thin fabric of my nightgown. My stomach churned, bile rising up to my throat.

"Let me go," I said. "When my father finds out about this, he's going to have you killed."

His hand returned to my throat, gripping it hard enough to deprive me of some breath. My eyes widened, and I sucked in more air rapidly in anticipation of having it further constricted.

"We have ways of making you forget. Did you know that, little dove? I could even make you beg me to fuck you. But where's the fun in that? I think I'll take what I want, then make you forget. You'll wake up tomorrow sore and satisfied, wondering why your dreams about me were so vivid."

I swallowed hard, his words hitting me like a ton of bricks falling onto my chest. Everyone knew the stories of the things the vampires could do, but I'd hoped they were stories. There was so much we didn't know. Did they have any weaknesses?

His grip tightened around my neck, cutting off my air. I sucked in nothing, my heart racing as fear sent my eyes wide. I struggled, trying to free my hands, my body moving, wiggling, desperate to break his grasp on my throat. Just as my vision darkened, he released his hold and air flooded my lungs. Stars danced before my eyes and I coughed. Relief mixed with anger and fear as I glared up at him. "Let me go. Now. Or I kill you myself."

He laughed, the sound mocking. "I'd love to see you try."

With another squeeze around my throat, he leaned down and pressed his lips to mine, taking a one-sided kiss while I struggled for air. After he removed his cold lips, he released his grip, and I sucked in air. His mouth re-claiming mine a second later.

I snapped my jaws, trying to bite him, but he pulled away too quickly, a wicked grin on his lips. "You want to bite?" His tongue rolled over the tip of one of his fangs. "I'll show you how to bite."

It was clear I wasn't getting out of this on my own. While I could still breathe, I took a huge breath, then with everything I had, I screamed.

Orion slammed his hand across my mouth, digging his fingernails into my cheek. Tears welled up in my eyes, making my vision blurry. I continued to kick and fight, but he was so much stronger than me.

I could keep moving, keep trying, or I could still and hope he let down his guard. With resignation, I tensed and stilled, peering up at the monster who looked like he was practically salivating at the sight of me subdued under him.

A shadow moved out of the corner of my eye before it

descended on Orion. He was hauled from me and tossed across the room, landing against the wall with a thud.

I bolted up and scrambled from the bed, adrenaline keeping me moving.

Ryvin stood in front of Orion, his hands in fists at his side. The temperature in the room shifted and my breath came out in clouds. I hugged my arms around my chest, trying to stave off the cold that was sinking into my bones.

"I told you not to touch her," Ryvin growled. Shadows swirled around him, moving and changing as if he was the flames of the fire. It was as if the whole room was enveloped in his power. Whatever dark thing he was, it was no longer sheathed away in the handsome human-looking form he possessed.

I should be afraid of the power of the shadows swirling around me, but I stepped closer. Teeth chattering, cheeks stinging from the cold, I pressed on, too curious to back down. I knew what was going to happen, and the thought made my insides squirm. There'd been so much bloodshed already, but this was different.

If he'd let me, I'd probably kill him myself.

Ryvin closed in on Orion, the shadows seething and twisting around him like a cloak of pure night. With his black tunic and dark hair, he was even more the dark prince I'd first seen him as.

He was death in physical form.

Time seemed to crawl, the seconds dragging into minutes. I watched as Ryvin closed the distance to Orion with graceful, fluid footsteps. Energy filled the room, sizzling and popping like static. My whole body felt alive and on edge.

"She's just a human," Orion whispered.

Ryvin stood in front of his companion, the two men staring at each other with disdain. Then, as if a switch flipped, time returned to normal, and Ryvin grabbed Orion. With a sickening crack, Orion's neck was snapped.

I turned away at the sound of breaking bones and tearing flesh. A thump, then another thump.

The contents of my stomach were threatening to spill, but I still had to look. I had to see that Orion was dead.

Just steps from where I stood, Orion's crumpled body lay on the floor, blood pouring from the stump of his neck where his head had been attached. I swallowed down the bile and let my eyes wander to the head. Eyes pale, fangs still extended, the face stared back at me.

Despite my churning stomach, I wasn't upset that he was dead.

I didn't even care that Ryvin had removed his head with his bare hands.

If anyone deserved it, it was him.

"I told him what would happen," Ryvin said, as if apologizing.

"How do you allow men like him in your company?" I asked, letting the fear I'd been feeling fully settle into anger.

"I don't. He had one warning. That's all they get," he said.

"Good."

"What are you doing in my room?" His eyes raked down my body, likely taking in my nightgown.

So I had chosen the correct room. "Why was Orion in your room?"

He stepped over Orion's corpse without flinching, moving closer to me in the flickering firelight. Red splatters dotted his chin and temple, and I was guessing there was plenty of blood hidden by the color of his tunic. He moved with ease, that same power about him I'd noticed earlier. Only this time, the shadows I'd seen were missing. Perhaps I'd imagined that. Or maybe it was the first time I'd truly seen him for what he was.

He stopped in front of me and lifted his hand. I held my breath as he brushed his fingertips over my throat. Those storm cloud eyes lowered, then darkened, fixed on something that made him scowl.

I peered down and noticed that my nightgown was shredded down the middle, the thin fabric only barely covering my breasts. With a gasp, I covered myself. When had that happened? And how had I not noticed?

"Did he...?" Ryvin began gently, letting the unasked question hang in the air between us like thick smoke, waiting for a gust of wind to blow it away.

"He didn't get as far as he would have," I said.

"I'm sorry I wasn't here sooner," he replied.

Where had he been? It was the middle of the night. My jaw tensed as jealousy flared, making me feel like I'd swallowed something hot. I shouldn't care. I didn't care. It didn't matter that my mind was racing, imagining Ryvin tangled with someone else. "Where you spend your time is not my concern."

It wasn't any of my business who he bedded. I shouldn't care, but in that moment, the thought of him with anyone sent me seething with rage. How could he? How could he be out fucking other women after everything we'd just experienced? After we'd nearly died?

That had to explain my emotions. It was the attack and the cavalier attitude he had toward his safety. Someone had tried to kill him and he was out wandering the castle at night.

"Asteri, you're not jealous, are you?" he asked, his playful tone a stark contrast to the killer I'd just seen unleashed.

I scowled, ignoring the nickname. "If you die, then it was

all for nothing. That attack, all the dead, David..." My voice caught in my throat. Hot tears prickled at the back of my eyes. "Why did you say that about him, anyway? That he'd tried to help us? That he was a hero? When it was my fault. Mine. I'm the reason he's dead."

I couldn't keep the guilt or grief contained. I'd tried to mask it, hide it, deny my emotions, but standing here with Ryvin, someone who had been there, it was too much. He knew the truth, and I couldn't hide it from him.

"I murdered him," I whispered, my voice laced with sobs. "He was my friend. And I killed him."

I was a monster. No better than any of the delegates from Konos. David hadn't been attacking me and I killed him in cold blood. How could I do such a thing to someone I cared for so deeply? All those years. All that time. I'd kept him at arm's length; I'd never told him how much I appreciated him. Something was wrong with me.

Tears slipped down my cheeks and I quickly wiped them away, hoping Ryvin hadn't noticed.

The ambassador gently caressed my cheek, the touch more comforting than I wanted to admit. "He wasn't a friend. If he was, he would have warned you at the very least. Not told his friends where you'd be."

"What if they didn't plan to kill me?" I asked, not caring at that moment that I sounded beyond selfish. It hurt too much now that I'd let it all come crashing down around me.

"You know the truth," Ryvin said. "Do you think they were going to let you live? Even if they killed me, do you think he'd have spared you?"

My mouth went dry and the tears welling up in my eyes made it difficult to see, but I could feel his anger. It was like the heat from a roaring fire, swallowing us whole. I knew the emotions weren't directed at me; they were aimed toward others, toward those who'd tried to hurt me.

"Would he have spared you?" Ryvin pressed, his voice firm.

"No." The word tumbled out on instinct and I knew it was correct. If I'd killed Ryvin, David would have turned his weapon on me. The tears stopped, but the sorrow hung over me, suffocating and oppressive. It mingled with the heat, making me feel sick.

"Why?"

"Probably the same reason you wish to see me dead." He took a step back, as if suddenly remembering that we weren't on the same side.

I opened my mouth to deny him, but it was true. I'd considered it, imagined it even.

"Why did you tell them he was a hero?" I asked.

"You asked me to help his sisters. Would they not be punished if your people knew the truth?"

"Since when do you care about humans?" I countered.

"I don't."

"So why did you do it?" I pressed.

"You asked me to help his sisters."

"I know that's not the reason you did it."

"You're right. If you'd died, I wouldn't have bothered."

"So why did you do it?" I tightened my grip around myself, suddenly feeling small and fragile.

"Because it changes how you view yourself. How others view you."

My brow furrowed.

"They don't have to know you ended his life." His tone was gentle, almost apologetic.

Suddenly, I understood. "Because I'm not a killer if he died a hero protecting me."

He nodded.

"But it's a lie."

"Sometimes lies make life a little easier to endure," he admitted.

"How do you do it?" I asked. "Continue after you've taken a life." It wasn't just David, but those other men. Their faces would haunt me until the day I died.

"It gets easier," he said. "Easier to remind yourself that it was you or them. Eventually, you stop seeing their faces."

I tensed, surprised that he understood so well. Part of me wanted to ask him how many he'd killed. How many it took until you stopped letting it eat you alive. But that felt too personal and honestly, I was afraid to know the answer.

"You should get back before anyone notices you're gone," he said.

"I have one more question." My heart raced and I could feel the blood rushing to my face as I thought about my injuries and how quickly they'd healed.

Ryvin was silent, waiting patiently for me to continue. There was a tired look in his expression that I'd not seen before. Perhaps a sense of resignation. A dead man lay on the ground behind him, one of his own, killed for touching me. I was an enemy or I was the daughter of an ally. It didn't matter how he viewed me, I wasn't one of his own. Yet, he'd killed a member of his own delegation for me.

Part of me was flattered, but mostly, I was reminded exactly how deadly this man - or whatever he was - was. I licked my lips, thinking about how to word this carefully. Instead, the words tumbled out in an ungraceful mess. "Why did you even bother to save me? I was dead. I should be dead. We both know that."

"I would never let anything bad happen to you," he said, as if it was the most obvious thing in the whole world.

My chest tightened, and a strange need ached between my thighs. The way this man got to me was dangerous. If I wasn't careful, I was going to lose myself completely. "You used magic."

"It was the only way."

"You shouldn't have," I said.

"I will do whatever is necessary to keep you safe. Now, you should go. The sun is about to rise and they're going to notice if you're not in your bed." He crossed the room, bypassing the body, and opened the door. "Get some rest, Princess."

Somehow, I made it back to my room. I tossed my torn nightgown into the smoldering embers of the fire, stoking it until the flames grew large enough to consume the fabric. Numbly, I made my way to my bathing chamber and scrubbed every inch of skin until it was red. Then I scrubbed some more until the pain helped wipe the memory of Orion's touch on my skin.

Head spinning, throat aching, I managed to pull on a new nightgown before burying myself under my blankets. My mind replayed the horror of what I'd endured over and over in an endless cycle. Shaking, I buried my face into my pillow, trying to send the memories away. It wasn't until I allowed myself to remember how Orion met his end that I finally felt some peace.

Ryvin's anger should have terrified me, but I knew he'd never harm me. *I would never let anything bad happen to you.* His words echoed in my mind in a constant loop. His deep, rough voice caressed my brain.

What did it mean when the person I thought was my friend would have killed me and the man I swore was my enemy was the one who'd saved my life?

CHAPTER 14

I woke with a pounding head and an achy throat. My fingers brushed across the tender skin on my neck and I dropped my hand quickly, scrambling up to sitting.

I almost died last night.

A vampire had nearly...

I pressed my palms against my eyelids, trying to force the memory from my mind. It was too much to consider what might have happened if Ryvin hadn't come into the room.

Ryvin, the ambassador from Konos. The man I hated. He'd killed someone.

For me.

I lowered my hands and blinked, letting my eyes adjust to the sunlight as the reality of the last few days hit me like a hammer.

I'd killed someone for him.

Since he'd arrived, it was like my entire world had been turned upside down. Everything was different. I felt different.

For the last few years, I knew my path. I fell into line when needed and avoided things I hated. Now, I was shoved into the forefront of the Choosing and no matter how much I fought the idea, I was part of the problem.

We all were.

"Ara?" Lagina's voice called as she opened the door. "Are you up for a visitor?"

It was the first time she'd come to visit and I couldn't let her see how confused and stressed I was. "I'm good, come on in." My voice was scratchy and speaking hurt.

If that vampire wasn't already dead, I'd demand his head.

I gritted my teeth at my own dark thoughts. Where had that come from? I didn't usually crave violence, but I couldn't help where my mind went. It made me feel wildly out of control.

She walked in, then stopped at my bedside, her eyes instantly finding my neck. "You're not healed yet. But I suppose that's to be expected. I heard how bad it was."

Perhaps the bruises on my neck were a blessing if the other injuries were too far healed to explain.

"I'm so sorry I didn't come sooner." She sat down on the edge of my bed. "How are you?"

"I'm doing better. I'm glad you came by. How are things?" I'd only been in this room for a couple of days, but I was already feeling disconnected from reality.

Her brow furrowed briefly, then she licked her lips. Her fingers played with the edge of a sheet.

It was the same tell she'd always had when she had bad news. "Gina, what is it?"

"It's fine, you're hurt, don't worry," she said.

I lifted my eyebrows. "Tell me. I can handle it. I'm not dead."

She chewed on her bottom lip, something I hadn't seen her do in years. It was a habit the queen had worked to break her from when we were kids.

I reached for her and set my hand on her knee. "Tell me. Whatever it is, I'm here for you."

"Things are a mess, Ara," she admitted, unable to hide the concern in her tone.

"The Choosing?"

"That's the easy part. Aside from your attack, that is." Her jaw tensed and in that moment, she looked like she'd aged ten years since we last spoke. She winced. "Sorry, I'm not trying to downplay what happened to you."

"I know what you mean. Don't worry about me. Tell me what's going on," I said.

"The dragons have stopped attacking the wall," she said.

"What? Why?" We both knew it wasn't because we'd won the centuries long skirmish at our border. The dragons were immortal and strong. In their human form, they could be killed like men, but they didn't attack our wall in their human form.

They used fire and flight. Their scales were like the strongest armor, which made them nearly impossible to kill. Mostly, we had to keep them away, knock them back until the next time they tried. Despite our efforts, we'd never found a way to truly defeat them.

"That's what we're trying to figure out. Two weeks of silence at the wall. We're in the dark," she said.

I sat up straighter, the pillows behind me falling around me like a barrier on both sides, a reminder of how coddled I'd been in this room. "Send me. I can go. Maybe they want to negotiate. Seeing a member of the royal family there will show them we're serious."

"That's just it," she said. "Aunt Katerina crossed the wall a week ago. Nobody's heard from her. We got the message the night you were attacked. We had no idea all this was going on."

I sucked in a breath as I thought of my aunt surrounded by enemies. Aunt Katerina was my inspiration for my own path. Her visits were rare, but each one had left such a lasting impact on me that I decided I wanted to be just like her.

I could picture her dark curls and hazel eyes as she burst into the breakfast room carrying gifts for my sisters and me. She was one of the few people who treated me the same as my sisters. I was just one of her nieces; it didn't matter if my mother wasn't important.

Her stories of battles on the wall were legendary. I still vividly remember the first time she showed me her dragon scale armor. It was the only time I'd ever seen it in real life. Few soldiers wore the iconic armor. It meant she'd taken down a dragon. Which, despite our years of conflict, was rare. Only those who'd made the kill themselves were permitted to wear such armor. Any extra went to the royal vaults to be saved in case of a full-on war. It was used to reinforce the most important parts of the armor.

"I'm sorry I didn't come earlier. I wasn't sure how to tell you," she said. "Especially after what happened to you. We were trying to deal with an attack on the Konos delegation and the issue at the wall. It's a lot, Ara."

"I know," I agreed. "How can I help? Is there anything I can do?"

She shook her head. "Not yet. I just wanted to tell you." She stood.

"You're leaving already?" I asked.

"I'm sorry. It's the Choosing feast tonight."

"You're still holding that after what happened to me? After what's going on at the wall? Aren't there bigger issues?" The Choosing feast was a banquet at the palace held for all the nobles and anyone my father felt was important enough to mingle with the Konos delegation. I knew it was a popular event and there had been rumors that if you attended, your children would be spared the Choosing. I wondered how true that was. None of us knew the methods used to select who would take that one-way journey to Konos.

"Father says we can't cancel and show weakness to Konos. They expect us to celebrate this the same as we would had you not been attacked," she said.

"What if the dragons found a way to attack here? Or what if the people who hurt me go after you or Father? What if they sneak in with the guests?"

"Then I suppose we'll see if all the new guards we've been hiring can do their jobs properly. You weren't protected out there. Father made a mistake by not sending any of our guards. He won't do that twice. We're prepared, Ara. We'll be okay."

I scowled. She didn't know that some of our guards had been among those who hurt me. I had to tell father. He couldn't go on with this event without knowing. We could all be in danger. "He hasn't stopped by, you know."

"I know," she agreed.

"Why?" I asked.

"You know why," she said.

I did. He never visited us when we were sick as children, either. He believed he would curse us if he begged for our lives. Apparently, he'd spent days at his mother's side when she fell ill when he was only a child. When she died, he vowed he'd never beg for another's life. He felt his prayers had cursed her. To this day, any time any of us had been injured or sick, he'd stayed far away until we were healed.

I shook the thought away. It was heartbreaking to imagine a child watching his own mother die. He must have felt so helpless and alone.

"Go see him tomorrow," Lagina suggested. "I know he'll want to see you."

"I'm not staying in tonight with that party happening," I warned.

"Yes, you are," she insisted. "Mythiuss said you needed your rest."

The only injury I could feel was the new one from last night. The worst of it was healed. I was recovered, but I shouldn't be. I knew the time in my room was more to give me a cover story than anything. "I'm fine."

"You were stabbed," she said.

I frowned. Unless I wanted her to know about the magic, I couldn't argue with her. "Fine. But take a weapon tonight?"

She grinned, then lifted her dress to show a dagger strapped to her calf. "Ryvin even showed me how to use it."

My expression darkened. "The ambassador?"

"Who better?" She shrugged. "I know you and David were close, but he's not here to ask."

My chest constricted. *David.* Every time his face filled my vision, I felt like I couldn't breathe.

"I'm sorry. I shouldn't have mentioned him." Lagina's expression turned sympathetic.

I swallowed hard, still so conflicted about how things ended. He'd betrayed me, but I'd betrayed him worse. He'd handed me off to people who wished me harm, but I'd been the one who actually ended him.

"It's fine. He knew what he signed up for," I said, trying to cover my reaction as purely grief at his passing. What would my sister think of me if she knew what I'd done?

"He'll be honored after the Choosing. Father is going to hold a festival in honor of those who defended you," she explained.

I tensed. A festival to honor a group of traitors. But what would be worse? A public hunt to find any conspirators, creating fear and anger, or a celebration for the brave men who gave their lives for the crown. One would sow mistrust and fear; the other would give the people hope and demonstrate a powerful monarch.

Suddenly, I understood the real reason Ryvin had said what he did. It was all politics. Appearance.

He'd understood the unrest the truth could cause.

Which made me wonder how deep it ran.

Would any others believe they'd truly stepped up to defend us and feel like they'd been betrayed? Or would they be emboldened by knowing they got away with it? Was pretending like everything was fine keeping them from acting rashly? Or were they about to kill us all?

This was why I hated politics. The truth was rarely what was presented.

"The funeral?" I asked, mostly because I needed to change the subject. But also because I wanted to know.

"Istvan says it has to be a private funeral at the temple. Something about the stars on the day he died." Her mouth twisted to the side in annoyance.

I tried not to let my relief show. At least I wouldn't be expected to attend.

"You should rest," she said. "I'll come check on you later."

As soon as she closed the door behind her, I jumped from my bed. There was no way I was staying in this room while a banquet was being prepared for tonight.

My sisters would all be in attendance, and while there would be guards, some of those guards had been part of the group that attacked me. They couldn't be trusted.

Mila walked into the room and I paused to cover my chest, my nightgown already discarded on the floor. When I saw it was Mila, I let out a relieved sigh. I didn't need my sisters or Mythiuss telling me to stay in my room.

"You're supposed to be resting," she said, her eyes drifting to my injuries.

"I'm doing much better. The wound wasn't as bad as they thought," I said.

"I saw it when they brought you in. I cleaned the blood myself. You were pale as death, muttering incoherently."

That was new information. "I guess I'm a fast healer."

She grunted, then walked to my wardrobe. "I take it you need something for the party tonight?"

"I will," I said. "But trousers and a tunic will do for now."

"Everyone expects you to be resting," she said without looking at me.

"I know," I agreed.

"Whatever was done that makes it so you're still alive, I'm grateful," she said.

"Thank you," I replied.

"But please, promise me, you'll be careful tonight. I think there's something brewing. Something big. And I have a feeling you're right in the middle of it."

It reminded me of Istvan's warning. "What have you heard?"

She shook her head. "Murmurings. Strange injuries. Missing staff. General fear. Nobody can pinpoint a reason, but since that delegation arrived, nothing's been quite as it should."

CHAPTER 15

"You're alive," Queen Ophelia said flatly.

My father stood, the servant behind him scrambling to move his chair back for him in time. I ignored the disappointed tone in Ophelia's voice and enjoyed the sour expression on her face as she watched my father race toward me.

He swept me up in his arms, squeezing so hard I gasped. Quickly, he pulled away, holding me at arm's length. "I'm sorry. I'm sure you're still hurting. I shouldn't have hugged you."

"I'm fine," I assured him. "Ready to leave my room."

His brow furrowed as he inspected me, his gaze lingering on the marks on my throat. Rather than try to hide them, I figured they'd be viewed as remnants of my attack. It was the only injury that wasn't healed.

"Did Mythiuss agree?"

"He thought I should stay in bed longer," I admitted. "But how will it look if I'm not at the party tonight? Those who attacked me will think they won. That they killed me, or that I'm afraid."

My father grinned. "And you're always saying you didn't have the heart for politics."

I could feel the tension rising in the room without even having to look at the queen. "You know I have no interest in any of that. You asked me to step up, to do my part for the family, so I need to be there."

My father patted me on the shoulder, then pulled his hand away quickly. "Sorry. I'm not sure where you're healed. But I'm proud of you. If you feel up to it, I think it'll send a very clear message to our enemies."

"Do you have any leads on it yet? Any possibility it could be bigger than it was?" I asked.

"Nothing yet, but our best men are on it," he said.

"There's something you should know about what happened." My eyes darted toward Ophelia. I didn't really want to talk in front of her, but I knew this was important. "About the people who attacked us."

"I don't want you to worry about any of that right now," he said. "You'll overexert yourself if you relive it all now."

"It's really important," I pressed.

"Later. Eat. Regain your strength." He led me to a seat at the table and a servant quickly set a plate in front of me and began serving me food. In the breakfast room, things were less formal, and we were able to serve ourselves. Whenever we ate here, it was a production, even if it was a quick meal.

My father sat down and resumed eating the salted fish and vegetables on his plate. Ophelia was pushing her food around, not actually eating anything. It was awkward sitting between them, but I made myself eat the food that was on my plate while my father asked me casual questions about my training sessions and the weather.

I wanted nothing more than to tell him about David and the other guards, but any time I tried to mention my trip to the city, he quickly changed the topic. It took a few times for me to realize that he might have been keeping me from speaking in front of Ophelia. I was going to have to find him later to let him know the information I wanted to share.

The food was cleared from my plate, and I was anxiously awaiting dismissal. My father finished his last bites, and I was thrilled when he declined the offer of more food. The dishes were cleared away, Ophelia's untouched.

"What are your plans for the rest of the day, Father?" I asked, trying to be cheerful but hoping he'd realize it was time to release us all from the table.

"Well, Ophelia is overseeing the banquet for tonight, so I have only my usual meetings with advisors this afternoon. Nothing too dramatic. I imagine you're feeling restless already," he said with a knowing smile.

I laughed. "I don't know how anyone could sit in a room for so long."

"No training yet," my father warned. "I want to hear from Mythiuss myself that you're clear to fight. Promise?"

"I promise," I said.

"Don't forget you have to meet with my uncle today," Ophelia said suddenly. "He wanted to speak with you before the feast tonight."

"Of course," my father replied.

"Ara, I'm guessing you will need a dress for tonight." The queen turned her attention to me.

"I'm sure I have something suitable," I said.

"Nonsense." She waved her hand. "Your sisters are with the seamstress now. I didn't order a dress for you, but perhaps she brought options for your sisters to try. Maybe one of their unwanted dresses will fit you."

"Wonderful idea," my father replied, rising from his chair. "Ara, I look forward to seeing you and your sisters in your finery tonight."

"I'll see if the seamstress has anything that will work for me." I stood. "Thank you for lunch."

My father kissed the top of my head. "I'm glad you pulled through."

The glare coming from Ophelia told me she didn't share the sentiment.

I found my sisters getting last-minute fittings with the palace seamstress, a woman not much older than us, named Magda. Lagina was standing on a stool, the seamstress pinning and marking the hem while Cora and Sophia waited their turn. The peplos dresses they wore were elegant, yet simple. They were made with luxurious fabric in traditional designs. The added elegance would come from stylized fibulae used to pin the fabric in place at the shoulders and any jewelry added.

"What are you doing up?" Sophia snapped as soon as she saw me.

Lagina spun to me, her lips pursed. "You were to rest longer."

"Stop moving, your highness." Magda poked Lagina playfully in the side.

"Sorry." My sister straightened and returned to her previous position.

"You look better," Cora said.

"I feel fine," I said.

"You're still supposed to rest," Lagina hissed.

"And let you three have all the fun?"

"Did you tell our mother you're attending?" Cora asked, a note of mischief in her tone.

"Oh, I bet she's mad," Sophia said.

"She wasn't happy," I agreed. "What did I miss?"

"She invited several wealthy noblemen to meet at the palace and accompany us to the party," Sophia explained.

"I welcome any and all distractions you can provide," Cora added.

"Stop it," Lagnia said. "You know how important this is tonight. With the attack on Ara, we need all the support we can get."

"And how do we know they weren't involved?" I asked.

"Don't be ridiculous," Lagina said.

"You're done, my dear, step down," Magda said.

Lagina gathered her skirts, then stepped down from the stool. The sea green fabric made her long gold hair and aqua eyes even more stunning. She was by far, the most beautiful of the four of us and I had no idea how she remained unmarried. Especially with the position she'd inherit. Though, I supposed that made it more of a challenge. There had been offers, but she was quiet about details.

It made me sad to consider how much she hid from me over the last several years. I hadn't stopped to think about it much. We each had different paths. She would be queen, and I'd be nothing more than a soldier.

Cora stepped up onto the stool, her sunshine yellow dress a reflection of her energetic personality. "Though I'm not sure the other men will have any chance to get to you, Ara. Not if the ambassador is as protective of you as he was while you were injured."

"What are you talking about?" I said, defensively. Of course, after last night's events, I'd had too much of a demonstration of what he'd do to protect me. But that was an extreme case, and I was trying to not let it into my thoughts. My skin crawled as I recalled the feel of Orion's hands on me and I had to resist the urge to reach for my neck.

"He waited outside your room the first two days," Sophia said quietly. "I don't think he even ate or slept."

"You mean his men waited," I corrected her.

"No, it was him. He said he didn't trust anyone else to watch over you while you healed," Cora said.

"I didn't know that," Lagina said. "He wasn't there when I visited."

"He left after she woke," Sophia said.

"You must have made quite the impression," Lagina said.

"I'm sure it was guilt at the fact that he nearly got me killed during our little outing," I said.

Magda made a strange noise, and I looked at the seamstress. She'd been making clothes for us since I was a child. First, she'd come with her mother, still a child herself, then she'd taken over the family business about the same time that Lagina had started training to be queen.

"You heard something." I walked over to Magda. "What did you hear?"

"Nothing," she said, the word muffled by the pins she held in her lips. She stared at the dress, adding a pin to the hem.

"Magda," I pressed. "What did you hear?"

She sighed, then dropped the fabric before pulling the pins out of her mouth. "I don't want to speak out of turn."

"Please," I urged. "Tell me. Whatever it is."

"There's rumors, I don't believe them," she said.

"What rumors?" Lagina asked.

"They say you were in the Opal with him, the one who chooses the tributes," she said.

"I was," I admitted. That was never going to remain secret. Even if he didn't choose from the people he saw there that day.

"There are always rumors about all of us," Lagina said.

"This is nothing new." She ducked behind a screen to change, effectively ending the conversation.

Magda returned to Cora's dress and pinned the last few places, but she moved stiffly, the tension obvious. Even without the physical reaction, I could practically feel her discomfort. There was more to this story, but she wasn't about to tell us.

"You're all finished," Magda announced. "I'll have the dresses ready in an hour."

I noticed that Sophia had already changed, her new dress carefully laid out on a table. Lagina emerged from behind the screen, fabric draped over her arms. "Thank you, Magda. They are beautiful, as always." She laid her dress on top of Sophia's.

"They really are," Sophia added.

"Thank you, ladies." She turned to me, a bundle of dark fabric in her arms. "I made this for you, just in case. Why don't you see if it fits?"

I accepted the peplos, then stepped behind the screen to change.

"Girls," Queen Ophelia's voice carried into the room and I winced, not up for another interaction with her so soon.

"I need you to start getting ready. The nobles will be here in a few hours. Magda will have your maids bring your dresses, right, Magda?"

"Of course, your highness."

I stayed frozen in place, not wanting to draw attention to myself. Once I heard the footsteps fade, I began removing my clothes to try on the dress.

My eyes caught on the new injuries. They'd leave scars that would be a permanent reminder of what I'd been through. The fact that I should be dead.

Eager to cover the ugly marks, I pulled the peplos over

my head. The soft fabric enveloped me, hanging loose around my waist and hips. The color was a deep midnight. So blue it was almost black. Like the sky before dawn. Or the sea from my window at night. It reminded me of the black dress I'd worn the night I met Ryvin and of the dark colors he always wore.

"I'm not sure this is the best color," I said as I stepped out from behind the screen.

"It's the right color. Defiant, but not so much the queen can comment on it," she said. "I heard what you wore the other night. I know there's nothing most of us can do about the Choosing, but at least you're not pretending you like it."

"Is that what people are saying?" It was true, but I wasn't sure what the gossip would say. Especially after I'd been out with the delegation from Konos at the Black Opal. I wasn't sure what the people knew about the attack. Or the role I played. The only witnesses, as far as I knew, were the members of the delegation themselves. There must have been others who saw the whole thing. Onlookers drawn in by the sounds of a fight.

Guilt swirled and I had to force back the memory of David's expression as he took his last breath. I probably deserved to be hated. I had done terrible things.

"Don't worry about what they're saying," she said. "Those of us who know you see your heart. And we're grateful you survived. Sometimes, that's all we have the power to do. Simply living to see another day has to be enough."

"I shouldn't have," I admitted. "I shouldn't have survived, I mean. I should be dead."

"I know."

I wondered how much she knew. Or what she suspected. I knew the maids and servants heard everything, and I knew they often shared the gossip with others. Was Magda part of that network?

She quickly got to work pinning the dress in a few places, tightening it around my waist to accentuate my figure. Sometimes I preferred loose-fitting gowns, but my sisters had been in similar dresses, so I let Magda choose what she thought was best.

Finally, she removed the extra pins from her lips, then nodded. "You're good. Remove it carefully so you don't get poked."

I walked back to the screen and quickly changed. Magda was waiting with her arms outstretched to accept the dress from me when I emerged.

"Thank you," I said. "I know it was last minute."

She shrugged. "It's good practice for my new assistants. I'm training three girls from the village. They're doing well so far."

"That's wonderful. I'm glad you're getting some help." She didn't only serve the palace, Magda's skills were in demand with anyone who could pay. It was nice to know she was able to expand so she could take on more customers.

"You know, I've always wondered why you so often avoid these events." She picked up the bundle of dresses.

"You know why," I replied.

"Perhaps."

I didn't feel like explaining how much it had bothered me as a child to attend events alongside my sisters. They were treated so differently than me by visitors. I was made all too aware of how my status as a bastard impacted my position.

As I got older, it didn't bother me as much. I didn't want to rule, but I also didn't want to attend events full of people who'd scowled at me as a child. Now that I was older, some of those same people were interested in thrusting their sons my way in the hopes of a marriage. I was accepted by my father, and they figured if they couldn't have my sisters, I was a decent consolation prize. The whole thing made me feel sick.

"You should know what they're saying before you go," Magda said.

"About the Opal?"

She nodded, then lowered her voice, "They're saying you two were alone in the pools."

I knew it wasn't going to stay a secret. My cheeks heated. That was true, but I didn't like what her tone was implying. "I haven't slept with him."

"I believe you," she sighed, "I knew about you and David."

My throat tightened, and I swallowed hard. Thinking about David was so painful and complicated.

"But you should know that many think you did." She walked over to where the other dresses were and laid my dress on the table next to the others.

"So that's why you chose this color for me," I said.

She grinned. "Show them you don't agree. The people will believe you."

"Thank you for letting me know."

"I'll send the dresses up soon," she said, her voice loud enough to carry from the room. I knew she anticipated that we had company, so I took that as my warning to leave.

Sure enough, two of my father's guards were standing in the hallway as if waiting for me. I halted in front of them. "Were you sent for me?"

The guard closest to me, an older dark-haired man named Argus, nodded. "We were told to accompany you back to your rooms."

My brow furrowed. "What happened?"

"There's been an incident."

"What kind of incident?" I tensed. Something was very, very off.

"We were instructed not to discuss this with you, your highness."

I looked at the second guard. I'd seen him around but didn't know his name. "You know anything about this?"

"We can't speak on it," he said.

I rolled my eyes, then marched past them. If something was going on, I was going to find out what it was.

"You must go to your room," Argus called.

I ignored him and continued on, back to the dining room where I'd last seen my father. A group of guards was gathered outside the entrance and I broke into a run, my heart racing. What if something happened to my father? Or to my sisters?

"Come back!" Argus shouted, the sound of his boots hitting the marble floor behind me.

I picked up the pace, pushing past the bewildered guards until I was inside the dining room. Panting and breathless, I slid to a stop, my eyes widening at the sight. The table had been cleared of food, but on top of it lay a female maid, her head turned away from me. Blood dripped from the table, adding to a sizable puddle on the floor.

"Your highness, you shouldn't be here," Argus's voice was soft this time, and his hand touched my shoulder gently. "Please, come with us to your room."

"What happened?" I could tell the incident was recent because she was still losing blood. "My father?" I spun to face Argus, fear squeezing my chest.

"He's fine. He and the queen were not here when it happened. They'd already cleared away the meal. Nobody knows why she was in here."

I turned from him, then walked closer, avoiding the blood.

Taking careful steps, I walked to the other side of the table. My shoulders sunk in disbelief and my heart felt like it fell into the pit of my stomach.

"Mila," I whispered her name, my hand covering my heart as the reality of this situation crashed in around me.

My maid, Mila. The woman who'd helped me with everything for the last two years. Her eyes were open, glassy and lifeless; her expression frozen with fear. "Who did this?"

"We don't know," Argus said.

"Your highness," another voice called, and I looked up to see Belan. "You shouldn't be here." The young guard's face was pale as he took a few steps toward me. "Please, go."

"Back to your post," another voice snapped. Belan reluctantly stepped back to where he'd been stationed next to the door. I hadn't even noticed he was there when I'd entered.

I reached for Mila and brushed a lock of her brown hair from her brow, then I closed her eyes. "Rest easy, dear friend."

"Princess," Argus's voice was pleading. "Please. If your father knows, I let you see this…"

I nodded, then took one last look at my friend. Through my blurry vision, something caught my eye, and I noticed something odd. Carefully, I moved her hair off her neck.

Two small round marks were caked in blood.

Bite marks.

I balled my hands into fists and clenched my jaw. Tears still stung my eyes, but now my sorrow was replaced by rage.

Someone had killed my friend. And it sure looked like it wasn't a human who did it.

CHAPTER 16

"Princess, wait!" Argus shouted after me, but I ignored him, racing down the hall toward the guest wing.

I weaved around bewildered maids, but didn't slow down. I knew the only reason I wasn't on the ground was that the guards weren't permitted to lay hands on a member of the royal family. As long as I kept moving, I could reach my destination.

Black-clad guards came into view, the men drawing weapons and forming into a line to prevent me from passing. I skidded to a stop, my sandals causing me to slide across the polished marble floor.

Breathing heavily, heart aching with grief, I stared down the men blocking my path. "Move."

"Your highness, I'm to escort you to your room," Argus said, his words coming between huffing breaths.

"I will see the ambassador." I moved closer to the Konos guards, chin high, daring them to use their weapons on me. "Let me through."

"I'm afraid the ambassador is occupied," one of the guards said. "But we will deliver a message for you."

"You will let me pass." The words came through clenched

teeth. My hands squeezed into fists and I welcomed the anger. It was better than feeling the pain of losing Mila.

"We can return later," Argus said. "Your father insists you wait in your room until he determines that everything is safe." He lowered his voice, "you shouldn't be here. Not with *them*."

My eyes flicked over to the older guard and I noted the very real look of concern in his expression. He was visibly uncomfortable around the Konos guards.

He was the smart one.

I should be concerned. I should worry about the fact that they'd drawn weapons on a member of the royal family.

But I was too angry.

Too hurt.

Too heartbroken.

Mila had been taken from me, and I knew someone from Konos was involved. The ambassador needed to answer for the crime and I refused to wait and allow my father to brush it aside in the name of peace.

I swallowed hard at that realization. That was the truth of it; the reason I was here. I knew in my heart that nothing would be done about Mila's death. She was a maid. She had no status. Nobody would mourn her. She wouldn't get a funeral as determined by the high priest.

David had died a traitor and would get more recognition and honor in death than Mila.

I couldn't allow that to happen.

"Please, Princess," Argus pleaded.

I nodded, allowing my shoulders to slump as if I'd conceded. Letting out an over-dramatic sigh, I slowly turned away from the guards. The rustling of fabric and movement of feet told me they were returning their weapons and standing down. I took a cautious step forward. "Lead the way, Argus."

He let out his own relieved breath and turned away from me, heading back to my room.

Quickly, I spun on my slippery sandals and bolted through the line. The guards shouted after me and I heard grunting and yelling, but I didn't turn back. When I reached the ambassador's door, I pounded on it as hard as I could. "Get out here, you coward!"

Someone grabbed my upper arm, and another arm crossed over my throat. I gasped as I was pulled against a firm chest, in the solid grip of a Konos guard. "I told you to leave."

"Let her go, the king will hear of this!" Argus shouted.

I glanced over to see that he was bound by two Konos guards. A third had their weapon drawn, the sword pointed at his throat.

"You will leave our wing. This is our space, and it is ours to do with as we wish per the treaty," my captor hissed.

"She is a member of the royal household. You will remove your hands from her," Argus snapped.

"Her rank has no status here," the guard said.

"What is going on here?" A calm, deadly voice filled the hallway, sending a shiver down my spine.

The guard holding me tensed and nobody spoke. I was dragged so I could face the newcomer, but I already knew who'd joined us.

But I hadn't expected him to be undressed.

My cheeks heated and my eyes dropped, confirming that he was indeed completely naked. Hair mussed, a slight sheen of sweat making his bare chest and shoulders gleam, he no longer looked like the dark prince I'd thought him to be. No, now he looked like a god.

My knees buckled, but thankfully, the guard holding me kept me upright.

"Take your hands off her. Now." His tone was harsh and dripping with command. Fear spider walked down my spine.

The guard released me, and I stared at Ryvin, my heart thundering against my ribs.

His gaze met mine and something seemed to snap between us, like a tether holding me in place, frozen in his stare.

I'd never seen him quite like this, radiating power and authority. It seemed to flow from him effortlessly. He didn't need the uniform or a weapon; he *was* power. I knew instinctively this was who he was. Dangerous. Raw. Beautiful.

Like a creature that lured you in, then snapped off your head like the top of a flower. He reminded me of the sirens we'd been warned about. So dangerous we couldn't even swim in the sea. They'd lure you in with their beauty and song, then eat your flesh while you were still screaming.

I knew Ryvin was dangerous. I'd seen it firsthand. Watched him end the life of a vampire; a creature far more powerful than me. My insides felt wobbly, and I realized that I'd made a mistake coming here.

For the first time since we met, I felt afraid of Ryvin.

"Ambassador, please forgive us," Argus said, finally breaking the silence. "She's distraught. She just lost someone close to her."

Ryvin's brow furrowed slightly.

He didn't know.

"Release the guard," Ryvin said. "They aren't our enemy."

The guards holding Argus stepped back and re-sheathed their swords before standing at attention, facing their leader.

"Return to your posts," Ryvin said.

Movement caught my eye, and I glanced toward the ambassador's open door. A woman filled the frame, a sheet wrapped around her torso, shoulders bare, long auburn hair tumbling down to her waist. "Is everything okay?"

My chest felt like it was on fire. Who was this woman? And what was she doing in the ambassador's room?

"Go back inside." Ryvin's tone was softer than it had been.

"I can see why your guards were so eager to prevent us from interrupting." I was seething. He was in his room fucking someone while one of his men was draining the life from my friend. "Maybe if you did your job, Mila would still be alive."

"Who's Mila?" he asked.

My eyes dropped again, and I huffed in frustration as I had to force myself to focus on his face. "Can't you at least put some clothes on?"

A robe flew from his open door and my jaw tensed, knowing it was the girl he had in there who was helping him. She'd sure made herself comfortable if she thought she'd just toss him a robe.

Ryvin slipped the robe on and moved closer to me. "What happened, Ara?"

"My maid is dead. She had puncture wounds on her neck and was laying in a puddle of her own blood." I let the words sink in, the accusation hanging in the air between us.

Ryvin's expression darkened, and his jaw tensed, making a vein in his temple bulge.

"I know human life means nothing to you, but Mila wasn't just my maid, she was my friend," I said. "She wasn't even eligible. And you already took her sister from her. But that wasn't enough, was it? It's not enough to come here and put the fear of the gods into us and take our people at random.

You ruin lives, families, whole futures, just to feed the monsters on your island. We're nothing more than lambs waiting for slaughter to you. I know that. But you could have at least waited until you were gone. At least let us have the illusion of your false promises of safety for our people."

My cheeks were wet, and I knew I sounded hysterical, but this was too much. All of this was too much. Since the delegation had arrived, I'd lost David and Mila. If not for Konos, they'd both be here.

"My men didn't kill her," Ryvin said. "I promise you. They know better."

"Like Orion knew better?" I shook my head. "You're nothing but a bunch of murderers and liars. Hurry up and choose your lambs, then leave us be."

I spun on my heels and walked away, the guards parting quickly for me to pass through them.

"Ara, don't go," Ryvin called.

I froze, but didn't turn. "There's a naked woman waiting in your room."

"She means nothing," he said.

I turned. "Why would I care what she means to you?" But I did care. Even as I said the words, an ache that wasn't the same as the one I felt for Mila filled my chest.

I cared.

And I hated that I cared.

None of that mattered, though. It didn't matter if I'd felt something inappropriate for the ambassador. It wasn't real. And it was wrong. It was some odd reaction to sharing a life or death experience with him. Or it was because he was inhumanly handsome.

Emphasis on the inhuman part.

He was a monster, and I wanted nothing to do with him.

He should fuck the other woman. He should fuck as many other women as he wanted.

As long as he stayed away from me.

"I swear to you, my men would never do something like that," Ryvin claimed, as if looking for my approval.

He wasn't going to get it. "Keep your men in line or I will find a way to do it myself."

We both knew I was useless against the men from Konos, but I was furious. And I knew that if it came to it, I would do everything in my power to fight them. I loved my people, and I'd already done enough damage to them to protect this delegation. To protect and uphold a treaty I hadn't signed.

"Don't speak to me again," I warned.

It didn't matter what my father asked of me. With Katerina missing and the dragons pausing their attack, I knew it was unlikely he'd agree to allow me to serve at the wall any time soon. All my plans were on hold and I couldn't help but blame Konos for everything. Nothing had gone right since they arrived.

"I'd like to return to my room," I said, facing Argus.

He nodded. "Of course, Princess."

When I reached my room, I allowed Argus to open the door for me. I stepped inside and the guard followed me, closing the door behind him.

My brows lifted. "Is there something I can help you with?"

"I wanted you to know that I was wrong about you," he said.

"What do you mean?"

"Can I speak freely?" he asked.

I nodded.

"I've watched you train with other guards, and I thought it

was all a joke. A spoiled princess who was bored," he admitted.

My mouth twisted to the side. I wasn't surprised. Many of the guards weren't willing to spar with me and I wasn't permitted to join in actual training sessions.

"But you really mean it, don't you?"

"Mean what?" I asked, a little more forcefully than I meant.

"That you'd defend your people," he said. "Hearing you threaten the ambassador," he chuckled, "that was either incredibly brave or incredibly stupid."

"Which one do you think it was?"

"Probably both," he said. "But I want you to know, I'm going to talk to the other guards. You're welcome at our training any time. And if any of them give you shit, they can bring it up with me."

I sucked in a breath, letting my chest expand. His words gave me hope. "Thank you."

He nodded, then opened the door. "I'll see you around, Princess."

CHAPTER 17

"Mila?" I called out her name on impulse as I stepped into my bathroom, then winced when reality flooded in. She was gone, and she was never coming back. It didn't feel real. I almost expected her to walk into my room.

But she'd never walk into my room again. My throat burned and tears welled in my eyes. I'd been so full of rage when I'd gone to Ryvin's room that I hadn't let myself feel the pain of her loss. First David, now Mila. I sank to the floor and hugged my knees to my chest. It was too much. This was all the fault of that stupid delegation. Ryvin and his men caused all of this. Mila would never see her mother again. David wouldn't get to be at his sisters' weddings. Their lives were cut short unfairly, and it all felt like it was my fault.

All of this connected to me as much as it did to Konos. I killed David. And Mila was my maid. What was she even doing in the dining room? Had she gone looking for me? Had she walked in on something she shouldn't have?

If not for me, she'd still be here. I knew that in my gut.

Tears slid down my cheeks and my shoulders shook as silent sobs racked my body. My heart ached so much I thought it might explode in my chest. How was I supposed to continue on as if nothing had changed?

I let the tears flow. I let myself release all the anguish and pain and sorrow. We'd been taught to maintain composure at all times; to never let our emotions win. But I couldn't hold it back any longer. These were my friends. Or the closest thing I had to a friend. Regret swirled at how closed off I'd been with both Mila and David. I was so worried about feeling this kind of pain when I left that I never wanted that connection. Now, it was them who'd left me and I felt like I missed out on so much. I didn't even know their families. I didn't know where they lived or what they needed. They gave so much to me, but I'd kept them out. And now they were gone.

The tears fell until there was nothing left. My head throbbed and my body ached. There had to be something I could do to honor their losses.

Sniffing, I wiped my eyes and swallowed against the lump in my throat. I wasn't going to participate in this anymore. After a few shaky breaths, I regained my composure. Mila deserved better. Even David had. Sure, he had betrayed me, but he was willing to do something about the tribute situation. What had I ever done?

After splashing some cold water on my face, most of the evidence of my crying was gone. My father did not bend to emotion. He only listened to reason. It was time to tell him what really happened when I was attacked.

David's sisters and mother would lose out on survivor benefits, and I hated that, but there was too much at stake. There were probably other guards involved and it wouldn't take long for word to spread about Mila. If they suspected that Konos was involved, there was a good chance they'd strike them again. And this time, they might not wait for them to leave the palace.

What if they attacked while one of my sisters was in the way? They had no problem sacrificing me. I couldn't allow anyone else I cared about die.

Argus and another guard were stationed outside my door. I frowned at them, but adjusted my expression quickly. "Remain in your posts. I won't be gone long."

Argus nodded, the two of us having reached some kind of odd understanding. The other guard was young, probably younger than me. His eyes darted from me to Argus a few times, clearly confused. He lowered his voice, "I thought we were to keep her inside."

"You heard the princess," Argus said. "As far as either of us know, she's still in her room."

I nodded at Argus, then left before either of them could say anything else. My bare feet padded along the polished marble floors. At some point, I'd removed my shoes, though I didn't recall when that had happened. It didn't matter. I wasn't about to risk turning back in case Argus changed his mind.

Several guards were stationed at various points along the halls, their presence indicating the fact that my father must feel we're still at risk. The problem was that the threat was already here. From our own guards and from the Konos delegation. It was like having a cloth barrier between tigers and wolves. The predators only held off on attacking one another because it wasn't quite the right time. As soon as that barrier moved in the breeze and both sides realized how fragile it was, it was bound to be a bloodbath.

Dark clouds were blowing in over the sea, making their way toward the palace. Wind whipped my hair as I walked through the open-air corridor. I could smell the incoming rain and almost feel the charge of lightning nearby. Thunder rumbled, low and ominous in the distance. It wouldn't be long before the storm arrived.

More guards watched me with silent judgment as I passed. I wondered which side they were on. Would they be loyal to my family? Or would they strike us down if it meant having a shot at someone from Konos?

My father's study was like a fortress. Six guards stood outside the door, glaring at me as I approached. These were my father's most loyal men, and I knew each of them by name. They were with him daily, but usually they were not waiting outside his study. It was rare that this many would stand here. I knew I wasn't the only one who was nervous about what was coming.

"I have urgent news for my father." I waited for them to shoo me away or offer to take a message. To my surprise, the door opened before any of the guards could respond. Istvan peered out, his mouth twisted to the side at the sight of me.

"You didn't heed my warning, girl," Istvan hissed. "And you nearly got yourself killed."

In all the chaos, I'd forgotten about the vision he'd claimed he had. "Well, perhaps your vision has come true and now we don't have to worry about it anymore."

"You mock me, but things are changing and your status here is slipping." Istvan was smug, the look of someone ready to burst with information they had to hold back.

"Who is that, Istvan?" My father's voice called.

The priest stepped back. "Ara, your highness."

"Come in, darling," my father called without hesitation.

I threw Istvan a dirty look as I entered the room. At least I was pretty confident now that his vision had been self-serving and designed to throw me off rather than being authentic. How it benefited him, I wasn't sure, but he was always out for himself.

Istvan backed away from me, retreating to the corner where my father was standing. It was a flurry of activity within the sprawling study. Advisors huddled around my father, their white hair stark against their blue tunics. Wind whipped in from the open window, making the maps strewn around on tables ripple and flap in the breeze. Carved ships and figurines of soldiers dotted the maps, all of them centering around Konos.

In all my visits to his study, I'd never seen anything like this. There was only one reason I could think of that he'd have maps and ships placed like this.

Relief and fear twisted together, making me feel overwhelmed and satisfied at the same time. They were going to attack Konos. After all this time. All these years of sending our people to die, my father was finally going to do something about it.

Our navy was small, though, and it had always seemed an impossible task to take on the fae. But something must have changed to make them think we finally had a chance.

"You shouldn't be here, Princess. Your father is very busy," Istvan said, his tone condescending.

I lifted my hand to silence him in a move I'd seen Ophelia use a thousand times. To my surprise, he pressed his lips together and stepped back, as if I'd physically pushed him.

I was going to have to start using more of what I'd learned from Ophelia. As much as I couldn't stand the woman, she knew how to command.

"Istvan, Ara is welcome to visit me," my father said warmly. "What can I do for you?"

One of the advisors slowly closed the book they'd been looking at and flipped over some of the documents. As if I would read them from where I stood in the center of the room. While my father didn't seem concerned that I was here, everyone else seemed uncomfortable. It wasn't often that I'd entered this room, but I'd never seen a reaction quite like this. Though, as far as I knew, they'd never been planning something so important.

"I'm sorry to intrude, but I need to speak with you for a moment," I said.

He nodded, then looked to his gathered advisors. "Let's reconvene in ten minutes."

The men broke away from the table, speaking amongst themselves, and my father led me out of his office. We walked down the hall, our footsteps falling into line. His sandals made a flapping sound as they moved over the marble floor, but my feet were silent. The guards straightened as we passed, lifting their chins higher and keeping their gazes focused ahead of them, careful not to stare at the king.

It was odd walking with him now and seeing the turmoil unfold. When I was a child, he was simply my father. I had no concept of the power he could wield. As I grew, I came to resent his role and the time he spent with his job. My sisters and I were raised by household staff, a new nanny every year or so, nobody ever able to hold down the position. It wasn't that we were bad kids, there was always some other reason. Often, we were told the nanny was pregnant and had to leave, or had to go to care for her own family. Oddly, I can't recall any of them clearly enough to know if I've ever seen them in town over the years. It wasn't like they could go far. Athos was all we humans had.

We turned into the library, passing another pair of guards on our way in. This was one of the darkest rooms in the palace. No windows, no airflow. A few lanterns flickered and glowed on the small wood tables in the center of the room. On each wall was a bookshelf that spanned from the floor to the ceiling. Ladders had to be used to retrieve any of the books on the higher shelves.

I knew the books here were some of the most priceless artifacts in Athos. A few of them had even come here in the packs of refugees when the city was founded. Those were locked away in a hidden safe behind a painting of the rocky coast. The books were only allowed to be viewed with my father's permission. They were too precious to risk opening often, the pages already crumbling with age.

I'd seen them once, when I was around twelve. I'd been fascinated by the prospect of learning from those who'd come before us, but the language was different enough that it was a challenge to read them. Add in the fading and smeared ink, and it was too intense for a child to interpret. I'd settled instead on the history books written by the priests and priestesses in the temples. Fresh copies were added annually to make sure our history was available to be read.

An odd hollow sensation filled my chest as I recalled what Ryvin had said about my city's past. I wondered if I should take another stab at reading those ancient texts when this business with Konos was settled.

"What can I do for you, dear?" My father asked as he settled into a carved wooden chair with a plush green cushion.

I sat in the chair's twin, a small table with a flickering lantern between us. Glancing around, I looked for the librarian. The space wasn't huge, we had shelves on each wall and a second adjoining room with shelves on each of those walls. Somewhere around a thousand books that were maintained by a priest who'd transferred to the palace after serving at the temple of Athena for a decade.

"Theo has returned to the temple," my father said, as if reading my mind. "What is troubling you, Ara?"

Librarians at the palace never lasted long. The priests and priestesses serving in the position often missed their old life and asked to return. I had liked Theo and thought he'd stay a while, but I supposed life in a palace was very different from the isolation of one of the temples to the gods.

"I kept something from you, Father." I looked down at my lap, my hands entwined so tightly they were starting to hurt.

My father set his large hand on my knee. "Tell me, daughter."

With a sigh, I looked up. His forehead was wrinkled, his thick brows close together as he stared at me with concern. His deep blue eyes, so intense and clear, were still as sharp as ever. Despite being near his seventies, he still looked as I remembered him from my youth. I wondered if I'd always see him the same way I do now.

"I killed David."

He moved his hand from my knee, and his brows lifted in surprise. "That's not what I was expecting you to say."

"He wasn't helping defend us, Father. He, and likely a few other guards, were part of the attack. They were trying to take out the Konos delegation. And me." I swallowed hard. "David was going to kill Ryvin, the ambassador, I mean, and I had to make a choice."

"You chose to protect the ambassador?" He seemed surprised. Leaning back, he tapped his index finger on his chin, his eyes unfocused, deep in thought.

"Father?"

He blinked, then lowered his hand to his lap. "I did ask you to entertain him. I suppose I should have expected that you might come to care for him."

"No. That is not what happened." My face heated and my eyes widened. "I can't stand the man. Or whatever he is. I made a choice. At that moment, I was dying. David was dying. I was certain that if I killed the ambassador, we'd have war."

"I think that's inevitable at this point," he said.

I'd seen the evidence in his office, but hearing him say the words made it seem so real. "You're going to attack Konos? Can we win that battle?"

"We're still working on it, Ara. There's a lot to consider," he admitted.

My conversation with Lagina flashed in my memory. We'd always been short on soldiers with our fight at the wall, but the dragons had stopped attacking. What if those men were on their way home? "Does this mean our war with the dragons is over?" Flutters of hope filled my chest. What if we had a chance to finally stand up to the fae and end the Choosing?

He chuckled. "Lagina. She told you?"

My stomach tightened. I shouldn't have said that. The last thing I wanted to do was get her in trouble. "Only that Aunt Katerina was missing beyond the wall. Is there news of her?"

"She's safe. And she'll be here soon with information that might change everything." He smiled, then patted my knee.

"An alliance?" It seemed too good to be true. If we'd ended the war with the dragons, we'd have more resources for other things. But if we worked with the dragons, it could change everything.

"Perhaps." He leaned forward and lowered his voice. "I'm glad you came by. I was going to come find you after my meeting. I have something to ask you."

I listened intently.

"Everything could change once your aunt arrives. But it won't happen if Konos gets word of it. We intercepted their spies on their way to report the changes at the wall. We bought ourselves a few weeks before they realize they've had no correspondence. The timing isn't ideal. The dragon king refused to wait on an official visit, so they're on their way here. We must prepare for them in the background without anyone from Konos discovering what we're doing."

"How would they find out?" I asked. "It's not like they're going into your private office."

"We aren't sure how their magic works or if they had spies in the palace," he explained.

"What exactly are you asking of me?"

"I need the ambassador occupied. Distracted. He can't have time to explore the grounds or get into anywhere he shouldn't. I know it's probably not necessary, but I need you to get closer to him. Make him think he has a friend in this court," my father said.

"You want me to distract him?" My heart fell into the pit of my stomach. I wanted to avoid Ryvin, not spend more time with him. Besides, I'd just come from threatening him and his men. There was no way he was going to let me cozy up to him again. "I think it's too late for that. I accused him of killing Mila."

"Mila's death is being investigated," my father assured me. "But it is not to be discussed with anyone, you understand?"

"You know it was one of them and they should be punished. Mila was important to me. She can't just be swept away," I said.

"We can't afford to make enemies of the delegation," my father warned.

"They already are our enemies," I pointed out. "And if they killed her, what's to stop them from killing others?"

"I will figure it out. We can't let them know we're on to them. We must keep them distracted and happy. The

Choosing has to go on as usual and then we can finally make progress toward ending this once and for all," he said.

"You really think the dragons will help us? You really think it could stop the Choosing?" I wanted to end it now, to save my people from this fate, but I'd take hope wherever I could get it.

"Sacrifices must be made for things to change." His expression turned stern. "Mila's family has been taken care of and she will be given full rights in death. But we must not speak of it again. I'm asking you to not think of it, please."

"First David, now Mila..." I fought against the threatening tears. "I don't know what you want from me. I killed David for them and they returned the favor by killing Mila. How am I supposed to ignore this?"

"By serving your people. Your kingdom. Your family."

"I thought that was what I was doing when I saved the ambassador." My chest ached and I couldn't shake the look of betrayal in David's expression as I watched him die. He deserved better. He was the one who stood up to the Konos delegation, and I'd chosen them over my own people.

"Don't ask me to choose them again," I said. "I can't."

My father reached out and stroked my hair like he did when I was a child. I pulled away, feeling unworthy of the kind touch. "I made a mistake." I hadn't even let myself think those words, and now that I'd said it out loud, my chest felt like it would cave in from the grief.

"I understand why you did it. And why you didn't tell me." He sighed. "I am sorry to admit, I already knew." He offered a weak smile.

"How?"

"The ambassador told me what happened. Told me he promised you he'd make sure David's sisters were cared for as you were taking what he thought were your last breaths," he explained.

"You already knew about our guards?" I confirmed.

He nodded. "It's taken care of. And I will keep David's secret, unless you'd like me to change his status to a traitor and expel his family?"

I shook my head. "That explains the private funeral."

"Istvan knows the truth. I couldn't allow a public ceremony to honor him, but I couldn't bring myself to deny your request while you were unconscious in your room. When I thought you might not wake..." his voice constricted and he cleared his throat. "We will move on from this topic. It's done."

"What if there are more of them? More traitors?" I asked.

"I told you, it's taken care of. You have nothing to be concerned about," he said. "You will continue to do your duty. Entertain the ambassador to distract him until they leave. It's vital they are unaware of the changes at our border."

"I told you, it's too late for that."

"No, it's not. The ambassador could have let you die. He carried you here himself. He stood vigil at your door. A man doesn't do that unless he has certain feelings for a woman," he explained.

I lifted a skeptical brow. He'd obviously been with someone else when I'd found Orion in his room, and today, he'd had another lover with him. Perhaps the same woman both times. Either way, his affections were not aimed at me. "You misunderstand. He must have been trying to prevent the death of a royal on his watch. I'm sure that wouldn't look good for our alliance. Besides, he was with another woman when I saw him today."

"Only because he can't be with you."

I swallowed hard, and a tiny part of me rejoiced at the notion. I shoved the feeling down; deep, deep down. I refused to allow myself to let physical attraction cloud my judgment.

"He will forgive you for yelling at him," my father said confidently. "You're the only one who can do this. Men will abandon all reason for a woman they desire. If he's chasing you, he won't be looking for anything else."

"You're asking me to seduce him." Something strange gripped my insides. Fear mixed with giddy desire. How did I fight the strange feelings I had for the ambassador?

"Do whatever is necessary. We'll have one chance to convince the dragons, but if their convoy is attacked by fae before they arrive, it's all over."

"This is terrible timing." Why did the dragons have to be on their way right now?

"We've been working on this for years. Why they finally agreed to meet now, I'll never know. But we won't get another chance."

"You do realize what you're asking me." It was one thing to feel pulled to the ambassador, it was another to be pushed toward him by my own father. "I don't like the idea of being a pawn in this game."

"We all play our part in the game of blood and salt." He grabbed my hand and squeezed.

It was a stark reminder of duty, and the fragility of humanity. We were the last survivors, bound by our shared human blood and protected by the sea. Our history was full of strife, but the stories of us coming together, of sacrificing, were what kept us alive.

"What if he doesn't want to see me again?" I asked.

"Then the duty will pass to one of your sisters," he said.

"No." I stood. "Not my sisters. They stay far away from

all the Konos delegation. Swear to me. I will do this for you, if you promise me you won't ask this of them."

He stood, his face hardening. "I will do what I must for my kingdom, Ara. You are not the ruler here."

I overstepped. Something I rarely did. Most of the time, I could get away with anything. I wasn't in line for the throne and I stayed out of the way. But there were rules, protocols, expectations. I wasn't immune to his status. None of us were. Lowering my eyes, I nodded. "I'm sorry, Father." Looking up at him, I met his gaze. "I will do this. But please, keep them out of it."

"Then do it well. Don't make me resort to other means."

I hated this. I hated what he was asking me to do.

"Do your duty. Keep him distracted so he's watching you instead of Athos," he said.

I nodded, understanding my role. I had said I'd do whatever it took to save my people. This was my chance to prove that I would follow through. For the first time, there was hope for Athos to find a way out of the treaty with the fae. If it meant ending the Choosing, I'd do anything.

Even if it meant that to do so, I had to sacrifice myself.

CHAPTER 18

I sipped my wine, letting the familiar taste coat my tongue. It was my third glass, and I was already feeling a little lightheaded. I may need even more to pull off what my father had asked of me. It was better if I didn't remember it. Or if I wasn't aware of my own body when the time came.

The courtyard was stunning tonight. Decorated even more lavishly than the welcome reception we'd hosted a week prior. Lanterns with colorful paper covers hung from the trees, casting lights in a rainbow of colors. They were a recent import from the east, brought over by one of the brave traders who risked traveling through the fae lands of Telos.

Long tables were covered with gold silk tablecloths, more goods imported from the fae territories. I'd never stopped to consider just how much of the luxury I was surrounded by came from trading with our enemies across the sea. I supposed that was as much the driving factor for why we sent tributes as the prevention of war. We'd grown accustomed to the finery, though I doubted it affected the regular citizens in any way.

I ran my fingers over the tablecloth, appreciating how the fabric shimmered under the pink light of a lantern above me.

It was beautiful, but the cost was far too high. None of this was necessary.

The scents of exotic spices caught my nose as servants carried in platters of food. I backed away from the table, giving them space to set the impressively overflowing dishes. How many of those spices came from beyond our kingdom? How much of what I'd grown up with was due to the sacrifice of our people?

The traders risked their lives to purchase these goods. It wasn't just Telos, it was the sea itself. Beyond our shore were sirens, sea dragons, and monsters who lurked in the depths. Half the ships that risked the voyage never returned. Then there was the Choosing and the tributes. How much of that was to allow us access to their shores?

More visitors were arriving, and I made my way through the thickening crowd, keeping a lookout for Ryvin. If my father was right, he might forgive me for my actions today. If he was wrong, I was going to have my work cut out for me.

I hated that I was seeking him out like this. I hated going back on my words. But I was determined to do my duty. If we had a chance at peace with the dragons and a way to challenge the fae, my small sacrifice would be worth it in the end.

With the news of the dragons and my father's plan, I had to wonder how much would change for Athos. Would we be able to defeat the fae or would they use force to establish a new treaty? Would it end our trade routes or would it finally be enough to establish a true peace? One where we weren't sending our own to their deaths?

It seemed like an impossible dream. Generations of Athonians had watched helplessly as their children and loved ones were sent away. After the attack in the city, I knew they weren't going to allow it to continue forever. They'd reached their breaking point and my father had seemed to come to the same conclusion.

What had caused the change with the dragons, though? And how would that impact our future? We'd been at war with them since Athos was founded. What had finally brought an end to the fighting?

I couldn't even imagine what Aunt Katerina had done to convince them to talk, but I was very curious to see a dragon shifter up close. I wondered if they were like the wolf shifters, flawlessly blending in with us humans when they weren't in their dragon form.

The energy of the crowd changed, drawing me from my thoughts. Little gasps and the rustle of fabric made me turn to see the king and queen joining the reception, followed by my sisters.

The queen had insisted on using traditional protocol for this party, arriving in ruling order, which meant I was omitted. I didn't even argue when Lagina had stopped by my room to inform me. It was better this way. I could hide in the shadows in the hopes that nobody would even notice I was here. Maybe fewer people would notice when I dragged the ambassador from the party to entertain him, as my father had requested.

My stomach tightened, twisting in anticipation and dread. If I was honest with myself, I wanted more from the ambassador. But not like this. Not as a tool to subdue him. It felt dirty, wrong. But then again, every interaction with him was wrong, wasn't it?

It didn't matter if my body responded to his touch, he was still my enemy. I had to remember that. Sex was a tool. A weapon. Just like a sword. It was something I could wield for the sake of my kingdom.

I sipped my wine, watching as my father, the queen, then

my sisters walked past me. My father caught my eye, hesitating for a moment in front of me, the heavy weight of understanding passing between us. The interaction was so quick, I doubt anyone else noticed, but I could feel the meaning behind his gaze. I was to fall into line, do my duty, distract the ambassador.

Ophelia kept her face forward, aiming toward the throne without so much as a glance at any of the sycophants bowing in her wake. I had to admit, she radiated power. Nobody would dare cross her when she carried herself this way. I made a note to add that to my growing list of things I'd learned from her. Maybe it would come into use one of these days.

Lagina nodded, offering a sympathetic smile as she passed me. As if to say, *sorry I'm here and you're there.* I inclined my head, giving her the closest thing to a bow I'd allow, and her shoulders seemed to visibly relax, satisfied that I wasn't upset. How could I be? I had no desire for her role and welcomed my place in the background. I never enjoyed being stared at or whispered about. Lagina handled it beautifully, and I knew she'd be an amazing queen when the time came.

Perhaps helping her was an option for me instead of the wall. With the possibility of peace, there was likely no need for me to head to our border. I'd need a new plan. Serving Lagina would give me purpose. I'd never seen a woman as a royal guard, but why not let me protect her? After I proved myself with the ambassador, I'd ask my father. He was going to owe me after this.

Cora winked, then reached her hand out, brushing against my fingers as she passed. Sophia brought up the rear, looking stunning in a silver peplos. She was like the sea under the moonlight, radiant and peaceful.

She stopped in front of me, then threaded her arm through mine, dragging me toward her before walking again.

"Sophia, no," I whispered, pulling my arm away from hers.

"I'm not going up there without you," she said.

Murmurs sounded around us, and I knew we were causing a scene. The rest of the family was already on the dais and Ophelia was watching me through narrowed eyes.

"Go, Sophia." I gave her a little push.

"You are my sister. I don't care what protocol says." She tugged my arm.

So much for fading into the background tonight. I glanced back up at the thrones where my father and the queen were standing in front of theirs, waiting for the entire family to be in position before taking their seats. Lagina and Cora were standing next to them, both of them incredibly tense looking.

Then I caught sight of Ryvin, near the dais, head tilted to the side just slightly, as if studying the interaction between Sophia and me. Nervous flutters filled my chest and I couldn't stand the thought of him gaining anything from this interaction.

Fixing a smile on my face, I linked my elbow with Sophia's. She wore a self-satisfied expression as we continued toward the thrones and the two of us ascended the dais arm in arm. I remained next to her as she took her position beside Cora. My other sisters kept their faces forward, looking out at the crowd, but I could practically feel their anxiety and desire to turn toward me.

My father smiled warmly at me, then lifted his arms toward the gathered crowd. I looked ahead, still awkwardly clutching a wine glass in my hand. My cheeks felt hot, and I wondered if I was red from the alcohol.

"Welcome, honored guests. All of you are our dearest

friends and greatest allies. At the end of this week, we will celebrate another successful Choosing, solidifying our alliance with the Fae King for another nine years. Tonight, we celebrate the peace of the last nine years with the delegation from Konos." My father gestured to where Ryvin was standing. Several of his men were behind him, all of them looked like they were miserable. There wasn't even an attempt to appease the crowd staring at them.

Ryvin's gaze met mine, and I swear those gray eyes of his looked darker than they ever had. He looked positively furious. Apparently, he wasn't over our confrontation earlier today.

My job might be more difficult than I anticipated. I took a long slug of my wine, unconcerned by the fact that I was breaking protocol. I had already broken it enough by simply standing up here with my sisters.

Ryvin's lips twitched, and I got the sense that maybe he found me a little amusing. Perhaps there was hope that I could undo the damage I'd done earlier today.

I wanted to continue to hate him. I wanted to avoid him. But I wouldn't. For my people, I would do what was required. My stomach tightened as I considered my next steps. I swallowed down the rest of the wine in two huge gulps, then lowered my hand so the cup was dangling by my side. This was how I could help Athos. It wasn't the way I imagined I'd be saving my people, but I was going to take this chance.

My father was still speaking, but I didn't hear anything. My head buzzed from the wine, my vision a little fuzzy. At least Ryvin was handsome. Undressed, he was the ideal man. I'd be lying to myself if I said I wasn't at least curious about him as a lover.

There was no way my face wasn't flushed now because heat was rapidly growing low in my belly.

The wine was doing its job, and I was struggling to recall why I hadn't just fucked Ryvin. Sure, I hated everything about him, but he was gone in a week. If I was stuck entertaining him, I might as well get some pleasure out of it. Then I'd never have to see him again. Plus, anyone who knew what I did would forget as soon as better gossip came around.

Ryvin lowered his head into a bow and I tore my gaze away, realizing that my father was done speaking. The gathered crowd, and my sisters, were all bowing to their king. I followed suit, inclining my head in a demure way, just as my sisters were.

My father took his seat, then Ophelia sat. Each of my sisters kissed my father's cheek, one at a time, then moved to kiss their mother's hand. Reluctantly, I followed.

When I held Ophelia's hand, she grasped my wrist and yanked me forward so her lips were near my ear. "I'm watching you. Step one toe out of line and I will ensure you're sent to a temple so fast it makes your head spin."

"That's not your decision to make," I replied.

"I'm with child," she cooed. "Your father will do anything I ask to keep me happy."

My eyes widened, and I glanced at her stomach as if I could see some visible signal of the child within her womb. She grinned, the smile of someone who knew she'd won. "Take care of the ambassador, just like your whore of a mother took care of your father."

I gritted my teeth and had to bite back the urge to slap her across her pretty face. Hitting her while all the nobles in our kingdom were watching was dangerous enough. If my father knew she was pregnant and I struck her, I was sentencing myself to a temple for sure.

"Careful, Princess, if I have a boy, your father will forget all about you," she hissed, then she released my grip.

I stood, not bothering to kiss her hand, then marched off the dais. Music started, and the crowd rose to their feet, the official ceremonial greeting complete. I was certain people had watched the interaction between me and Ophelia, but she'd been quiet and careful with her words. Even my father hadn't seemed to notice what was said between us.

The worst part was, she was right. If she was pregnant, my father would dote on her and do anything to appease her. Not out of love for his wife, but out of love for a future child.

The part about having a son also stung. While my father loved his daughters, I knew it pained him that he didn't have a boy to carry on the line in the traditional sense of the word. Lagina could be queen, but she'd be the first woman in our family history to rule. I was certain that my father wouldn't love us any less if he had the son he always wanted, but a baby boy would be a distraction. Enough that it's possible Ophelia could get exactly what she wanted in regard to me.

The only thing that kept me from spinning out of control was the fact that I knew something Ophelia didn't. We were about to be at war. And war would surpass all else. Including the arrival of a prince.

CHAPTER 19

Ryvin wasn't waiting near the dais, and his men had managed to blend into the crowd. The room was awash in color. Many of tonight's guests were in purple, the rarest and most expensive dye, to show off their wealth. The midnight blue fabric of Magda's design made me stand out. A night sky among a rainbow sea. It was a fitting visual for how I felt about everything around me. A shiny round gold fibula clasped at each shoulder stood out like a pair of moons against the dark fabric.

Figuring I'd run into the ambassador eventually, I looked around for my sisters. Lagina was surrounded by a group of men of varying ages and importance. A quick glance told me they were all unmarried. Despite the fact that she was past the usual age of marriage and had never announced an intention to wed, she was still in high demand.

She'd once told me she was holding out for true love. It was insane to think she'd have a chance at that. I think we both knew it was a matter of time before she'd be forced to marry so she could produce an heir. If our father showed any signs of illness or slowing down, I think she'd be married within a fortnight.

I caught sight of Cora sneaking off with a dark-haired

male, Tomas, I think, but they were already in the shadows when I found her. She was the smart one. Getting away from the party as quickly as possible. The queen had publicly announced the intention for Cora to marry, so she was often a hot commodity at these events.

It took a minute to find Sophia, but I finally found her near a bubbling fountain at the other end of the courtyard. My pulse kicked up when I noticed she was speaking with Ryvin. I didn't want her anywhere near him. I didn't want her anywhere near any of the delegates from Konos.

Quickly, I cut my way through the crowd, apologizing when I bumped into someone but not stopping my progress. Sophia's laughter was light and musical, the kind of laughter that made even the grumpiest people smile. Except for right now, it made me scowl. I didn't want *him* to make her laugh.

"What do you think you're doing?" I demanded, stepping in front of my sister so I could get closer to Ryvin.

His lips quirked in an amused smirk. "I'm having a conversation with a lovely woman. You're being rude."

"Ara, Ryvin is being nothing but a gentleman," Sophia said.

I ignored her, keeping my eyes fixed on the ambassador. "I thought I told you to leave my sisters alone."

"I thought you said you never wanted to speak to me again," he countered.

"If you have to speak to anyone, I'd rather it be me. Leave her out of this," I said.

"Ara, you are being ridiculous." Sophia pushed me aside in a more aggressive move than I'd ever seen from her. It startled me and I stepped aside so I could see her better.

"Soph, please. There are plenty of other people to speak to here," I said.

"We're supposed to be diplomatic and welcoming, remember?"

"I will be diplomatic. You go find some of your friends," I said.

She sighed. "I love you, Ara, but I'm not twelve anymore. Haven't been for a long time." She slipped her arm around Ryvin's. "Shall we?"

"Nice to see you again, Ara," Ryvin said before leading my sister away.

I was going to kill him.

It didn't matter what my father wanted; I was going to murder him. If it meant keeping him away from my sister, I would risk the wrath of the Fae King himself.

"Wine, your highness?" A servant asked.

I grabbed the glass and took a huge gulp. I was already feeling the other wine I'd had, but at the rate things were going, I was going to be in much better shape if I just forgot all about whatever happened tonight.

Several nobles asked me to dance, but I turned them all down. All I could do was stare after Sophia and Ryvin as they spun around the dance floor. She looked radiant. Happy and full of life. My insides felt like molten lava.

Ryvin was going to get bored of Sophia and when he did, I would spring. I was supposed to distract him tonight, but my new goal was to keep him away from my sisters.

"How many glasses is that now?" Someone grabbed my wineglass and I turned to see a man in the familiar crimson tunic indicating that he was from Konos. He set the glass down on the tray of a passing servant. "You're going to be too drunk to dance if you keep that up."

"Maybe that's what I'm going for," I said.

He extended his hand. "Well, then you won't mind that I'm a terrible dancer."

I frowned, then looked back to see that Ryvin and Sophia were still moving gracefully across the dance floor.

"He's only dancing with her to piss you off after what you did today."

My head snapped back to the guard. "He was the one who answered the door naked. And one of your people killed my maid. Don't you dare act like it wasn't a big deal."

The man pressed his lips together into a line, making him look like he was holding back from speaking. My eyes narrowed. "You know something."

He shook his head. "All I know is that none of our men killed your maid."

"You're all a bunch of liars," I said.

He extended his hand again. "Liars can be found in all kingdoms, in all creatures, my lady."

"Are you saying it was someone here?" I set my palm in his automatically, too focused on the conversation to resist proper etiquette twice. By the time he swept me onto the dance floor, I realized what I'd done. I stopped moving. "I don't want to dance."

"Dance. Talk. It's harder for people to overhear," he said. "Plus, we'll piss off Ryvin."

That got me moving again. "Only because I want to hear what you have to say. It better be good." I wasn't about to admit I liked the idea of angering the ambassador.

"I'm Vanth, by the way." He moved his hand to the small of my back, flawlessly falling into the steps of the dance.

"Ara," I responded. "I don't need the titles."

He grinned. "I like you."

"Don't get any ideas," I warned.

"I don't have a death wish. We all know what happened to Orion," he said.

I hummed. That was surprising. Usually those kinds of

things were covered up. I didn't realize Ryvin would use it as an example.

"What did you want to tell me, exactly," I pressed, eager to end our dance. I was already feeling a little dizzy as we went through the motions, the alcohol making a dance that was usually as easy as breathing a little more difficult.

"I watched you comfort Adrian after we were attacked," he said softly.

"Adrian?" My brow furrowed.

"The wolf," he explained.

"Adrian." I said the name softly, like a prayer. He'd defended me. Saved my life. And I hadn't stopped to mourn his loss. Guilt squeezed my insides. I'd been so busy worrying about David, then Mila, I'd forgotten about him. I was terrible. He might have been from Konos, but he'd treated me with more care than my own people.

"He was a good fighter, a good friend," he said.

"I owe him my life," I said. "I have no way to repay that."

"Your presence with him as he entered the Underworld was payment enough, Princess." Vanth spun me, not missing a step.

"You lied," I said. "You're not a terrible dancer."

"You're drunk," he pointed out. "You are in no position to judge."

I smiled, dropping my guard a little with him. "Tell me about your friend, Adrian. Was he a shifter?"

Vanth nodded. "As am I."

I flinched, having to force myself not to step away. "You are?"

"You realize none of us in the delegation are human."

"I figured that, but I have no way of knowing, do I?" I replied.

"I forget how limited human senses are," he said. "I

thought for sure you'd be able to figure out what each of us was."

"Why would I have such a skill?" I asked.

He shrugged. "Something about the way you didn't panic when you calmed Adrian, I suppose."

"I'm sorry about your friend. He was very brave."

"One of the best men I knew," Vanth said.

The song ended, and polite clapping sounded around us. I stepped away from my partner, then inclined my head in a gesture indicating that I was finished. "Thank you for the dance."

Before I waited for Vanth to reciprocate, I was already on the lookout for Sophia and Ryvin.

They were gone.

I rounded on Vanth. "Where is he? Where did he take my sister?"

He shook his head. "I don't know."

"You were sent to distract me." I scoffed, irritated that I'd fallen into the exact same ploy I was supposed to provide.

"I simply wanted to dance with a beautiful woman," he claimed.

"Don't patronize me," I snapped. "I know the leash Ryvin keeps on all of you."

"You don't know anything about him," Vanth said. "If you're smart, you'll take this reprieve and celebrate that you got away."

"But my sister didn't," I hissed. "Where is she?"

"I really don't know. But please trust me on this, if he's moved on from you, let him. The last thing you want is to be something he desires."

"It would be a nice warning if I could make peace with allowing my sister to go in my place, but I can't. Do you have siblings, Vanth?" I asked.

He shook his head. "It's rare for a shifter to have even one healthy child."

"Would you have taken Adrian's place?" I asked.

Vanth tensed, his expression turning stony. I took a step back, concerned that I'd pushed too far. Then he nodded once. "I would."

"Then you understand why I need to know where my sister is," I said.

He sighed through his nose, then lifted his chin toward the gardens.

Fuck.

If she was alone with him in there, I might already be too late.

CHAPTER 20

The scent of sage and thyme perfumed the air, overtaking the smells of food as I strayed farther from the party. There were no lights out here, the moon my only illumination as I made my way toward the overgrown hedges.

The garden was divided into three parts. The first was a sitting area with a fountain at the center. Several stone benches were scattered throughout, beautifully framed by large trees. Flower beds were artfully arranged to enhance the space. It was beautiful during the day, but in the evening, it felt depressing. The color was leached from the flowers, leaving everything in muted duller hues by the light of the moon.

The fountain bubbled, and the breeze rustled the fabric of my peplos. My sandals crunched over the gravel path, alerting anyone who was within earshot of my approach. I pulled off my shoes and set them near the fountain. The small pebbles weren't the most comfortable to walk on, but I wanted silence. I had to know what Ryvin was doing with my sister, and I wasn't about to give them advance warning.

My mind whirred, playing the possibilities in an endless loop. Was Sophia taken by the ambassador's looks and going of her own free will, or was this retaliation against my actions? Worse, had my father lied? Had he set all of us on Ryvin as distractions? Four women throwing themselves at one man would certainly make it difficult to concentrate. Especially if you were hiding them from each other. Had he already been with one of my sisters? Was this his plan? Get each of us in his bed?

I made my way through the second part, which was mostly used by the staff. Most of the herbs and vegetables for the kitchens were grown here. It was so well tended and thriving that the scents of the herbs overpowered the flowers. I didn't venture this far often, but it was connected to the orchards, which was where most couples went to get away.

Hundreds of trees loomed ahead, looking like dark sentinels against the starry sky. Olive trees, fig trees, and peach trees filled my vision. During the day, they seemed so peaceful and open. Now, I wondered how I would find anyone among the branches and the odd shadows they cast in the light of the moon.

Growing up, we'd all heard so many stories of wild rendezvous in the palace orchard. The thought of my sister joining that list was too much. At least not with Ryvin. She deserved someone sweet and caring. She wasn't wild like Cora, or impulsive and detached like me. Sophia was the one who was most likely to find a love match. Could she live with herself if she was acting on our father's orders? She was so delicate, so optimistic about the world. I didn't want her out here doing something she wasn't interested in doing.

But what if she wanted this? What if she thought the ambassador wanted her? What would she do after he seduced her, then left to return home? Would she feel betrayed? Would she try to go with him?

My chest tightened. That was my worst fear. I didn't want

to lose any of my sisters. Especially not to Konos. Especially not Sophia. She was like sunshine. She'd wither and die under the gloomy cloud cover of Konos. Lagina could handle it. Even Cora could probably survive there. Not Sophia. She was made of pure joy; the antithesis of everything I was.

Wandering between trees in the dark was more difficult than I imagined. I walked for a while before stumbling across a couple entwined. They weren't who I was looking for, so I continued on. After several more encounters that weren't what I was seeking, I was starting to wonder if Vanth had given me bad advice. A bubble of relief floated up inside me. Maybe they'd not come out here at all.

That's when someone grabbed me from behind, their hand closing over my mouth before I could scream. I shoved my elbow back, nailing my attacker in the stomach, then twisted, trying to free myself.

"Stop moving, Asteri, and listen to me." Ryvin's rough voice was in my ear, his breath hot against my neck.

I struggled, and he pinned my arms to my side, holding me impossibly tight with one arm. Frustrated, I tried to bite at his hand, but he had it cupped enough that I couldn't do any damage.

"I told you to stop moving. For once in your life, just listen," he hissed.

Furious, I stilled, then glanced around for my sister. If she was here, she wasn't in my line of sight.

"I am done fighting with you." He took his hand from my mouth.

"Let me go," I hissed.

To my surprise, he released me. "Where's Sophia?"

"Why would I know?" He shrugged.

"Because you were dancing with her, then you both vanished."

"I danced with her because I knew it would infuriate you," he said.

"You're an asshole." I shook my head, then walked by him, making sure I shoved my shoulder into him as I passed him.

He grabbed my upper arm. "Where do you think you're going?"

"As far from you as I can." I knew I was supposed to distract him; to play nice, but there was something about him that made me so angry. I couldn't trust myself to stay. Tomorrow I could face this with the cool disinterest I needed to be smart around him.

Strong fingers closed around my upper arm, pulling me to a stop. I glanced back, eyes narrowed. I opened my mouth to curse at him, but was quickly silenced by his lips claiming mine.

I pushed away, but he wrapped his arms around me, pulling me closer. For a moment, I was stunned still, then I reacted, kissing him back, matching his hungry, frantic pace. Then I realized what I was doing and pulled away. His mouth crashed into mine again, his tongue darting into my parted lips.

My blood was molten, my skin tingled, wetness grew between my thighs. My body wanted this so badly, but I knew it was wrong. I knew I'd already crossed too many lines with him. Pushing back, I tried to break the kiss, but he leaned in, increasing the pressure. I struggled, squirming my way out of his grasp until I was finally free.

Then I slapped him across the face.

It didn't matter what I was supposed to do. He drove me insane. I couldn't do it.

Mostly because I knew if I started, I wasn't going to be able to stop. I was supposed to distract him, but I wasn't in control when I was with him. If I allowed this to happen, I'd get lost completely.

I wanted him more than I'd ever wanted to be with anyone. My whole body burned with desire, but I had to fight it.

He chuckled, a low rumbling kind of sound, and stared at me. His eyes seemed to glow in the moonlight, reminding me of a cat. I suddenly regretted not asking Vanth what exactly Ryvin was. Was he also a wolf? It would explain the lack of fangs.

He rubbed a hand over his cheek, then across his chin. He was looking at me as if I were his next meal. The expression was so intense I almost groaned.

I hated that I wanted him. It was so hard to resist him when every fiber of my being was crying out to touch him. To beg him to touch me.

I was broken.

I wasn't supposed to want him.

Seducing him was one thing, but the desire coursing through me was unbridled lust. It wasn't the curiosity turned pleasure I had with David. With him, there'd been no strings. No emotions. It was fun, detached, empty. It was never real. And I was always in control.

Somehow, in the few short days I'd spent hating Ryvin, I'd grown to crave him. If he asked me to, I'd let him break down all my defenses. I'd give everything over to him. It scared the shit out of me.

"I told you I wanted nothing to do with you," I spat. "And I told you to stay away from my sister."

"I danced with your sister, nothing more. And just so you know, she's an absolute delight," he said. "I have no idea how the two of you are related."

"Why do you continue to torture me like this?" My heart

hammered in my chest and I felt like I was burning up from the inside out. A gust of wind swept past, sending a rush of goosebumps down my bare arms, but I didn't feel cold.

He leaned in so close to me that I could smell him, despite the fragrant blossoms around us. His words came out so quiet, his gravelly whisper like a stroke of his fingers down my spine, "You are my favorite person to torture."

Something snapped.

I lunged for him, grasping his cheeks with my hands and pulling his face into mine. When our lips met, it was like an explosion, all that pent up desire mixing with unbridled rage. I hated this man, but I couldn't get enough of him. I couldn't stay away.

His hands slid down my body until they came to a rest at the small of my back. He pulled me against him, our bodies pressed so close I could feel that he was already fully hard.

"This doesn't change anything," I said between pants.

"Stop fighting what you want, Asteri." He bit down on my lower lip and I moaned, tipping my head back.

I tangled my fingers into his hair and pulled myself even closer to him. It was as if I couldn't get him close enough. Our kiss continued, frantic and angry. His stubble scraped across my cheeks and my lips already felt swollen, but I needed more. His tongue darted into my mouth, lightly testing. I responded aggressively, our tongues meeting and tangling just as brutally as our lips.

Fingers dug into my ass, unrelenting and forceful. There was need behind his grip; a need that I understood. I dropped my hands to the edges of his tunic, then broke from our kiss so I could help him out of it.

We were both breathless, moving wordlessly as we stripped our clothes as quickly as possible. For a moment, we stood there staring at each other in the moonlight. His body was just as perfect as I remembered. He was strong and lean, elegant and brutal. Like he was carved from marble before one of the gods breathed life into him.

I covered my chest, suddenly feeling like I wasn't enough compared to him. I was less soft curves and more muscle than a woman was supposed to be. There were scars from old injuries and I was no match for his beauty.

He stalked toward me like a panther, his eyes glinting in the light. Hungry, assessing, taking in every inch of me. Gripping my wrists, he lowered my arms to my sides before scanning my body. His tongue darted out, licking his bottom lip. "You are so fucking beautiful."

My breath caught in my chest and I met his gaze, searching for signs of lies; for the pretty words of a practiced courtier.

He gripped my chin roughly, lifting my face so I was looking up at him. "I am going to taste every inch of you and leave you in a shaking puddle when I'm done with you."

His lips were on me before I could respond, and all lingering self-conscious thoughts melted away. Our hands worked in a frenzy, touching and caressing and clawing at any bit of skin we could reach, while our kiss reached an angry crescendo.

Ryvin's hands moved from my cheeks to my hips. They trailed across my ribs and finally made their way to my aching breasts. He was rough and possessive, squeezing and kneading. He pinched each nipple, and I gasped. When he deepened the kiss, I groaned, the pain mingling with pleasure making everything feel so much more intense.

Tension wound tight low in my belly and I wrapped my leg around his waist, desperate to feel more friction.

He broke from the kiss, his lips moving to my ear. "Naughty girl, not so fast."

When he removed my leg from his hip, I whined.

With a chuckle, he stepped back from me, leaving me feeling empty and frustrated. "I told you I'd have you begging."

Clenching my jaw, I glared at him. I refused to beg. I refused to give him the satisfaction. It was taking every fiber of my being to not launch myself at him. If he walked away now, I might chase him.

I might even beg.

My body was desperate to touch him again. To feel his skin against mine. To feel him inside me.

"I think that look in your eyes might be the most deadly I've seen from you," he teased.

I moved faster than I knew possible, leaping onto him, wrapping both legs around his waist. He gripped my ass, his mouth finding mine with a moan that told me he wanted this just as badly as I did. I dug my fingernails into his back, holding on so tightly he couldn't let me go.

I didn't recognize myself. I was a woman possessed; desperate, insatiable. I needed everything he could give me.

When my back hit the soft earth, I finally released my grip. Ryvin was on his knees between my thighs and I got the sense that this was a man who was never on his knees for anyone. My chest swelled and something warm seeped into my very soul.

No.

I might not be able to fight the physical attraction, but there was no way I would allow him into my heart.

"I'm still not begging," I said.

"I'm not finished yet." He lowered his head and then I felt his tongue brush against the sensitive nub between my thighs.

I gasped. "What are you doing?"

"Stop talking, Asteri." It was an order.

He licked me again, and I flinched, the sensation pure pleasure but nothing like I'd ever experienced before. I lifted myself to my elbows and pulled away. "Stop it."

His brow furrowed. "You don't like it?"

"I don't know." It was confusing. I'd never experienced anything like it.

"Did your past lovers not take time to pleasure you?" he asked.

I enjoyed sex with David fine. It was fun and easy, but it was never about me. I found pleasure in it often, but not always.

"Let me make you feel good," he said softly.

His change in tone took me off guard. It was too intimate, too familiar. "Why?"

"Because how else am I supposed to ruin you for other men?"

There he was. There was that asshole I knew.

Dark shadows slithered around us and I sucked in a breath, recalling the shadows I'd seen around him before.

"Do you trust me?" he asked.

Did I trust him? He was my enemy. He wasn't even human.

"Say the word and we stop right now," he offered.

Panic rang out. "No. Don't stop."

His grin was feline. "Then stop fighting me or I'll have to make you stop."

"You can try," I challenged.

He reached between my legs and brushed his thumb over my clit. I tensed, unused to the sensation. How had I never felt anything like this before? My past experiences were rushed thrusts. Nothing like this.

Ryvin continued to stroke and circle the sensitive nub, and I bit down on my lower lip to keep from moaning.

"Now, be a good girl and let me worship this magnificent body." When he lowered his head again, I tried to still, but the sensation was so overwhelming that I sat up again.

"Naughty girl," Ryvin chided. "You want me to stop?"

I shook my head. It was so different, but it felt so good. I didn't want him to stop.

The shadows swirling around us closed in, several of them slithering across my torso and arms like serpents of smoke. My heart raced, and I tried to move, but they were holding me in place. Eyes wide, panic made my pulse race, but his mouth was on me again, distracting me. I tensed again, but the shadows held me in place. My body tensed, writhing as he licked and sucked.

Panting, my fingers dug into the earth, eager for anything to grip as pressure built. Slowly, he slid a finger inside me and I gasped, the dual sensations chasing away my resistance.

I gave in, my mind relaxing as I welcomed the pleasure.

"That's it, Asteri, give in to me." Another finger slipped inside, curling until it hit a place that made my back arch. His tongue teased my clit, fingers pumping. Pressure built, winding tighter as my breathing grew more rapid.

"Stop fighting me."

It was too much. My body was overwhelmed, the building pressure too intense. Suddenly, it was as if an explosion tore through me, sending a shockwave of pleasure that made my whole body quiver. Sweaty and panting, I had to close my eyes to recover as waves of tiny aftershocks rolled through me.

I shuddered, then opened my eyes, meeting Ryvin's pleased expression. He was on his knees again, caged in by my legs. "Good girl."

The shadows receded, and I pushed myself to my elbows. "I've never felt anything like that before."

"We're just getting started."

He grabbed my ankle and pulled, my bare ass dragging over the earth, until my entrance was nearly touching his knees.

I knew he'd be looking for his own release, and that was something I was far more experienced with. While no man had never had his mouth on me so intimately, I'd certainly learned how to please a man with my lips. I reached for his cock and Ryvin grabbed my wrist. "I'm not done with you yet."

Hazy with need, heat swelled between my thighs at the promise of more. "Then let me touch you."

"That sounds a lot like begging." He nipped at my earlobe and I groaned reflexively.

"Not begging," I panted. "Returning the favor. It's called being polite."

"Since when did you care about being polite around me?" His lips moved to my neck. Lips and teeth and tongue making their way down to my collarbone.

My chest heaved, and I could feel the wetness pooling between my thighs.

His hands were on my hips and he lifted me without effort, setting me down on his lap. Now I was the one straddling him. A little rush of power flickered inside me. I could take some control in this position. I ground against him, eager to feel his cock inside me.

"Not yet, Asteri." He grabbed the back of my head and pulled me toward him until our lips crashed together again. I met the kiss eagerly, unable to get enough of him. My hips moved, grinding and undulating against him.

He moaned into my mouth. "You are going to undo me."

"Then let me," I breathed. On my knees, I lifted myself so I could reposition. He didn't fight me this time as I hovered above him. The tip of his cock brushed against my entrance, and it was like time slowed. Using my hand, I guided him to me, keeping my eyes locked on his.

His chest rose and fell, his hands still on my back. It was as if he was committing this to memory, taking it all in. Or maybe that was just me. I wanted to retain this moment forever, burn his silver eyes and his handsome face into my memory.

Alarm bells rang in my mind, a keening, deafening warning that I was getting too deep. This was quickly becoming too personal, too intimate. I wanted him. I wanted all of him. And not because of how good he was making me feel, but for reasons I wasn't willing to admit to myself.

It wasn't supposed to be that way. I was losing control.

Losing myself.

"Asteri..." His brow furrowed slightly, and I caught a glimpse of concern. Vulnerability.

There couldn't be any of that. This was just sex.

I lowered my hips quickly, and his cock slammed into me. He groaned, his back arching, fingers digging into my hips. I sucked in a breath as he stretched me in the best way. Slowly, I began to move, rolling, lifting and lowering, each movement drawing pleasure that continued to build.

His hips worked with mine, his hands exploring my skin, his mouth leaving a trail of kisses over every sensitive part.

He was impossibly warm and cold at the same time, his body moving with mine as if we were in a dance only the two of us knew. It was so different from anything I'd experienced in the past. It was as if all of me was responding to him on instinct. As if I could anticipate his every movement.

We moved in unison, touching and tasting. My senses were in overdrive; hyper aware of the way his fingers left a trial of tingles across my skin, tasting the wine he'd had in his kiss, catching that sea salt scent of him. I was consumed, experiencing too much all at once.

His fingers trailed along my back, sending shivers down my spine. Then he pulled me closer, his hands rough and demanding. Our mouths met in a frenzy; colliding together with desperation that matched the rising tension in my core. Pressure built, and I gasped and moaned as he deepened the kiss. Our tongues met, tangling together, fighting for dominance. We kissed like we fought. That push and pull; the hate mingling with something else, something I didn't want to give a name to.

Suddenly, he gripped my hair and pulled my head away. Gasping, I looked down at him, noting the heavy look in his eyes. He was pure predator. The gaze was intense and claiming. I could feel the power behind that look and it terrified me.

"Ara..."

I didn't let him finish. I leaned down, silencing him with my mouth and moving my hips faster. He groaned, his hands gripping fistfuls of my hair, pulling slightly as our tongues resumed their battle.

The pain mixing with the rising pleasure was driving me insane. My breath came out in short bursts, my body like a firework ready to ignite.

"Come for me," he coaxed.

I gave in.

And I exploded.

My back arched, and I cried out as my orgasm ripped through me, sending waves of pleasure radiating from my core. It was impossibly intense, making my eyes roll into the back of my head.

Strong hands supported my back, the only thing keeping me from falling. Gasping and tingly all over, I opened my eyes, and he lifted me so I was sitting upright again. With a satisfied grin, he leaned close until our foreheads touched. Everything around me faded. It was just the two of us here, everyone else in the world no longer existed. Silently, we stared at each other, our breathing the only sound.

"I'm not finished with you," he growled, breaking our silence.

I wasn't sure how much I had left, but I wasn't about to turn down more.

Suddenly, I was on my back with Ryvin between my legs. With a wicked smirk, he stretched my arms out above my head. A trail of cold drifted across my wrists and I startled, surprised by the sensation. I tried to lift my arms, but they were pinned to the ground.

I opened my mouth to say something, but his lips closed around my nipple and I moaned, too distracted to care. His fingers slid down my stomach until they reached my clit. Between his lips, tongue, and fingers, he had my hips bucking and back arching over and over. I was dying to touch him, the inability to use my arms driving me insane.

Panting and riding the wave of another orgasm, I had to resist the urge to beg. "Release my arms."

"I don't think I will," he said.

"I want to touch you."

"Not yet."

He was such an asshole.

When his head went between my legs again, I almost lost it completely. The desire to run my hands through his dark hair, or dig my fingernails into his back was making me ravenous.

His tongue teased my clit, fingers thrusting into me. Gasping and moaning, I fought the rising orgasm until I couldn't anymore. I cried out, my hips bucking wildly as I climaxed again.

Ryvin hovered above me, his hips settled between my thighs, his arms caging me in, those silver eyes locked on mine. I was going to break in two if I couldn't feel him. "Release me," I repeated. "Please."

He smirked. "That sounds like begging to me, Princess."

It was. I was desperate to touch him. But I couldn't tell him that. "I just don't like feeling trapped."

"You're even more beautiful when you lie."

I felt the cold dissipate, and I tested my arms. They came free, and I wasted no time in grabbing him and pulling him to me. We met in a ravenous kiss, my hands gripping and stroking and touching every inch of him I could. Then he plunged his cock into me and I moaned into his mouth.

Chest to chest, I held him against me, feeling his hot breath against my neck as he lavished kisses on me. The hunger we'd started with returned and our hips and hands moved in greedy movements, as if we couldn't get enough of one another. As if we had to take everything we could get. As if this was our only chance.

My breathing grew rapid, tension building. I dug my fingernails into his back and just as I lost control again, I felt him thicken inside me. With a groan, he found his release.

Panting and sweaty, Ryvin leaned down and kissed me gently. Tender, soft, intimate. My throat tightened, and I cupped his cheeks, drawing out the kiss before making myself turn away.

I couldn't let this mean anything, but it felt like everything had changed.

CHAPTER 21

"I'm going to bed. Alone," I said, even though I desperately wanted to grab his hand and haul him to my bedroom for another round. You'd think that would have appeased me, but all it did was make me crave him more. I knew if I didn't get away, I'd fall into his embrace all over again.

"After all that, you still want to keep me at arm's length?" Ryvin asked with a laugh.

"This doesn't change anything between us and it can't happen again," I warned. "I still don't approve of what you're doing here, and I never will."

"You've made that abundantly clear," he said.

"Have you already decided who you'll take back?" I hated that we'd have to watch a group of our own leave the city, but if my father could ensure this was the last time, maybe their sacrifices would be worth it.

"I'm actually not the one who chooses." Ryvin stepped into his trousers and my eyes dropped to catch a last glimpse of his still enlarged cock before he tied up the drawstring.

I forced my gaze back to his face. "Who does?"

"Morta knows what we're looking for," he explained.

"How does she choose?" Was it random then? Allowing a

blind woman to point to people? Was that better or worse than if Ryvin did it himself?

"It's her gift. She knows who should go," he said.

I shuddered, not sure I wanted to know what kind of magic was lurking under that childlike façade.

"It's all outlined in the original treaty. We just follow the rules established by your king." He pulled his tunic over his head.

"And yours?"

"Your people got the better deal, believe it or not."

"How is that possible? I don't see you sacrificing your own to whatever beast lurks on Konos," I said.

"We lose too many in our own way. Often, to put down rebellions driven by a desire to claim your city."

"Why not just let them have their way so you don't have to protect us anymore?" I asked.

"I've considered it, but the tributes are necessary and good for morale," he said, his expression completely blank. He had no emotional response regarding the slaughter of human lives.

It was a reminder of how dangerous he was. Suddenly feeling cold, I wrapped my arms around myself, my thin dress doing little to shield me from the chill of the evening air.

"What are you?" The words came out without thinking, without any sugarcoating.

He smoothed his tunic, then slipped his feet into his sandals before walking over to where I was standing. With a gentle movement, he stroked the back of his hand from my temple to my chin. "Don't you worry about me. I'll be out of your life in a matter of days. Sometimes it's better not to know certain things."

I pulled away from his touch, then frowned. "I can handle more than you know."

"I know you can. But I like the way you look at me. Like you're trying to decide if you want to drive a sword through my chest or stick your tongue down my throat."

He summed up the way I felt about him better than I could. Even now, as my body was still basking in the afterglow of orgasm, I was contemplating if ending his life would benefit my people.

"Ara, what are *you* doing out here?"

I spun, my cheeks heating, to face Cora. She wore a knowing grin. "Well, well. This is a surprise."

"It's not what you think," I said.

"I guess you took father's request to keep the ambassador busy to heart. He'll be pleased." Cora stumbled, giggling as her partner caught her.

"Nice to see you again, Ara," Tomas said, his words slurring slightly. They were both drunk, and I was hoping they didn't recall this meeting in the morning.

"I was just leaving. Have fun, you two." I turned away from my sister and walked toward the palace. I heard her giggles receding as I hurried away from the ambassador.

"So that's what this was all about?" Ryvin said from behind me, his tone amused. "You were distracting me? From what, I wonder. What could the King of Athos want to hide so badly that he'd send his daughter as my whore?"

My eyes widened, and I whipped around. "How dare you!"

"Am I wrong? Were you asked to use your body to entertain me? What kind of father would request such a thing? Especially when you make it so clear you despise me."

Jaw clenched, hands balled into fists, I glared at him. He was right. My father should never have asked this of me. But

I knew that I would have refused if there wasn't a part of me that desired Ryvin. "You don't know anything."

"I know you're fighting your own nature. I know there's darkness in you, desperate to get out. It calls to you, and you're suffocating every time you resist."

"Don't you put your Konos bullshit on me. There's nothing going on with me. I'm just doing what I can to help my family and my people," I said.

"You call me the monster, but your own father sends you to seduce me." He shook his head. "Humans act like they're better than us, when they're just as corrupt and immoral."

"You kissed me first." I stared at him, daring him to challenge me.

"You wanted me. If I had known it wasn't free will, I never would have proceeded," he said. "I may be made of darkness, but I swore to you that I would never hurt you, and I will honor that oath."

My breath was ragged, my emotions a tumultuous, tumbling mess. How was it that I could look at him and believe him? Anger radiated from him like dark waves, making the air around us feel heavy. He was furious, but I didn't feel like any of it was directed at me. I should be terrified, but I wasn't. I knew in my gut he would never harm me, just as he claimed.

But this couldn't be. I had gone to him out of duty. Nothing more. Anything I was feeling had to be false. It was self-preservation's way of helping me do what I needed to do. I couldn't trust my own emotions. Not where he was concerned. This wasn't going to go well for either of us now that the truth was out there. I'd have to tell my father that he must find a way to hide what he was doing better. The ambassador was going to be looking for anything out of the ordinary now.

"When you're ready to admit what you are, I'll be waiting," he said.

"I don't owe you anything," I said, my voice shaky.

"You certainly do not, your highness," he said.

I tensed, hating the use of my formal title on his lips. I probably wasn't going to hear the annoying nickname again. "Goodnight, ambassador." I turned and walked away before I said anything I'd regret.

Disappointment sunk like a weight in my stomach, but I shook it off, reminding myself that I hated him in the first place. Why should I care if he knew the truth? That was the reason for all of this, wasn't it? I'd figure out a way to help my father keep Konos from discovering anything. There had to be another way. I supposed the only good thing to come of this was that Ryvin wouldn't trust my sisters, either. He'd suspect if any of them threw themselves at him.

When I reached the fountain, I paused to slip my abandoned sandals back on. Ryvin wasn't anywhere in sight.

Good.

The last thing I needed was a man getting emotionally attached to me. I should probably thank Cora. If I had continued with this plan, I might be the one having to turn down a trip to Konos.

So why did it hurt so much knowing that I'd likely not speak to Ryvin again before he left?

As I made my way back to my room, one thought floated into my mind over and over. Ryvin was right about one thing: My father never should have asked this of me in the first place.

My head throbbed, and I pressed my palm to my forehead, groaning as I recalled exactly how much I'd had to drink last night. Then I remembered what else I'd done last night. "Fuck."

Carefully, I rolled out of bed and noticed a maid was in my bathing chamber filling the tub with water. She worked quietly, moving slowly, probably trying not to wake me until everything was prepared.

It was the opposite of Mila. She'd have already woken me with a knowing expression. She'd have heard the rumors about last night already. Somehow, Mila knew everything about everyone. She never asked outright, but I could tell she always knew what I had been doing.

My heart hurt worse than my head.

And last night I'd been with the enemy. It didn't matter if Ryvin swore his men never touched Mila, I knew what I saw. Those puncture wounds weren't natural.

"Good morning, your highness," the maid said. "Did you sleep well?"

I made a grunting kind of affirmative sound then rubbed my eyes before pushing myself to standing. The room spun and a wave of nausea rolled through me. I covered my mouth with my hand and closed my eyes until the sensation eased.

"My name is Clara," she said. "I'll be looking after you while Mila is away."

My brow furrowed. Mila wasn't away, she was dead. And she was never coming back. I knew my father didn't want anyone to know the circumstances of her death, but why would he claim she was away? It wasn't like the city was so large she could hide forever. People would notice her missing. "Did they say how long she'd be gone?"

Clara shook her head. "No, your highness."

Of course not. I had a momentary recollection of all the

nannies from my childhood. Always gone to visit family or ended their position for one reason or another. But none of them ever returned. What if Mila wasn't the first to have such a gruesome death? I tried to pinpoint when the Choosing was and if it lined up with the never-ending parade of nannies.

My head ached, and I pressed my palm to my forehead. I was too hungover to think about such things. I'd try to ask Lagina later. Maybe she'd remember more details.

"At the risk of overstepping," Clara said, "I brought you a draught that might help your head. If your head is sore, that is." She held up a small glass vial with a pink liquid inside.

"You heard?" I asked, knowing she was referring to the wine I consumed, but wondering if the news was out that I'd been in the gardens with the ambassador. Anyone could have walked by and we'd never have noticed.

Her cheeks flushed, the color spreading to her neck and ears. "I just know how much drinking happens at those kinds of events."

I took the vial from her. "I know you heard. I know how quickly word spreads." I uncorked the bottle, then knocked the liquid back. "Thank you."

"Would you like me to wash your hair?"

Most of the time, I requested to bathe alone, but today, it was probably a good idea to accept the help. "Thank you."

Clara guided me into the tub and I sank gratefully into the warm water. She poured in some oil, then scattered the surface with flower petals. The familiar scents of chamomile and lavender soothed me almost instantly.

I dragged my fingertips across the water's surface, letting my body relax. Tension eased, and my arms felt too heavy for me to lift. I lowered them into the water, watching how the dried petals drifted in the current, swirling and floating around me like little clouds.

Whatever was in that drought had eliminated my headache and my mind felt gloriously empty, all the worry and stress melting away. I couldn't remember the last time I'd felt this relaxed. Slumping deeper into the water, I let my body go limp, resisting the urge to hold myself up. Warm water lapped against my chin and something in the back of my head was trying to claw its way out, like a muted warning, but I couldn't be bothered right now. It was too peaceful; too calm. My eyes felt heavy and I couldn't think of a single reason they should stay open.

With a sigh, I let them close. I no longer felt in control of my own limbs. I was simply floating here and all I could think of was how light I was. And how sleepy I was.

Clara poured warm water over my head and began to work soap into a lather. "I don't know if you remember me, but we've met before."

"Hmmm?" I hummed, speaking felt like too much work.

"David introduced us. He's my cousin. Well, was my cousin, I suppose, since he's dead now."

A little flicker of panic tried to flare to life, but faded quickly. Her words felt so far away. As if they were being spoken from the other side of a long tunnel.

"Good night, Princess."

I felt pressure on my shoulders, and without resistance, I sank below the surface.

"I can't leave you alone for a second, can I?" The voice was familiar, but so far away. Angry. Why was he so angry?

My eyes fluttered, but I couldn't open them fully. Head lolling to the side, I tried to move, but I couldn't control myself. A moment of terror was quickly squashed by a sense of calm. Emotions clawed at the back of my mind, trying to make their way to the surface, but all I could do was slump forward as someone dragged me out of the bath.

Water sloughed from me, making a puddle on the floor, my feet finding the hard surface of the porous stone, but I couldn't make myself stand. Leaning forward, all my weight was against a firm chest, my arms limp at my side.

"Kill the maid," the voice ordered.

A whimper, then a cry quickly silenced before the sound of a body hitting the floor.

That seemed like it should be bad, but I couldn't bring myself to care. I tried to open my eyes again, but it was too difficult, so I stopped bothering. Instead, I let myself melt against the warm embrace of whoever was holding me.

I knew he was familiar. I knew I knew him, but everything was too fuzzy. But it didn't matter anyway. Thinking took too much effort.

My legs went weightless, and I was moving. Someone was carrying me.

"Get Ahmet, now. We need his blood before the princess dies."

My eyelids felt like they were sealed shut and I could tell I was somewhere new now. Maybe my bed? Letting go of all resistance, I sunk into oblivion.

CHAPTER 22

Everything hurt.

My whole body felt like it was burning up from the inside out.

I wanted to scream, but all I could do was curl up on my side and grasp my churning stomach. Something was wrong. So very, very wrong.

Panting, soaked in sweat, I turned to the other side, trying to find any position that might ease the agony I was feeling.

Nothing helped.

Then everything came up. I turned over the edge of the bed and retched, over and over, until there was nothing left.

A cool cloth wiped the sweat from my brow, then wiped my mouth. I relaxed a little, finally feeling some relief. I could hear someone moving around, possibly cleaning up the mess I'd just made. How many people were in my room?

My eyes fluttered open, and it took a moment for them to focus enough to see around my darkened room. A lantern flickered and glowed on my desk, casting dim light on my bed. I didn't need the light to know who was wiping my brow. I could feel him. It didn't make sense, but I knew it was him before I opened my eyes.

I looked around for signs of Mythiuss or my sisters. They

were absent. Ryvin dipped the cloth in a bowl of water, then rang it out before applying it to my forehead.

At my door were two guards, both his men. I recognized one as Vanth, the man I'd danced with last night. Had that been last night?

"What happened?" My voice came out like a croak.

"An attempt was made on your life," Ryvin said.

"What?"

"Your maid. She gave you something to drink, do you remember?" He was quiet, his tone more gentle than I'd ever heard.

"I do. Something for my head. From the wine the night before." My brow furrowed as I tried to recall what I last remembered. "She helped me into the bath, then I went under, didn't I? And you - how did you know?"

"I came to speak to you about something and found you," he said.

"I should be dead." If he hadn't come to my room, I would be. What about the maid? She seemed so nice. How had I misjudged her so terribly?

"She's dead, if you're wondering about your maid," Ryvin said.

I rubbed at my temples and closed my eyes. My emotions were a tangled mess. I hated that she was dead, but she had tried to kill me. And I'd already seen Ryvin kill someone on my behalf once before. This was becoming a habit I didn't care for.

"Why is it that people keep trying to kill me since you arrived?" I asked, attempting a joke, but my tone came out serious.

"You won't have to worry about that much longer." Water splashed, and I knew he'd dropped the cloth back into the basin. "I've asked your father to move up the Choosing ceremony. We're holding it tomorrow night, then we're gone."

I opened my eyes. Wasn't that exactly what I wanted? I'd failed at maintaining my composure around him and after Cora's words, he knew I was trying to distract him. Having him leave early was even better than trying to appease him while he was here. I should be happy I had a solution. It solved everything. The issues of my confusion regarding Ryvin and the promise I'd made to my father.

So why was my pulse racing in panic at the thought of watching him sail away?

"Where are my sisters?" It should have been my first question. If someone was trying to kill me, they had to be after my family as well. "My father?"

"And why are you and your men with me? Why don't I have palace guards?" I swung my legs over the bed, realizing that I was in my nightgown, which meant someone had dressed me. There were bigger problems right now, though. Who had seen me naked was the least of my concerns. Especially since I had a feeling it was likely Ryvin who'd dressed me.

Ryvin backed away, giving me some space. I stood, then swayed, a wave of nausea forcing me back to sitting. I closed my eyes until it passed.

Finally feeling like I regained control, I looked at the ambassador. "Tell me what the fuck is going on here."

"Your father doesn't know about the attack," Ryvin admitted. "We sent word with another maid that you weren't feeling well and wanted to be alone. Nobody knows we're here."

"My family?"

"They're fine. Going about their usual business," he said.

"Nobody else was attacked?" I asked.

He shook his head.

"I still don't understand why you're here," I said.

"Now that you're awake and passing the poison, I don't need to remain," he said.

"Poison." I shook my head. "I still don't understand."

"I think someone found out the truth about David."

My eyes widened. "I told my father, but he already knew. Maybe someone heard us?"

"Well, don't tell anyone else and you should be fine." His eyes seemed to flash before getting darker than I'd seen in a long time. "I took care of the problem."

"What did you do?" I shouldn't have asked.

"I told you I'd protect you." He stood. "You should rest. I'll tell your father you were distracting me all day. Just as you were instructed. He should be pleased with you."

My jaw tensed. There was hurt in his tone, but I shouldn't care. I couldn't care. Everything between us had been what it needed to be. It wasn't like it was a new idea to use your daughters as bartering chips with powerful families. The only difference was I wasn't being sold into marriage. At least that's what I kept telling myself as I tried to justify my father's actions.

"Don't drink any more poison. I can't guarantee I'll be here next time." He walked to the door, his guards parting to allow him to exit first.

As soon as they were all gone, I burrowed under my blankets, unable to resist the exhaustion tugging me under. His presence and what I'd just been through added so many new questions to my mind, but I wasn't sure I wanted to know all those answers.

Sunlight streamed into my room and I could hear the sounds of someone moving around. I sat up too quickly, tossing my sheets to the side and leaping from my bed. Lightheaded and slightly off balance, I had to use my arms to steady myself for a moment before turning to see a woman retreating from a tray she'd set on my desk.

"I didn't mean to startle you, your highness." The servant bowed, keeping her eyes downcast.

"Who are you?" I asked.

"I'm Iris. They sent me to care for you while Mila is away with her sick mother."

So that was the excuse they'd given. And that was about Mila. What about the other woman who'd been here last night? Had she even been sent by the staff? Or had she snuck in with the intention of harming me?

"I brought you some tea. How are you feeling? I was informed that you'd taken the day to rest yesterday and that you might need help preparing for the day."

"I was," I said, my words coming out too quickly, "sick, that is. I'm better today. I can take it from here."

"Of course, your highness." Iris curtseyed, then retreated, leaving me alone in my room.

I eyed the tea suspiciously and avoided it, heading straight to my bathing chamber. Deciding I wasn't up for a bath, I washed and dressed quickly so I could leave the confines of my room. Ryvin had said my sisters were safe, but I needed to see them for myself.

To my great relief, all three of my sisters were sitting in the breakfast room when I arrived.

"Welcome back, Ara," Cora teased. "Nice to see it wasn't me this time."

"I'm glad you had some fun for a change," Sophia said.

Lagina was chewing slowly, watching me with a look that

said more than any words. She knew exactly what I'd done that night. And exactly who I'd been with. I could tell she was trying desperately not to judge me, but it was tearing her in two.

I settled into the chair across from her. "Just say what you need to say before you explode."

She swallowed, then took a sip of water. "I'm not saying anything."

I reached for the smallest honey cake. My stomach felt strange. I wasn't quite sure if I was hungry or if I needed to throw up again. "Get it over with now. While it's just us and there's nobody else around."

"Yeah, Gina, do tell," Cora encouraged.

"Ara didn't do anything wrong," Sophia said, ever the mediator.

"I can't believe you fucked him," Lagina spat, the statement coming out much in the same way someone who'd been deprived of oxygen would suck in their first breath of fresh air.

I pulled a small piece from my cake and popped it in my mouth, waiting for her to say more.

"After all your talk, all the judgment about the Choosing, you let him have you? The ambassador? Their leader. I mean, I could see maybe one of the guards…"

"There are some attractive ones," Cora added with a shrug.

"I mean, Father had to ask Sophia to step up because you couldn't keep him busy so you decide the only way to do it is to fuck him? What is wrong with you?" She dropped the roll she was holding onto her plate.

"Are you finished?" I tore off another piece of my cake and rolled it around in my fingers, too distracted to eat.

"I just can't believe you did that. Aren't you still mourning David?"

Now I dropped my cake, and my hands clenched into fists. "First of all, don't bring him up with me ever again."

Her lips parted, and she sucked in a slight breath of surprise at my tone.

"Secondly, who I bed is none of your business. And how I fulfill my duties to our family is not up for debate. I was tasked with distracting him. I did my job." I couldn't bring myself to admit that our father had asked me to take things as far as needed. Or that during the party, in the gardens, I needed Ryvin as much as I needed air. I'd had a choice and now I had to live with that.

"I could have continued dancing with him, Ara. You didn't have to do that," Sophia said. "I'm happy to help."

"I don't want you anywhere near him," I snapped.

She tensed.

"I'm sorry, Sophia. But Lagina has every right to be upset about any of us being around him. Better me than any of you." I stared at each of my sisters in turn. "You hear me? Let me do this for our family. Let me be useful for once."

"You are useful, Ara. You're preparing to go to the wall," Lagina said gently, her typically calm demeanor returning. "I'm sorry for what I said. I was out of line."

I looked at her, searching for any signs of dishonesty. She didn't look like she was hiding anything. She didn't know. She didn't know about the dragons or what was coming. She didn't know that he'd asked me to occupy the ambassador to this extent. Father was planning for war and he'd left her out of all of it.

I stood. "Excuse me. I'm afraid my stomach isn't quite up to breakfast yet."

"Don't go, Ara. I'm sorry. I didn't mean it," Lagina said.

"I know and I understand." Probably more than she'd ever know. She was only pissed because she was worried about me, and I loved her for that. The two of us were so different in so many ways, but we were both bound by a strong sense of duty and we both worried about each other. One of these days, perhaps we'd reform the connection we'd had when we were younger, but for now, we were in different places, even if our goals were the same.

Before I could change my mind, I made my way to my father's study. I wasn't sure what I was going to tell him. Would I tell him what I'd done with Ryvin? Or how I'd ended things with him or that he'd been back in my room last night saving my life? Should I let him know that Cora spilled about my intentions? Did any of it matter now that they'd requested to move the Choosing?

I had no idea what I should say, but I knew I had to do something other than sit in the breakfast room waiting.

The study door was closed, several guards stationed outside. Most of them were newer again. That had been the pattern lately, so many new guards. Was this because they'd all left the wall and come here? It explained how disheveled many of them appeared. Standards must be different at the wall.

"How can we help you, Princess?" One of the guards asked. He was older, with a full dark beard streaked with white. Most of the guards were clean-shaven or kept their beards short. He must be one of the new recruits, but at least he knew who I was.

"I need to speak with my father," I said.

The guard nodded, then knocked on the door twice. It opened quickly, Istvan's face peering out through the small gap. "Princess?"

"I need to speak to my father," I repeated.

The door closed and my nostrils flared as anger surged. Then the door opened wider and Istvan inclined his head while sweeping his arm into the room in welcome.

I would have been less surprised at being kicked out.

Inside, my father was hunched over his desk while advisors stood on either side of him. They were staring at piles of documents, some of them yellow with age. The door closed hard behind me, making everyone in the room look up at me.

My father's wrinkled brow softened, and he turned over the document he'd been reading. "Ara. My darling girl, what can I do for you?"

"I just need a minute," I said, glancing around at the others in the room.

"Is this about David's sisters and mother?" he asked.

"What about them?" This wasn't what I'd come for, but my stomach twisted into knots in response to the sympathy painted on my father's face. "What happened?"

"Terrible tragedy. Their home burned down last night. There were no survivors."

"What?" Suddenly, a foggy memory materialized. The maid who'd poisoned me. Hadn't she said something about David? I could feel the color draining from my face. Ryvin. He told me he'd taken care of things. Was that what he meant?

He did this. Or his men did this.

"I'm sorry, dear. I know you were worried about them after David's death."

"I was," I said. But perhaps I hadn't been worried for the right reasons. Was it possible they were behind the attack on me? Ryvin certainly thought they were connected, or at least a threat.

The worst part was that I knew if it were reversed, and someone had killed one of my sisters, I'd do the same thing. I wouldn't hesitate. I would want vengeance on their killer. And that's what I was. They'd come after me for taking the life of one of their own.

My chest tightened. I deserved it, didn't I?

"What did you wish to speak to me about?" My father asked, breaking me from my ruminations.

"The task you gave me," I said, my mind returning to the request my father had given me. I didn't want to share about my near-death. Not now. Not when I knew the culprits were already likely dead. "He knows."

My father stood. "Everyone out."

I waited silently while the room cleared. My father walked around his desk so he was standing next to me. "He knows what exactly?"

"That I was tasked with distracting him," I said.

"But that's it?" He asked.

I nodded. "Cora found us together in the garden…"

"I see." My father cleared his throat, clearly uncomfortable with the topic. "You did well and I'm sorry I put that burden on you."

"I can't distract him further," I admitted.

"Is that why he requested we move up the Choosing?"

I nodded. "You'll do it, right? So we can be done with Konos for now?"

"Preparations are already underway. The ceremony will happen tonight," he confirmed. "You did well, Ara. Better than I could have hoped for."

His praise felt hollow. Empty. There was so much conflict in my heart. All of my interactions with the ambassador were a ploy; but it didn't feel that way if I was honest with myself.

"What about the tributes? Please tell me there's something we can do to stop it." If we were so close to starting a war, why not risk angering Konos now? We could spare so many innocent lives.

"I'm afraid that can't be helped this year, but you understand what their sacrifice will bring to all of us," he said.

"Why? Why can't we refuse? Send the delegation back without them. Let them come with their armies if that's what's going to happen, anyway."

"We need more time and the tributes gain that for us. I know it's not what you want to hear, but remind yourself that they will be the last," he said.

I swallowed against a lump in my throat. His words made sense, but I couldn't help but feel I was no better than those I stood against if I allowed this to happen. Was there anything I could do? What if I had taken things even further with Ryvin? Would he have turned down the tributes for me? What if I offered myself in their place?

It was too late for any of that now. There was no way the ambassador would want to see me again. Why he'd bothered to save my life was a mystery.

"You don't have to stay for the ceremony if it's too much," he offered. "Do you want to go for a while? Stay at a temple?" His tone was gentle, and it made me stiffen. It felt like I'd just leaned up against jagged pieces of broken glass. Every bit of me was on high alert.

"Is that what you want from me? To send me away?" I asked.

"Of course not. It's just that Ophelia mentioned that you might want to be away from men for a while after what we asked you to do," he said.

"We?" Since when was Ophelia part of his plans?

"What *I* asked you to do," he clarified.

"I will never serve at a temple," I said.

"There's no shame in a quiet life."

His words made my head swim. Was this the plan for me once this was over? The wall was no longer an option, and I wasn't needed. What would become of me after the Choosing? If we went to war, everything was going to change.

"We can discuss it more later," he said. "Get some rest today. After the ceremony tonight, everything will be much more clear."

CHAPTER 23

The morning was a haze. I wandered the palace, my mind at war. Logically, I understood the sacrifice the tributes were making, but it still felt wrong. The palace was a flurry of activity. Everyone was preparing for the ceremony tonight. They'd been preparing for this for months, but with the sudden date change, all the careful plans were in upheaval.

My stomach twisted at the thought of the people who would have their names called. While moving up the ceremony helped my father's goals, it gave all those tributes less time to say goodbye. How many of them had plans for this week? Last visits to family and friends? Favorite meals planned, outings or activities... anything to enjoy what might be their final days in Athos.

All the tributes had that stripped from them. Their families would go home tonight to empty homes, knowing they'd never see their loved one again. Those who were spared would spend the night indulging in luxuries and dancing until sunrise. How could I be a part of this?

Maybe I was just as bad as the men who attacked me had claimed. What had I done to help them? I'd bedded the Konos ambassador.

If we did make an alliance with the dragons, this could be the final Choosing. It would save so many of my people, but I was helpless to save those whose names would be called tonight. Maybe there was something I could do. Maybe I could have one final word with Ryvin and ask for a loophole. There had to be one, right? In all the stories of the fae, there was always a loophole.

On my walk to lunch, I caught sight of people already flooding into the palace grounds, hours ahead of the Tribute Ceremony. The guards would pass out food and gifts all afternoon, leading up to the main event at sunset when the Konos delegation would announce the names of the tributes. I didn't know if it would be fourteen, or a hundred. All I knew was that it felt wrong.

"You should eat, Ara," Sophia encouraged, breaking me from my thoughts.

I tore my gaze away from the window where I'd been staring, unfocused, at the blue sea beyond.

"Still hungover?" Cora teased.

"Just distracted," I said as I reached for the pitcher and poured myself some water. "It's not a day I'm thrilled about, you know."

"It's almost over," Lagina said, her tone soothing. She set a honey cake on my plate. "Sophia's right, you should eat. There's only so much you can control."

"At least the ambassador will be gone tomorrow," Cora said, her mouth full of food.

I hummed, the thought causing mixed feelings I wasn't thrilled about. There was a part of me that wasn't looking forward to saying goodbye, but I knew I'd get over that once he was gone.

"Listen to your sisters," my father said from where he sat across from me.

I offered a smile, reminding myself that at least we were free of Ophelia's presence. My father had announced that the queen wasn't feeling well when he entered the room. He usually had lunch with her, leaving my sisters and me to have the midday meal ourselves in the breakfast room. It was rare we got to eat an informal meal with him. I should be enjoying his company, but I couldn't get myself to enjoy anything today.

I made myself take a bite of the cake. It tasted like ash. "How do we just do this? How did I sit by and say nothing last time this happened? How do any of us sit by and do nothing?"

My father stretched his arm across the table and patted my hand. "Patience, daughter. Things will be better after sunset."

Clenching my jaw, I nodded, unsure of how that could be. Perhaps he'd share more good news about the dragon alliance once the red sails of the Konos ships melted into the horizon.

"Did you hear that someone spotted turtle eggs?" Sophia asked. "Can you imagine, we might see turtles again."

"I'm not sure I'd believe the stories of fishermen," Cora warned.

"They are saying the seas are calmer, less monster attacks and siren sightings," Sophia countered.

"It's possible. There were sea turtles before the monsters," my father explained. "But nobody's seen one in hundreds of years."

"What if they really were turtle eggs? And they hatched, and we got to see all those cute babies," Sophia said.

"If they begin to hatch, we'll go to the shore and see it for ourselves," my father promised.

"That would be proof that our agreement with the Fae

King was worth it, wouldn't it?" Lagina asked. "If there are less monsters in the sea, wouldn't it show that they were doing their duty to protect us? Perhaps we can go on a boat someday."

I gazed longingly at the water. I'd never been on the shores, let alone a boat. It was considered too dangerous. What would it be like to feel that water on my fingertips? To dig my toes into the sand? To rock and sway among the waves from the deck of a ship? It seemed like an impossible dream.

My father changed the subject quickly. "Did you hear that your mother is planning a ball for you girls?"

I shoved another bite of food in my mouth, knowing I wasn't part of the conversation or the planning.

"That's because she's preparing to marry us all off," Cora said darkly.

"It's important to unite you with a strong family," Lagina said.

"I don't see you heading to the temple to say your vows," Cora accused.

"I think it's very romantic," Sophia said. "Look at the love story our parents had."

I nearly choked on my water. Coughing and sputtering, I turned away from the table, trying to get myself under control. It was well known that my father and Ophelia weren't in love.

Cora patted me on the back, and I caught my breath. "Sorry."

Lagina scowled at me. "There are many kinds of love, Ara."

"I didn't say a word," I managed, still feeling a tickle in my throat.

"I'm happy to do my duty to the family when the time comes," Sophia added.

"Well, I might consider Tomas," Cora said.

"We'll see," Father said.

The conversation continued, moving into decoration ideas and reminiscing on past balls. It was a good attempt at distraction, but my mind still wandered to the day ahead.

Finally, my father stood. "I must prepare for tonight. I'll see you all at the ceremony."

We rose, letting our father leave the room before we made our way from the table.

"Do you really think my mother is going to marry me off soon?" Sophia whispered to me as we headed to the door.

"I don't know," I said. "She might have given up on Cora."

"I hope whoever it is, he's kind," she said.

"I'll make sure he is," I promised.

Going through the motions, I allowed my new maid to dress me in a shimmery gold peplos. Feeling numb, I sat in silence as she braided and twisted my hair into an elaborate style.

My mind whirred, thinking about the coming ceremony. I half hoped I'd have heard something by now from my father. Something to stop the whole thing. But we were still moving forward as if everything was as it always was.

"How about the gold tiara to match? The one with the blue jewels?" Iris asked.

"No crowns."

"You are still a member of the royal family," she said. "It does us good to see you take your place."

"I don't have a place here," I said before I could stop

myself. Until I'd said the words, I hadn't realized that I'd been feeling that way.

Everything had been turned upside down in my life in the last week. All my careful plans, gone.

Was this what was in store for me? Acting as entertainment and distraction for anyone my father pointed me toward?

I shuddered.

"We'll skip the crown, then," Iris said softly.

I knew she was trying to be kind, possibly even trying to get to know me or connect with me. But I wasn't about to let anyone else close. Losing Mila was too fresh, too painful when I let myself think about it.

"All ready." Iris took a step back. "You look beautiful. That ambassador isn't going to be able to keep his eyes off you."

That was the game, wasn't it? What was expected of me. I was done playing everyone else's game. "I don't think I'll be spending time with the ambassador tonight. I just want this whole thing over with."

"It's a shame, how it works," Iris said. "It's all about luck or stars, isn't it? Some of us are never even eligible. Like you and your family. Or me. I was too young last time, too old now." She shook her head. "It's a heavy feeling, isn't it? The guilt."

I looked into her eyes for the first time all afternoon. She was genuine in her expression and she'd articulated something I'd never been able to pinpoint. There was a sense of guilt attached to the Choosing. Guilt over not being able to do anything about it, and despite the fact that I'd never acknowledged it, guilt for not being eligible like all the others my age.

"We can't help the stars we're born under, your highness," she said. "All we can do is make the best of what the gods have given us."

I wasn't very good at speaking to the gods. There were times I called on them, and I made offerings on feast days. But it had always felt empty, and I'd be lying if I said I'd ever felt their presence in my life. It never made sense to me that the gods would care about human problems. They were immortal and had everything they needed. When the monsters came and nearly wiped humans from the world, the gods were silent. They could have saved us. They chose not to.

I scowled. "I'm not sure the gods have anything to do with my life."

"That's even better, then. It means you get to forge your own path."

"Perhaps you're right, Iris. Perhaps it's best if they ignore us. The gods seem to bring humans nothing but trouble," I said.

"There is strength in fighting things on your own. It might not be easy to follow your own stars, but in the end, that's how we shine the brightest," Iris said.

I smiled. "Thank you for the reminder."

CHAPTER 24

Palace guards stood in a circle near the entrance. I turned, bypassing them in favor of another exit. My sisters were still preparing and would attend the gathering with my father and Ophelia. At the last Choosing, Sophia had remained behind, being too young to attend the ceremony. I'd been stuck on the heavily guarded platform where my father and Ophelia sat in thrones carried out to the lawn for this very occasion.

I wasn't making that mistake again.

If I was to endure the Choosing, I'd do it on my own terms. I knew I couldn't stand there and wear an expression of disinterest, as was expected of me.

The kitchen was abuzz. Kitchen staff chopped and prepped. Some were sliding trays of dough rounds into the massive ovens, making more bread for the people.

All the bakers in the city had been hired to provide goods for this event, but the palace also added as much as they could create. The feasting would go on for hours after the tributes had been hauled away. The somber tone of the ceremony giving way to a celebration.

During the last Choosing, I had thought it was out of kindness. Now, I was old enough to realize it was a way to ensure complacency. A token to appease the people who were about to witness too many families make the ultimate sacrifice. The party after didn't celebrate peace as I'd been taught. It was a relief for those who weren't selected.

I slipped out the kitchen door unnoticed among the busy servants carrying platters of food to the open space near the orchard. I quickly turned away from the trees, forcing away any memories of what I'd done there with the ambassador. A dull ache occupied my chest, and I knew there was still a part of me that wanted to be around Ryvin. Writing the feeling off as dread for the upcoming ceremony, I continued forward, telling myself I wanted nothing to do with the ambassador.

Even as I made my way from the palace, I could already see the crowds descending on the event. There would be thousands of people here tonight. Anyone who was of age was required to attend, but most of the city would be here to see the spectacle and partake of the feast.

The open stretch of grass that spanned the distance between the palace gardens and the rocky cliffs was transformed. Torches burned along the perimeter and a platform had been erected in the center, complete with a pair of thrones for the king and queen. Long tables were heaping with food, luxuries that were beyond the reach of most of the citizens of Athos.

Music came in pockets from groups of musicians stationed around the sprawling space. Thousands of people mingled, ate, and danced. The atmosphere was energetic and optimistic despite the fact the sun was dropping lower into the horizon.

It wouldn't be long now.

"Your highness, you shouldn't be out here alone."

I turned, my lips already pressed together in a tight line as

I took in Ryvin. He was surrounded by his men, which caused me to take a step back.

He was wearing his signature black tunic while the rest of the men were in the crimson tunics of Konos. Behind them, I caught sight of Morta. She was wearing a flowy white dress constructed with layers of sheer fabric. It gave her the illusion of floating in a cloud. Out of all the gathered groups from Konos, she concerned me the most. I shivered.

"I'm not sure I'll be able to save you tonight if you find yourself in harm's way," Ryvin said.

"Is that a threat?" I spoke quietly, overly aware of the eyes of his entourage on me.

"You have nothing to fear from me or any of my men," he replied.

I glanced at Morta. Her head was turned to the side, her blank eyes fixed on some invisible point in the distance.

"None from Konos will harm you," he clarified.

Frowning, I turned back to him. I hated when he seemed to know exactly what I was thinking. "You'll be leaving after the ceremony?"

"At first light tomorrow."

"Good."

He chuckled. "It's a shame things didn't work out between us, Asteri. You need to learn to embrace your feelings rather than fight them."

"There are no feelings between us," I said, almost needing the reminder myself.

He straightened, the humor in his tone vanishing, "So you continue to say, Princess."

Heavy footsteps approached, and I spun to face the oncoming guards. My father, Ophelia, and my sisters were surrounded by them, all smiles and proper etiquette.

My father broke away from the guards. "Ara, you shouldn't be out here alone."

"I was keeping an eye on her," Ryvin said.

"You won't be here forever, ambassador," my father said, his tone cold. "Ara, you must stop being so reckless. Come with us."

He sounded concerned, but why shouldn't he be? Some of the citizens had wanted to end the Choosing so badly, they'd attacked me and the Konos delegation. Yet, we'd welcomed anyone who wanted to join us to publicly witness the announcement of the tributes. Besides, he knew Ryvin was aware of my orders to distract him. He likely thought I was in danger from the ambassador himself. Oddly, I believed that nobody from Konos would harm me. Had my father really cleared the guards of those who wished harm on Konos or my family?

As I fell into step alongside my sisters, anxiety and anticipation rolled through me like creatures slithering inside me. The Choosing was bad enough, but it felt so much worse this year. I hated that we were to watch our people as they were torn from their families, but I had to remind myself that this was to be the final year. It was the only way I was going to get through this.

I glanced around, involuntarily seeking Ryvin. My eyes found his, and I stared at him, feeling something heavy and uncomfortable in my chest. The sooner he was gone, the better.

I tore my eyes from him and followed my family toward the platform. With a glance to the sky, I blew out a relieved breath. The sun was making its descent. I'd dreaded this day for so long. Now, all I wanted was to get through it and move on to the next thing. Perhaps my father would allow me to help with the upcoming war. He'd shared more with me than he had with Lagina. Maybe he had plans for me that didn't involve having me sit on the sidelines.

Istvan waited for us on the platform and I went through the motions of falling into my place behind the thrones. It felt like I was wading through hip-deep mud, my movements stiff and slow. My mind was overflowing with thoughts and I was so distracted, I had to be asked several times to move or reposition.

"What's wrong?" Sophia whispered.

I shook my head, indicating that I wasn't in the mood to speak.

Her brow furrowed and her eyes lingered, but as soon as Istvan climbed onto the platform, she dutifully turned to watch the priest.

This would have been much easier to watch from the crowd where I wouldn't have to mask my reactions. But I was here now, so I was going to have to play the part. My heart raced, blood pulsing in my ears, blocking out the sounds of the people around me. Istvan was speaking, but I didn't hear a thing. It was taking all of my energy to keep my expression impassive. To distance myself from the humans who were about to be pulled from the crowd.

A bead of sweat slid down my back, and I could feel the tension around us. It was as if the very air I was breathing was too heavy. Something was wrong. "Can you feel that?" I whispered.

"Feel what?" Sophia asked.

"Hush," Lagina scolded.

I forced myself to focus, catching bits and pieces of Istvan's words. He spoke about our history, the treaty we signed with the Fae King, and mentioned things like honor as the reason why the tributes should go gratefully to their new homes.

We'd all been told the stories. Always conflicting. Never certain. The tributes would either live a life of luxury, or they'd die a gruesome death.

Perhaps they lived for a short time before being shredded to ribbons or drained of all their blood.

Nobody really knew.

My fingernails bit into my palm as I waited, feeling nauseous and overheated. This was so wrong. All of it was wrong.

Ryvin climbed the stairs, joining Istvan on the platform. All lingering chatter and conversation ceased. It was as if the entire crowd was holding a collective breath.

The tributes would be called by name. Having been selected at some point during their visit or perhaps today during the festivities leading up to the ceremony. For so many families, today would destroy them. I scanned the crowds, catching tears on more than one person. On other faces, I caught joy and anticipation. Some even appeared excited.

My chest ached. How could so many stand by and pretend this was a celebration while citizens of Athos were about to be ripped from their lives, taken from their families, and sent to that cursed island?

"With these tributes, the peace between our kingdoms will span another glorious nine years," Ryvin said.

Polite, awkward murmurs came from the crowd, but I was no longer listening. Movement caught my eye, somewhere near the back of the audience. People moved like rippling waves, the crowd beginning to split in two.

Startled cries and confused gasps were quickly replaced by anguished screams as a group of men burst through the crowd, heading right for the platform. Their faces were contorted into expressions of hatred and rage, their arms raised with whatever weapon they'd brought.

The Konos guards had been standing along the side of the platform and they moved as a unit to the front, while the guards around my father closed in, swallowing him and the queen. One of the guards shoved me aside, knocking me to the ground before moving toward my family. Pure chaos erupted, and I pushed myself to stand, intent on making sure my sisters were safe. The guards were turning on us. My father hadn't taken care of this. They shoved me out of the way so they could get to the more important targets, I was certain of it.

"Gina, Cora, Sophia!" I cried out to them, shoving through a tangle of bodies and dodging the attackers who were already on the platform.

Someone slammed into me, knocking me from the platform. I landed hard, half on top of another person.

"Get up." Ryvin pulled me to standing.

"What are you doing? My sisters are up there!" I turned back to the stage, desperate to enter the fray and find my sisters.

"They're already on their way to the palace. Along with your treacherous father," he hissed.

"The guards…"

"They're after my people. Your family is already safe," he assured me, his calm tone a strange contrast to the cries and chaos around us.

I noticed a blur of movement and, without thinking, I shoved Ryvin aside just as an attacker slashed a blade through the air. He missed us both, then spun around to face me. His blue tunic and leather armor were unmistakable as one of the palace guards.

Several more armed men came rushing forward and Ryvin was swept away, sword drawn as he fought his attackers.

Defenseless and confused, I stared at the palace guard. I knew him. He'd served my father for years. "Don't do this, Riks. We can't win this fight. It's just going to make everything worse."

"I wasn't sure I believed it when they said you'd turned on us." He shook his head. "Such a waste."

"I didn't turn on anyone. I'm trying to protect my people. Do you know what the Fae King will do if his men don't return? My father already has plans to help Athos. We can't risk that." I hated what I'd said, but I knew I needed to calm the guard down.

"Our priority needs to be making sure my family is safe," I commanded.

"They're already in the palace," he confirmed. "But it looks like they left you out here to die with an enemy you hold so dearly. I'm going to enjoy killing you, Konos whore."

The man made a gurgling sound and his blade fell to the ground. Eyes wide, he clawed at his throat. He was choking, but nobody had touched him. I caught the faint wisp of a dark shadow slithering around the man's body as he fell to his knees. The shadow faded just as the man slumped to the ground, eyes glassy and unfocused, chest unmoving.

"How…"

Ryvin was next to me again, yanking on my arm, pulling me away from Riks' bloody remains. "Run, Ara." Ryvin released me, already returning to the fray.

I knew I should head to the palace, especially if my family was already there, but I had to know for sure. Was Riks honest, or was he trying to get a rise out of me? I had to make sure my sisters weren't out here, abandoned like I was. What if they were hurt? What if they were dead? My chest constricted, and I pushed the thought away. They had to be okay.

I picked up a fallen sword, then headed back to the platform. I had to see for myself that my sisters were not among the fallen.

Palace guards, citizens, and Konos guards fought in a frenzied dance of bodies and movement. Steel clashed and blood sprayed. Panting and terrified, I wove through the fight until I reached the stage.

One of the thrones was on the grass, the other tipped on its side on the platform. Bodies littered the stage. I raced around it, taking in every dead face.

There was no sign of any member of the royal family. They were gone. Riks was telling the truth. They'd been shielded and removed just as the battle started.

And I'd been left to die.

Someone howled, and a battle cry ripped through the air. I moved on instinct, away from the sound as several figures leaped onto the platform. They kicked bodies aside as they fought, unconcerned with the dignity of the dead.

In a blur of crimson, one Konos guard fought bravely. He was surrounded by fighters in plain tunics. They were clumsy with their weapons, their footsteps heavy, their movements jerky and hesitant. But they had the numbers. Frozen in place at the base of the platform, I watched in horror as my people, citizens of Athos, surrounded the Konos guard.

Despite the numbers, the crimson clad guard was eliminating his opponents one at a time. I watched in impressed horror. The skills were like nothing I'd ever seen before. I knew what a strong fighter looked like. I'd watched countless hours of sparring and training over the years. This was on another level. He should already be dead simply based on the odds. Instead, he had a chance to get out of this alive.

One of the Athonian men charged the Konos guard, using his body as a battering ram. He was quickly eliminated, but distracted just enough that another Athonian was able to get close enough that he was able to shove his sword into his enemy's stomach.

I couldn't see the blood. It must have blended in with his tunic, but I knew the weapon had struck true. The Konos guard fell to his knees, and the Athonians surrounded him, stabbing him over and over until they were satisfied. I had to turn away.

When I glanced back, I realized I'd made a mistake. The man who'd made the killing blow was staring right at me. Holding a bloody sword and wearing a wicked grin, he leaped from the platform. "You're the one who keeps the enemy's bed warm."

Another man joined him, his uniform quickly identifying him as a palace guard. "Stand down."

"What? I was told we could take as many enemies as we wished," the first man said.

"The royal family is off limits, and you know it," the guard replied.

"She's a bastard, anyway. Nobody will miss her," the man said.

"We aren't to harm the royal family," the guard repeated.

My lips parted, and I sucked in a breath as the realization hit me. I took a step back. This was organized, just like the attack on the carriage. Had my father set this up? Had he sent them after me the day I was with the ambassador? Was that why only Konos guards joined us?

"She's a traitor," the man spat.

I lifted my sword, prepared to fight. "The only traitor here is you."

"Stand down. There's still more of them to kill," the guard said.

The man rammed his sword through the guard's throat, then pulled it out quickly. He turned to me before the guard even hit the ground. "Your turn, filthy whore."

Well, at least I knew what my reputation was in Athos. Lifting my weapon, I glared at the man. "I won't go down easy."

"I'd be disappointed if you did." He lunged forward, his sword slicing with brute force and no grace.

I dodged his attack, then spun, aiming my weapon at him. I managed to slice his arm, leaving a line of crimson beading with blood.

He lumbered toward me, his motions choppy and forced. He'd clearly had no formal training. He was stronger than me, and I knew I couldn't underestimate him, but he wasn't protecting himself. He was all strength and no finesse. I got the sense that the sword didn't even belong to him. In a fist fight, I'd likely already be dead.

I dropped to my knees, remembering to make myself smaller, as another sloppy pass of his sword arced toward me. He was unsteady, his balance thrown off each time he struck. I jumped back to my feet, then continued to avoid his clumsy attacks.

With each attempt to end my life, he grew angrier and weaker. He was panting hard, sweat streaming down his face. I could probably end him now, but I wanted to be smart about it. A few more dodges, and he'd be too weak to see me coming.

Suddenly, a blur of fur and teeth raced past me, landing

on the man. The sword flew into the air and my opponent was slammed to the ground, the wolf pinning him to the dirt.

"I had him," I shouted.

To my surprise, the wolf leaped from the fallen man, then growled at me, before turning back to the enemy. He bared his teeth, then snapped his jaws. He inched forward, haunches raised, looking every bit the monster we feared the wolf shifters were. The fallen man was weeping.

"Please, please, I don't want to die," he whimpered.

I walked over to him and looked down at him. "Make your peace with your gods."

"No, no, I have a family. A wife, children…" His eyes were watery with tears and he let out gasping, heaving sobs.

I hesitated, but caught movement out of the corner of my eye. The weeping man was reaching for his fallen weapon. It was all an act. He thought me weak. Rage seared hot in my chest. I was so tired of everyone making decisions about who I was and what I was capable of. I kicked the sword away.

His eyes widened in true terror, then narrowed. "You can't kill me. Hades will punish you in the afterlife."

"You first." I drove my sword into his chest, pushing past the resistance of bone, letting my anger fuel me. Blood sprayed, coating my arms in warm scarlet liquid. I didn't even flinch. This man would have struck me down with a smile on his lips. All I felt was indifference toward him and anger for everyone else.

When I tried to remove the sword, it was so jammed into the body that I left it there. I picked up the weapon the dead guard dropped, then looked around, preparing for another fight.

The wolf blocked my movement, growling at me.

"I have no quarrel with you, Vanth," I said, hoping it was

the same male I'd spoken to before. And that he could understand me while in this form.

He snapped his jaws, then tilted his head, as if signaling to me. I took a step forward, sword pointed at him. "Stay back."

It was clear the wolf was trying to get my attention. "What? It was self-defense. Mostly." Guilt twisted in my gut now that the anger I'd felt had waned. I'd killed him. While he'd been largely defenseless. The worst part was I felt guilty for not regretting my actions rather than for the life I'd taken. Maybe Ryvin was right. There was something dark inside me.

The wolf nipped at my dress, pulling on the fabric. There was no denying it wanted me to follow. "Alright. Let's go."

CHAPTER 25

Battle cries enveloped us as palace guards and citizens of Athos closed in. The wolf tugged on my dress, urging me away from the onslaught. The bravery I'd felt was wearing off as I took in the overwhelming odds against me. It was just like the attack on the carriage, only this time, there were hundreds of assailants and there was no way we were getting out of this alive.

"Get her out of here!" Ryvin yelled, seeming to materialize from nowhere. As quickly as he'd arrived, he vanished, swept into a mass of bodies that swallowed him up in a frenzy. The sound of clashing steel, swearing, and flesh against flesh sent every sense into overdrive. I stepped forward, clutching my weapon, feeling the overwhelming urge to help him.

The wolf cut me off, snapping his jaws in warning.

"What am I supposed to do?" Ryvin wasn't going to get out of this alone, and a glance around the chaotic scene showed that the crimson tunics of his entourage were scattered about, engaged in fights of their own.

The wolf tugged at my dress and I took a step back automatically, numbly taking in the attack. I couldn't follow

Ryvin; I shouldn't even be here. I should be in the palace with my family. They'd been swept away by guards, but I'd been shoved aside, unwelcome in the fold.

My throat stung as the painful understanding settled around me. As much as I told myself I was part of the royal family, I had always been an outsider. I loved my sisters, but there'd always been a barrier between us. Something I couldn't put my finger on that divided us. It had to be the fact that not all our blood was the same. I was only half royal.

But it had to be an oversight. Everything happened so quickly, they probably thought I was with them, right? My father would never allow me to be placed in harm's way, I was certain of it. While it was clear some of the guards had turned on me after what I'd done with the ambassador, I had to believe my father would clear that up after Konos departed. They couldn't hold that against me forever, could they?

There was a small part of me warning that I was never going to be safe again. If I was truly viewed as a traitor, what would stop others from seeking to harm me? I'd already had two attacks on my life. Was that how things would be from now on?

Shoving the thoughts away, I reminded myself that I couldn't change the past. All I could do was survive this moment and make sure my sisters were safe. Staying any longer would only solidify my status as a traitor to anyone who questioned my loyalty.

I couldn't stay here. This wasn't my fight. And the men from Konos weren't my concern.

Trying to push aside the heartache at being left behind, I turned back to Ryvin. He was drawing the fight away from us, his black tunic a blur of movement as he fought palace guards and citizens alike.

Every time he moved, every time he struck someone

down, another figure took their place, swinging at him. Each time, they failed, falling at his feet. I'd never seen anything like it. I'd watched in awe as the fallen Konos guard had felled several men, but even he'd met his end. Ryvin looked at home on the battlefield. Like he thrived on death and destruction.

The wolf tugged on my skirts and I walked backward slowly, following his urging while keeping my eyes on the ambassador. His skill was memorizing and I no longer felt like I was in danger.

Nobody was paying any attention to me, they were all too focused on the ambassador, coming at him in groups, weapons drawn. Anyone else would have been long dead. Ryvin didn't even look like he was breaking a sweat.

His movements were fluid and so fast you couldn't see how he made his opponents fall. They simply raced forward, then came up short. A trail of bodies led away from me as the distance between us increased. Part of me ached to run after him, but how could I put my enemy before my own people? How could I harm any other Athonians? I'd already ended too many lives with my blade. I was already walking the tightrope between traitor and self-defense. I couldn't afford to show any more kindness to our enemy.

The wolf tugged harder, pulling me away from the onslaught. It was time to go. Even if I wanted to stay and help, which side would I choose? The wolf was from Konos, and he was trying to save me. Once again, my own people had attempted to take my life.

I was more at risk from the people I was supposed to help than I was from our enemies. Bile rose in my throat. Maybe I wasn't balancing on that edge as much as I thought. Perhaps I already was a traitor.

No. I was my father's daughter. A daughter of Athos. I

knew my place. I just forgot for a moment. Whatever happened to Ryvin or his men was in the hands of my people.

Giving in, I followed the wolf, heading back toward the castle. The sounds of the fight played in the background like some kind of cruel orchestra, but I kept my gaze forward. There was too much chance that I'd double back if I took a look.

Suddenly, someone grabbed me and pulled me back. My dress tore, a piece of the shimmery gold fabric dangling from the wolf's teeth. I was roughly tossed aside, landing hard on the rocky ground. The sword I'd been carrying was thrown beyond my reach.

A palace guard crouched down, retrieving my weapon, before turning his attention to the wolf. He was a bulky man in a poorly fitting uniform. The leather armor over his chest and back was flapping around as he moved, the ties having come loose. I had a suspicion that they'd never been able to tie, considering his size. He'd have needed very large armor to cover his bulging stomach and wide build.

Scrambling to my feet, I ran toward him, then I slammed into his back with my shoulder, trying to knock him down. It was like running into a stone wall. He didn't budge, and I nearly ended up on the ground again, this time with screaming pain in my shoulder from the impact.

Hissing, I rubbed at my injury. The huge man turned, his eyes narrowed. "Whose side are you on, Princess?"

"This creature was helping me," I said. "It was leading me back to the palace."

"Well I can do that, so its services are no longer needed."

"You will not harm it," I ordered.

"It's a shapeshifter, your highness," he said. "One of the evils from Konos."

I knew I had to be careful how I spoke and how I reacted. Feigning surprise, I widened my eyes. "If that's the case, then it's clearly switched sides if it was helping me."

"Or it was trying to sneak into the palace to kill you all," he spat.

The wolf lunged, going right for the fleshy side that wasn't covered by the armor. I leaped back before the huge man could fall on me. His attention went right to the wolf, grappling with the creature while still holding onto both swords.

His movements were awkward and sloppy, the weapons in his hands hindering his ability to fight. Still, he tried to use them, attempting to stab or slice the lithe and flexible wolf. The shifter always one step ahead of the lumbering guard.

The cries he made drew attention our way, and I backed away more, knowing I wasn't going to be able to defend myself against the incoming fighters. Why hadn't I run to the protection of the palace walls as soon as the attack started?

I glanced toward the palace walls. I could probably make it if I ran, but I'd be leaving Vanth to his death. What could I do to stop it? I wouldn't be able to protect myself, let alone him, without a weapon.

I wanted to view myself as a fighter, but I knew I wasn't prepared to take on several angry men, even if they were poorly trained. The wolf wasn't going to fare much better without backup.

Fuck.

I turned back to the fallen wolf. This was going to end badly for both of us. I had crossed so many lines I didn't even know who I was anymore. But I knew I couldn't allow someone who'd saved my life die without making any effort to help them.

"Run, Vanth!" I screamed as I raced forward, hoping I was getting the right name. "Run, you stupid wolf!" I scanned the ground for any abandoned weapons, praying for something, anything to go my way.

Two of the men circling Vanth changed direction, coming toward me with looks of pure disdain. "Wonder if royal blood is the same color as everyone else's," one of the men said. He was shorter than me and had beady, dead-looking eyes. His long, sandy-colored hair hung in dirty strings around his red face.

My breathing already rapid, pulse racing, I stepped back again. "Stay back."

The short man advanced, his smile showing rotting teeth. Despite the fact that he was wearing a blue tunic, denoting him as a member of the palace guard, I knew he was either an impostor or he'd been one of the recent additions. Even without his appearance, the way he carried his weapon, loose in his grip, dangling at his side, gave him away.

"I'm warning you." I tried to stay calm, use that authority I'd seen demonstrated by Ophelia, but my voice wavered.

"I thought we were supposed to keep the royal family alive," another man said. He looked far too young to be fighting. I would guess he was in his early teens at the most. He was wearing a torn and bloody blue tunic, but the dagger he carried was poorly crafted, likely a personal weapon. It didn't look like something issued by the palace.

"The queen never said we had to keep her alive," the short man said as he approached. "She was very clear on her instructions. Her and her husband, and the three true princesses."

My chest tightened. So it wasn't a mistake when I'd been left behind. This was planned.

An anguished yelp sounded, and I turned to see the wolf

thrown to the ground, a group of men around him, weapons drawn.

No. This was not how it was going to end.

I ran right past the small man and the boy who'd been trying to decide my fate. They made startled sounds as I passed, but I didn't look back. Vanth needed my help.

Shoving a man in a bloodstained white tunic aside, I dropped to my knees next to the fallen wolf, draping myself over him. "Leave him alone!"

The wolf's chest rose and fell, the creature breathing slowly, shakily, but breathing nonetheless.

"He's a monster, get out of the way!" Someone shouted.

"You're the monsters!" I replied, not looking up. I didn't want to see my death coming. For some reason, I believed it would hurt less if it was a surprise. It wasn't like the pain would linger, with this many enemies, I'd be dead quickly.

Blood seemed to pulse in my ears and that word, *enemies*, played over and over in my mind. Is that what they were? My own people. Enemies.

I was protecting my enemy.

My thoughts were a swirling mass of confusion. Which side was I on anymore? Which side were any of us on?

"Just kill the girl so we can finish the beast," someone said.

Shouts erupted around me, the men arguing about their next steps. Was it right or wrong to kill an unarmed woman? Would they get in trouble for killing the king's bastard? Was the wolf a threat to them anymore, as injured as it was?

I moved my face closer to the wolf's ear. "I'm here," I soothed. "I won't let them hurt you." It was a lie. They could easily go right through me and kill us both, but I was too grateful to Vanth for the protection he'd provided earlier. My own family had left me for dead, but he'd stayed. He'd sacrificed to keep a human woman he barely knew alive.

My sisters hadn't even returned for me. Were they prevented from returning? Were they dragged away against their will? Had they looked to see if I was with them? Had anyone noticed as they were whisked away to safety?

Perhaps they were told I was already dead.

I was, wasn't I?

This was simply prolonging the inevitable.

"I'm sorry I didn't go with you right away," I said quietly.

The wolf whimpered, the sound sad and reassuring. It almost came across as an acknowledgement of my words, as if he was trying to comfort me. I didn't know what he could make out in this form, but at least he wasn't alone.

Someone screamed. Bloodcurdling and sharp before it turned into a gurgling sound. Shouts and cries surrounded me and I looked up to see the men around us falling, one at a time.

Blood streamed from their eyes and poured from their noses. They clawed at their throats, gasping for air before blood bubbled up from their open mouths, causing them to gurgle and sputter, seeming to choke on their own fluids.

Shaking and terrified, I watched in horror as the men who'd been surrounding me fell to the ground, their eyes wide with terror, their bodies convulsing a few times before going still. They formed a gruesome circle of death around me.

I looked down at myself, my hand going to my throat, then feeling my chest, then my arms, checking for injuries. How was I still alive while everyone else was dead? Turning to Vanth, I checked him. The wolf was taking slow breaths. He was still alive too. What had happened to the others?

That's when I realized the sounds of battle were gone.

Slowly, I stood. No new attackers charged. Nobody moved toward us. Not even the wind blew. All the men who'd been threatening us were on the ground, dead.

I stared out into a field of corpses. I was surrounded by death. Unmoving, bloody bodies dotted the landscape as far as the eye could see. It was as if the chaos had simply ended, leaving anyone with Athonian blood dead.

Except me.

The only living beings were clad in crimson tunics, the men slowly walking toward me from their scattered positions around the battlefield.

Sounds behind me pulled my attention away from the field of death. The fallen wolf was convulsing violently, limbs shaking rapidly. Panting and grunting, the poor creature appeared to be in intense pain.

"Vanth!" I ran to him. "What's wrong? How can I help?" I dropped to my knees next to him. Stroking his fur, I tried to soothe him, whispering calming words. "I'm here. It's okay. I'm not going anywhere."

Then I noticed his legs lengthening, arms breaking, bones cracking. My eyes widened as I realized what was happening. Scrambling to my feet, I gave him space and then watched in amazement as the wolf's body gave way to human form.

Vanth's human body replaced the fallen wolf. He stood, turned away from me. His flesh was scratched and scraped. Bruises already bloomed across his bare back and down his legs. But he was alive.

Overcome with relief, I blinked back the tears that formed in my eyes. It felt ridiculous to be so emotional about seeing him survive, but I felt as if we were old friends.

Swirling shadows swept past Vanth, the dark, ethereal quality an alarming contrast to the dim golden light of dusk.

"Did you see…" I didn't get the rest of the words out

before the shadows collided, morphing into the shape of a human figure. They solidified, their opacity increasing until the shadows began to pool into solid darkness that took on a human form. They dissipated, fading like smoke in the wind, leaving Ryvin standing in their wake.

"What?" I had just seen a wolf change into a man, but this was far more unsettling. The shadows had started like fog, transparent and moving on the wind. How had that become anything?

The wolf I could explain. I'd grown up hearing stories of shifters. We all knew they existed, even if we hadn't seen them. But a person who could become a shadow was not in any of my stories.

I backed away, finally understanding what Ryvin had meant when he warned that some things were better left unknown. His magic was terrible and more powerful than anything I'd ever seen. He could have killed everyone who attacked us outside the Opal without effort, yet he'd hidden it. He'd sacrificed one of his own to keep that secret. Whatever he was, he'd gone to great lengths to conceal it from all of us. "What are you?"

Ryvin glared at me, not a shred of kindness in his expression. I could practically feel the rage and hatred radiating from him. With a wave of his hand, he summoned more of those shadows until they too began to darken. When they fully materialized, he was holding a bundle of fabric.

He tossed it to Vanth. "Get dressed. We have a king to speak to."

"We lost one," Vanth informed Ryvin as he stepped into a pair of trousers. "Darius."

Ryvin nodded, then walked away. I followed, ignoring the stares from the other members of his entourage. I noticed that most of them were covered in blood, their clothing torn and mangled. But they were alive and standing; hundreds of humans were not.

Somehow, this small group of less than twenty had taken down ten times their number.

A lump rose in my throat.

I shouldn't be out here with them.

Ryvin stopped at the platform, his attention going to the fallen Konos guard. It was where it had all started. I'd seen him fall, surrounded by confusion and fear.

Holding back, I watched as all of the surviving Konos guards followed their leader, each of them bowing to their fallen comrade. After the last one had paid their respects, Ryvin placed a coin on each eyelid, then rested his hand on the man's chest.

It was the same tradition we held for our dead. Coins on their eyes so they could pay Charon to cross the River Styx. Without that, his soul would be condemned to wander for a hundred years; aimless and alone. Had anyone put coins on David's eyes? Or Mila's? Or any of the other trail of bodies that seemed to be growing around me with each passing day? Who would put coins on the eyes of all the fallen Athonians from this battle?

I felt like I was witnessing something I shouldn't. I was an outsider, catching a private, intimate moment between old friends. My throat tight, I tried not to think about how similar this was to our ways. The creatures of Konos and beyond were said to be so different from us, yet I was watching them honor their dead, just as we did.

Ryvin whispered some words, quiet and calm. I wondered if their prayers were the same ones our priests said for our dead. The shadows returned, engulfing the fallen man like blankets of smoke. Twisting and churning, the shadows billowed around him until they tightened into nothing, leaving the platform empty.

I sucked in a breath, feeling a sense of both terror and awe. This was powerful magic, and I knew my kingdom made a very big mistake by crossing Ryvin.

CHAPTER 26

"This is what you were trying so desperately to protect?" Ryvin asked as he walked toward me. "These cowards who attack unbidden?"

"You're taking our people." The argument was getting old, and it felt like sand in my mouth.

"And your family left you behind while they fled to safety." He grabbed my upper arm roughly and pulled me alongside him.

Head down, I bit back the tears. I wasn't about to let him see how upset I was. We marched toward the palace, my feet stumbling over the uneven ground, struggling to keep up with Ryvin's quick pace.

There was no gentleness, no concern. The world around me had melted away in an instant. As if everything until this moment had been pretend. As if his mask slipped and I was finally seeing him for what he truly was.

No words in my vocabulary could define his abilities. He wasn't a shifter or a vampire, that much I knew. Which meant he was fae.

Or worse.

Letting my mind consider the possibilities was too much.

A pair of guards moved to block our progress at the

palace gates, their well-fitted armor and disciplined demeanor instantly giving them away as experienced and dedicated members of the guard.

Of course my father had stationed the very best to protect him. He'd sent the new guards and anyone else he could find into the battle. They'd all been sacrificial lambs.

My stomach twisted as I realized how similar my father was to the Fae King. Our enemy asked for fourteen souls every nine years. My father had just risked the lives of hundreds to save so few.

Neither was good. Life should be treasured, I knew that. But I couldn't help but see the parallels between my own kingdom and that of the creatures I'd been raised to hate.

"You're not welcome here," one of the guards said.

"Step aside," Ryvin warned.

"Go back to your ship. Tell your king there will be no more peace between us," the guard said.

I tensed. No more peace? What had my father hoped to accomplish by this? He'd told me we were awaiting an alliance with the dragons. That had a possibility of success. This had been suicide. To what end? To prevent sending tributes? To instigate the fae? He'd lied to me. I'd played some strange piece in a puzzle I didn't understand. I'd blindly stepped in to help my family while I'd been left to my death.

"I don't have time for this." Ryvin sounded bored. He released my arm, then lifted his, making lazy movements with his hand. A swirl of shadows twisted around his wrist before snaking out toward the guards.

The startled men's eyes widened, then they started to scream. Blood poured down their faces, streaming from their eyes and noses. I turned away, knowing what came next. When their cries turned to gargled, suffocating sounds, I pressed my hands to my ears and squeezed my eyes shut.

There'd been too much death already, and I wasn't sure I could take any more.

For the first time, I was grateful that I was no longer headed to the wall as I'd hoped. I had seen enough bloodshed to last me a lifetime.

Ryvin's rough grip tightened around my upper arm again, pulling my hand from my ear just as the thud of the bodies hit the ground. I winced but forced my eyes open, careful not to look down at the guards. The bloody faces from when I'd been with Vanth in his wolf form were burned into my memory and would haunt my nightmares. The terrible things I'd seen today would be added to a growing list of atrocities that started when Ryvin and his men arrived. Many that I'd had a hand in committing myself.

Practically dragging me, Ryvin moved past the gates, his men fanned out on either side of us, walking silently with their leader. Each of them were more deadly than ten palace guards, but the ambassador himself was on another level. I wondered if he could have eliminated everyone on that field alone.

A shudder ran through me, and I was certain I knew the answer. The fighting had come to an abrupt stop the second he determined it was time to end it. The amount of power he held was terrifying, but right now, I was only feeling annoyed by his presence. I hated that I'd worried about him. Hated that I'd felt things for him.

Defiantly, I pulled my arm away. "I can walk myself."

To my surprise, he released me without a word.

I knew how I must look walking into my home with these creatures. Just like them, my clothes were torn, and I was splattered in blood that didn't belong to me. What did that make me? Whatever it was, I was not the same woman I'd been before they arrived. I wasn't sure what I would become after they left.

The next set of doors we approached took us into the palace itself. These guards backed away, not making the same mistake as the others. Silently, they let us pass, and I caught the scent of urine. My nose wrinkled. One of the guards had soiled himself.

To be honest, he was the smart one.

We should all be that afraid.

I knew I should be quaking with fear but it was locked away behind numb disbelief and an overwhelming urge to simply stay alive. Like an animal who knew she was cornered, my only option was to pretend I was more dangerous than I really was. I held my chin high and carried myself with as much dignity as I could muster.

Add in the fact that I had no idea what was coming and all I could do was shut everything down. Thinking about anything too deeply would send me into a spiral I wasn't sure I could return from. What kind of pain would I feel when I allowed myself to linger on the fact that my family had left me to die? What kind of madness might I succumb to if I didn't bury all the lust and tangled emotions I felt for Ryvin? How would I react when I finally let myself atone for all the lives I'd taken?

Shoving all my thoughts into the depths of my soul, I continued forward, focusing on the sound of our collective footsteps against the polished marble. I would become as cold and unfeeling as the ambassador.

We were heading right for the throne room.

The massive doors were closed, six guards standing in front of them. I watched, devoid of feeling, as they each clutched at their throats. One by one, they fell in bloody heaps, their skulls cracking as they hit the floor.

I didn't turn away. I didn't even blink. I no longer felt anything.

When the doors opened, I trailed behind the others, afraid of what I would see or what I would feel once I was reunited with my family.

Guards raced toward us, but they collapsed almost immediately, those dark shadows slithering around them, stealing their life without effort.

As the bodies hit the floor, I looked around for my sisters. It wasn't a surprise that Ophelia would want me dead, and as much as I hated to admit it, I could see my father leaving me behind. Not on purpose, but out of a sense of protecting his line. It hurt, but I could accept it.

What I couldn't accept was my sisters willingly walking away while I was left to fend for myself.

My father and Ophelia rose to their feet, startled by the sudden death of their guards. Perhaps even startled by the fact that their enemies had survived and made it to the heart of the palace.

"Guards!" Ophelia cried.

The side doors opened and more guards streamed in. The shadows returned. Ryvin didn't even flinch. His expression remained impassive, detached, vicious.

It was a side of him I'd failed to believe existed. But now it was on full display and I wondered how I'd missed it.

Then I realized my own expression was likely similar. I'd forced my emotions away, afraid to feel anymore. Was that what he'd done? Or did he simply not feel things the way humans did?

"Enough!" My father called.

The shadows dispersed.

Ryvin stepped over the fallen guards, approaching the thrones, his gaze unfaltering. "You betrayed us."

My father didn't even try to deny it. His jaw tightened and sweat glistened on his forehead.

"I should kill you and your entire family," Ryvin said. "Put new rulers in place who can abide by the treaty."

"You are bound to the treaty, the same as I am, so you will not harm us," my father answered, his tone resolute.

I glanced around again for my sisters, feeling the detachment I'd worked so hard to cultivate slip as worry crowded my mind. Where were they? If they weren't here, did that mean they'd been left behind too? Or were they swept off to a temple?

Footsteps made me turn, and I nearly cried out in relief when I saw my sisters being hauled into the room at the hands of Morta. It was short-lived, as I knew the woman guiding them was likely just as deadly as the men who'd been fighting on the battlefield.

My sisters held their chins high and though I could see the remains of tears streaking their cheeks, none of them were crying now. They stood silently, awaiting orders.

"Thank the gods," I breathed out.

"Ara!" Sophia cried, then stepped out as if she was going to run to me. Morta grabbed her and yanked her back.

"Just stay where you are," I warned.

"I found them in a hidden room," Morta said. "Not even a single guard on them."

"No!" My father stood. "Don't harm my daughters. They had no part in this. You have what you need for my end of the bargain."

Ryvin glanced at me, his expression flashing into disgust for a moment before regaining his stoic, unconcerned persona. He glared at my father. "You know the consequences of your actions."

"I already gave you my sacrifice," my father claimed. "If

I violate the treaty, the payment is clear. Did I not grant my daughter to you? Did she not warm your bed and offer herself to you?"

I stepped back, his words hitting me like a blow to my stomach. Holding my breath, I stared at him in disbelief. It couldn't be. This whole time, that was the plan? He'd asked me to entertain the ambassador the day he arrived. Was that why I'd been pushed toward him over and over?

"Father?" My voice was shaky. I felt like I was a child again. Being disciplined for making a mistake. I'd learned quickly that perfection was rewarded and mistakes weren't tolerated. I'd thrived on his praise, made sure I didn't do anything to let him down. But that hadn't happened in so long.

"Ara, it was necessary." There was no warmth in his tone.

"No." Disbelief washed over me like cold air, swallowing me whole.

"That's why you asked her to seduce me?" Ryvin's voice was amused. "So I'd take the child you were willing to sacrifice."

"How could you, Father?" Lagina cried.

The room felt too large and too small all at once. Everything that had happened since Ryvin arrived blurred together. My father had encouraged me to be with the ambassador since the beginning. He'd sent me out alone with him. We'd been attacked, yet he'd asked me to do more. To continue to pursue the ambassador. Why would he do that? How could he so easily sacrifice me? I thought he cared for me.

I stumbled backward as a million interactions with my father raced through my mind. Always kind, always understanding... as long as I played along. Was that really how it had been my whole life? I did what he asked, and I was rewarded with his love. None of my sisters had to perform for him. As long as I was serving my purpose, he let me do as I wished.

How long had he intended this? How had I missed the signs? "You planned this whole thing. You didn't even think you'd win. You were willing to send me to my death from the beginning." I was stunned. My chest tightened and my vision blurred as the betrayal grew until all I could see was my father's disappointed expression.

"It was a necessary gamble," he said. "Blood and salt."

"You humans and your blood and salt," Ryvin hissed. "Your blood is weak and disloyal, and the sea has never protected you. It bows to us. It consumes your ships, tears your flesh, batters your shores. You fear it, yet you call on it as your savior. Much the way you pray to the gods. You're nothing to them. Pawns. Entertainment."

"Guards!" My father called.

More guards rushed in but they instantly collapsed, wisps of shadows fading from their fallen bodies. Ryvin hadn't even moved.

"Leave this place. Take her and go. My advisors and I have studied that treaty. It's ironclad and I know you can't harm me. You can't retaliate against my family or Athos. If you do, the treaty is invalid and your king loses everything he gets from us."

My heart shattered. That was in the treaty? If that was the case, Ryvin was right when he said it favored the humans. Was that what my father was hoping for? That the Konos delegation would retaliate and break the treaty?

A tiny flicker of hope fluttered in my chest. Maybe it was all a gamble, and my father was counting on that. I'd be free, then. It would free us all. He knew the sacrifices I'd make for my people.

"You, of all people, know I won't cross the treaty," Ryvin hissed. "You've pushed us before and we've never broken."

"Then leave. Take your tributes, take Ara, and get out of my kingdom," my father said, his tone cold, emotionless.

"You used your daughter without any thought for her." Ryvin shook his head. "And you call me the monster."

Brow furrowed, I looked to my father for any response. Any kind word or sign of regret. There was none.

Was I always seen as a tool to get what he wanted? Had he always intended to throw me away as soon as it served him? I felt queasy. My whole life was turned upside down. I thought I'd meant something to him. I thought I mattered. But he couldn't even look at me.

My sisters were calling out to our father, begging him to reconsider. Begging him to stop. Tears slid down my cheeks. They weren't to blame for this. They had no idea what my father had planned.

"The tributes will be loaded onto the ship tonight," Ryvin said.

"Of course," my father replied.

I looked up, surprised at the turn in conversation. Was Ryvin going to let this go? I didn't even know if they were taking the fourteen or a hundred. Guilt made my stomach churn as I realized I hadn't even thought about what would happen to them. There were already so many dead and if we didn't comply, they'd wipe us out completely. The number of tributes was irrelevant now that I knew how fragile our city was at the hands of the fae.

"And I will take your daughter. But not Ara." Ryvin looked toward the doors where Morta waited with my sisters.

I stopped breathing.

CHAPTER 27

"No," my father commanded. "You will take Ara. This is not up for discussion."

"I'll go." My voice finally returned, and I forced myself to move closer to the ambassador.

"It's not your choice to make, Princess," Ryvin said.

"Please, there's no need to do this. I'll gladly go in place of my sisters," I said.

"I know you would, but it's not my decision to make." He turned to look at the doorway and I followed his gaze.

Morta stepped away from my sisters, moving to the center of the throne room with ease. The sheer fabric of her dress billowed around her, moving and flowing like waves in the sea. Her milky white eyes took in her surroundings as if she could see something the rest of us could not.

That was why she was here, but we never saw her. She was the one who chose the tributes. They weren't just taking one of us as a hostage, we'd join the tributes and face the same fate as them.

"There's no need to evaluate the others. I'll go," I repeated, this time speaking to Morta.

"Such a brave woman." Her words came out like a

chorus. As if she was speaking with multiple mouths at once. "But these decisions are not for you to make."

"You can't. Please. We didn't do anything wrong." Cora took a step away from the door, moving closer to Morta. Sophia was crying, Lagina holding her tight.

Lagina was silent, but her lower lip quivered. She was trying to hold her emotions in, to prevent herself from putting on a scene the way we'd always been instructed.

"Can you make an exception?" I couldn't allow any of my sisters in my place. What would even become of me if I stayed? My father didn't want me here. My own father had used me as a bargaining chip. Ophelia didn't want me here. And multiple guards had tried to kill me. As much as it broke my heart, if I stayed in Athos, I was as good as dead anyway.

"No," Morta said, turning her milky, empty eyes on me. "It is not your turn."

"I'm going," I insisted. "I will not let one of my sisters go to Konos. You'll take me or none of us."

"Stop talking, Princess," Ryvin hissed.

"That one." Morta pointed a long, pale finger toward my sisters. "The youngest. She's who we will take."

"No!" I raced forward, intending to position myself in front of Sophia, but I was suddenly frozen in place.

"She's not even of age!" Cora cried.

"That doesn't matter with the treaty," Lagina said flatly.

"Do something," I demanded. "Stop this. Sophia can't go."

Morta had materialized out of thin air and was now standing in front of me. Bony fingers locked around my wrists. "The fates have spoken."

I yanked my arms from her grasp. "And I have spoken. You can't have her."

"You will not touch her," my father commanded, but nobody even turned to him.

"You touch her and I'll find you, I swear to the gods, I will find you," I hissed.

"Ara, stop," Sophia said, her voice calm.

"Silence, Sophia," Ophelia called, joining the conversation for the first time. "Ara has volunteered. She is of royal blood and her father's favorite. She should be more than adequate to show our respects."

"The decision is made," Ryvin said.

My father took the stairs leading down from the dais, strolling casually toward Ryvin. He paused in front of the ambassador, his expression defiant. "The treaty clearly states that one of the king's children will be sacrificed as payment. It does not say you get to make that choice."

I tensed. *Sacrificed.* Not prisoner. He expected me to die. Something cracked inside me and I felt my limbs go numb. It was as if all the fight in me was gone. My own father wanted me dead. That was his plan all along.

"You're in no position to negotiate, old man," Ryvin said.

Suddenly, my father shifted his weight, and I caught the glint of steel as he unleashed a dagger hidden in the folds of his tunic. The blade flashed, and he took a step forward. "Don't make me do this. Don't make me complete the sacrifice myself."

He locked his gaze on me, his eyes burning with determination. "It has to be done." My father moved closer, intent on killing me, but I remained where I was, unable to move.

If there was anything left of my heart to break, it reduced to dust. He'd kill me to keep any of my sisters from meeting this fate. I stared at my father, the man who'd raised me. He knew I'd do anything for my sisters. That had always been the understanding. I was to keep them safe. It had been drilled into me since I was a child.

"Stand down," Ryvin said through gritted teeth. "Morta's word is final. There is no changing it."

"Do it," I hissed. If killing me was a loophole to save my sister, I wouldn't fight. "They can't have Sophia."

My father moved so fast and I gasped as I braced for impact, but instead of the bite of a blade, I was shoved to the ground, Ryvin taking my place.

In a flash of silver, the dagger found a target, my father shoving it deep into Ryvin's chest. I screamed as the dagger impaled the ambassador, blood pouring from the wound.

"No!" I tried to go to him, but some invisible force was holding me down. Fighting to break free, I desperately tried to reach him. "Ryvin!"

Pulse racing, breath coming out too fast, I struggled against my invisible bonds. Had Ryvin really stepped in front of a weapon for me?

The ambassador glared at my father, his expression pure rage. My father stumbled back. "That blade was not meant for you."

Screams erupted around us, but I couldn't see my sisters. The room was filling with shadows, snaking around us like ribbons of death. The temperature dropped and goosebumps shivered down my bare arms. My breath came out in clouds.

I was still on the marble floor, struggling to gain my freedom from my unseen bonds. A startled cry made me look up, and I sucked in a breath. My father was vertical, hovering above me, his toes inches above the ground. His body shook with silent sobs, his eyes brimming with tears. "I'm sorry, Ara. It had to be you. You were the only one who had a chance."

"Father!" My sisters cried out, the three of them yelling and crying. Their fear was palpable, and the shadows intensified. "Ara!"

Could they see us? Did they watch as our father tried to end my life? Panic gripped my chest, squeezing like a snake choking the life from its prey. "Cora? Sophia? Gina? Are you safe?"

"Ara? Where are you?" the voice was so far away I couldn't make out who it belonged to.

The shadows deepened, and I wondered if they were fed by the terror they sensed around them, growing stronger as they devoured our distress.

I could see Ryvin and my father. The three of us in a circle of faint light, surrounded by darkness. My father was sobbing, and he looked older than I'd ever seen him. He looked like he'd shattered under the pressure of everything that had passed between us.

My heart ached. He'd been willing to sacrifice me, but I'd gone along with it. I hated him for being so quick to throw my life away, but I understood that call to duty. That drive to give everything for those you care about. "Please, stop this. Let him go."

Ryvin's eyes found mine, and I searched for any spark of humanity, any sign that he could be swayed to find compassion.

Tears streamed down my cheeks. "Please."

The ambassador tore his gaze from mine. "He meant to kill you, yet you beg for his life?"

"He's my father," I said, but my mind was at war with my heart. The shadows closed in around us, a swirling cyclone around my father, Ryvin, and me.

My father wept, mumbling incoherently. Tears and snot

ran down his face. Seeing him like this was too much. I buckled, finding only sympathy despite what he'd done to me. "Please, release him."

"Ask him who killed your maid," Ryvin said.

My brow furrowed, and I noticed an immediate change in my father's reactions. The tears instantly stopped, and he turned his gaze on me. There was no indication of remorse in his dark eyes. In fact, it reminded me all too much of the detached look I caught on the ambassador.

"Father? What is he talking about?" I was still being held to the ground by an invisible force, unable to stand and face him. "Do you know who killed Mila?"

"Tell her," Ryvin encouraged. "Go ahead. Tell her."

"Father?"

Ryvin yanked the dagger that was still embedded in his chest from his body. Blood poured out, but he didn't even appear phased by the injury. He walked to me causally, then gripped my arm, pulling me to my feet, finally releasing me from whatever invisible bonds had held me down. Awkwardly, I stumbled forward, confused and afraid.

"Tell her," Ryvin insisted. "Or I'll show her myself."

"I don't owe you anything," my father hissed.

Ryvin sliced my forearm, and I gasped as I pulled my arm away. "What the fuck?"

Burning pain blossomed at the site of the injury, and I pressed my palm to the cut. Before I could get another word out, Ryvin grabbed my chin roughly and turned it so I was staring at my father. His other hand held the knife out, my blood and Ryvin's dripping from the blade.

My father's face was contorting, and he started to sweat. Eyes closed, he panted desperately, as if he was in pain.

"What did you do?" I turned to the ambassador.

He guided my head back. "Watch."

My father howled, an inhuman sound tearing from his throat that sent a shiver down my spine. But that wasn't what made me suck in a breath and back away, right into Ryvin.

No, it was something far worse. Something made of nightmares.

Two of his teeth elongated, sharp and dangerous. It was impossible to ignore what those fangs were. I'd seen them before. Too closely when I was with Orion.

My father had vampire fangs. "No."

It wasn't possible. How could my father be a vampire?

"Who killed her maid, your majesty?" Ryvin asked.

"You killed Mila?" I felt like I didn't know the man in front of me. What other lies had I been told? "Was that what happened any time a servant went missing? What about all our nannies? Maybe even the priests from the library." My stomach rolled, and I fought against the rising bile. "How many, Father? How many have you killed? How could I not see this?"

"You have always been too smart for your own good, but you only see what you want to see. It's your greatest weakness," he hissed. "Now, release me and get her out of my sight before I drain her dry."

"You will not touch her," Ryvin warned.

"You have no power here. If you won't take her, I'll send her to Hades myself and our debt will be paid," my father spat.

I didn't even recognize the creature in front of me. Hot tears slid down my cheeks, but I sat there numbly staring at the man who'd raised me. How long had he hidden this from us? Had he been born a vampire, or had he been turned?

And what did that mean for me?

I pushed the thoughts away. It was too much. I couldn't

let myself wonder. Not now. Not as my father bared his teeth at me and glared at me with such disdain.

In this form, he wasn't the father I'd always known. He was a stranger. A monster. One of the creatures we'd been warned about our whole lives.

"Father?" Was there anything left of the man I'd known my whole life? Was any of it real or had it all been lies?

He lunged forward, teeth bared. My eyes widened, and I screamed, pressing myself against Ryvin on reflex.

Shadows whipped past me, moving up my father's legs, holding him in place. He snapped his jaws and clawed at the air as if trying to make his way toward me.

Tears streamed down my cheeks, and terror made my breaths shaky and stilted. He was like an animal, desperate to devour his prey.

The shadows slithered up my father's legs, then wrapped around his waist before creeping their way up to his chest. They lingered around his neck, as if allowing me to look at his face one last time.

His pupils were blown wide, making his iris solid black. Red lines filled the whites of his eyes. He continued to growl and fight, those fangs glinting in the dim light like beacons of death.

"He won't hurt you again," Ryvin whispered, pulling me into his embrace.

I couldn't feel his arms around me. I couldn't feel anything anymore. I wasn't even sure I existed at all. My entire body was numb; my emotions a hollow shell.

A strange sense of calm settled around me as I watched the shadows resume their creeping progress until every inch of my father was claimed by darkness. The dark tendrils encased him like a cocoon. They pulsed and swirled as if they were a living, breathing thing. Tightening, the shadows compressed until they squeezed in, then they exploded, fanning out around us.

Everything went dark.

Startled, I pulled away from the ambassador, blindly reaching out in the darkness. Light returned as the shadows dissipated, and I had to blink a few times against the illumination. My father was gone. No body, no signs of where he'd been. It was as if he'd never existed.

My breaths came in shaky, stunted inhales. It didn't seem real. If I hadn't seen the evidence of what those shadows could do already, I'd believe it was a trick. I'd believe my father was still here somewhere, but I knew better.

The worst part was that I still felt nothing. My father was dead and I couldn't even find it in me to mourn his passing.

"It was the only way, Ara," Ryvin whispered. "And now you know the truth."

The ambassador had killed my father because if he hadn't, my own father would have ended my life. There was no good and evil anymore. There were no allies or enemies. I wasn't sure there ever had been. It was all an illusion. Nothing in my life was what it seemed.

Quiet cries broke me from my thoughts and I turned to see my sisters huddled together. Morta was gone, thankfully, and my sisters appeared unharmed. For now.

My senses flooded into me, relief at seeing my sisters alive chasing away the numb indifference. I knew I'd have to make peace with what I'd seen eventually, but I couldn't allow myself to consider it right now. My sisters needed me and I was going to be there for them.

Picking myself up from the ground, I ran to them, meeting them in a bone-crushing hug. The four of us held each other as we all shook from our tears. I held them until their cries began to ease.

"I'm so sorry, Ara," Lagina said. "I never knew. I never knew."

"We heard everything," Sophia whispered. "I'm so sorry."

"He can't hurt you or anyone else again," Cora said.

"I'm afraid we are short on time," Ryvin announced.

My sisters and I pulled apart, all of us still catching our breath and wiping our cheeks.

Ophelia was seated on her throne, shaking and pale as a ghost. Ryvin stood in the center of the room. To my surprise, he looked run down. His shoulders slumped, and he had dark circles under his eyes. The use of that dark magic must cost him.

I approached cautiously. "What do you intend to do?"

"I will have Sophia," he said. "The rest of you are free to do as you wish."

"You will take me," I offered again. "Not Sophia."

"I told you, I am not the one who makes those decisions," he said.

"Then change it," I demanded, then I softened my tone so I was pleading; begging. "Please."

Footsteps sounded across the marble floor and we both turned to see Lagina crossing the room. She approached the empty throne where my father had sat just a few minutes ago. Hesitating for only a moment, she faced us, locking her eyes on the ambassador before sitting down.

"With my father gone, I assume his title. My first order of business is to ensure continued peace between Athos and Konos." Lagina held herself like a queen. The way I'd seen her mother act my entire life. It was as if she'd been born into this role and had always been queen.

"Your majesty." Ryvin bowed, low and reverent.

The numbness returned. What was going on? How could

she step into this role so quickly after everything that had just happened?

Ophelia stood, then dropped into a curtsy and I noticed my other sisters following her lead. It felt wrong to be moving into this new era without acknowledging the reason why it had happened, but I joined the others, bowing low to my sister, the new queen.

"We will send the tributes as requested and continue to welcome your delegation to our city every nine years, as outlined in the treaty," Lagina said.

"You can't mean –" I looked from her to Ryvin, then back again. "You mean the tributes that were selected. Not Sophia."

"The treaty is clear, Ara. And he is within his right to request a member of our household for our disgraceful behavior," she replied.

"But you took father; you killed the king," I said. "Surely that's enough."

"I've read the treaty," Lagina said. "It is clear that it must be the offspring of the king."

"I killed the king because he tried to hurt you, Ara," Ryvin whispered. "I told you I'd protect you."

"Ara, it's okay," Sophia said, reaching for my hand. "Let me do this for our family."

I sucked in a breath, silenced by the use of my own words against me.

"My men will retreat to our rooms to rest," Ryvin said. "Princess, you have until morning to prepare for the journey. We'll leave at sunrise."

"Soph…" my throat was tight and I couldn't get any other words to flow.

"Come, ladies," Ophelia said, her tone more gentle than I'd ever heard it. I hadn't even noticed her approach, but she set her hands on our shoulders and guided us from the throne room. "The new queen has a lot of work to do, and we must help Sophia pack for her journey."

I'm not sure how I ended up in Sophia's room while Ophelia began the process of procuring trunks to pack her youngest daughter's things. Cora sat on the bed, her eyes glazed over and unfocused. I understood what she was feeling. It didn't seem real.

We'd all lost our father, most of our guards were dead, and now we had to say goodbye to Sophia. There wasn't even time to process the magic that had been used or the fact that my father had been a vampire. Had he always been a monster? Or had he been turned later in life? I wasn't sure I even wanted to know the answers to those questions. It didn't change the fact that he was dead. Or the betrayal I'd faced.

How could Lagina move right into her new role with such ease? The only thing I could think of doing was taking my anger out on everyone from Konos. If they'd never come here, my biggest concern would be avoiding marriage or preparing to serve at the wall. Their insistence on taking human lives rather than letting us be was to blame.

But that would be a suicide mission.

Still, how was I to pretend things would work out? How was I to go about my days knowing what Konos had cost us? Every time I looked toward the sea and saw that cursed island, I would mourn my family. I would wonder if Sophia's heart still beat or if she'd been fed to the vampires or dropped into their maze to entertain the fae and appease the beast that lurked within.

Sophia was in better spirits than I anticipated, wearing a

bright smile and helping choose her favorite dresses and jewelry to bring. As if she were going on a trip rather than sailing to her demise.

My only chance of making progress to reverse this nightmare was Ophelia. She loved her daughters, and she'd have gladly sent me to my death years ago. The chance to see me go to spare Sophia was a dream for her. I approached the former queen and sat down next to her. "You know this is wrong."

Ophelia smoothed the fabric of the dress that was draped across her arm. "You know the solution, Ara. And you're the only one who can make it happen."

"What are you talking about?" I replied. "I'm not in charge here. You heard me get shut down. How can I fix this?"

She carefully set the dress into the open trunk. "Sophia, why don't you ask your maid to bring us some lunch?"

Ophelia had immediately dismissed all the maids when we'd arrived in the room, but Sophia didn't seem to think her mother's sudden change of mind was unusual. She nodded brightly, then left the room.

The former queen pulled me close, her tone low and conspiratorial. "The ambassador is still in our palace and the tributes are already on their ships. If something were to happen to him, it's possible they'd leave with what they have. He was the only one in that room. None of his men stayed. They don't know Sophia is to join them."

"You want me to kill him?" My chest tightened. "Is that even possible?" My father had stabbed him and he didn't even flinch. He'd taken out hundreds of fighters with his magic. Could he even be killed? I didn't know what he was or what the extent of his power entailed.

"Do you want to save your sister?" Ophelia asked.

I nodded. If there was a chance Sophia could be spared, I had to try. "They'll never let anyone close enough."

"They'll let you. They won't suspect if you're visiting tonight to say goodbye." She shrugged. "Everyone knows what happened in the orchards."

My lips twitched and guilt swirled. I couldn't deny that I'd wanted him that night, but I hated what it made people think of me.

"What if he can't be killed?" I asked.

"You'll think of something," she said.

There was no need for me to respond. If there was a chance at sparing Sophia's life, we both knew I'd take it.

"For what it's worth, I didn't know about your father. I never knew he was a..." She shook her head, unwilling to say the word aloud. None of us had spoken a word of what we'd learned. There were no witnesses aside from us and the ambassador. I think we were all wondering what it meant for our family. If he'd always been a vampire, what did that mean for his daughters?

"I need time to find out more discreetly," Ophelia said. "It doesn't change the line or how I feel about my children. But if the people find out, they will come for us. All of us." She rested her palm on her stomach protectively.

I reached out my hand, covering hers with my palm. "You know I would never do anything to put my sisters," my eyes dropped to our hands, then I looked back to her, "or my brother in harm's way."

She nodded, her eyes misty with tears. All these years, she'd treated me terribly, and I had hated her for it. The only place we saw eye-to-eye was regarding my sisters. I always figured she saw me as a threat, but I realized I was also a reminder of her husband's infidelity. Whenever that thought would cross my mind, I'd vilify her for her treatment of me.

It wasn't my fault; I hadn't asked to be born. But I could see how difficult it might be to live with that constant reminder of how little she meant to the man she'd married.

"I'm sorry, Ara," Ophelia said.

"I am too," I replied.

She squeezed my hand. It was the most comforting and maternal thing she'd ever done. A silent understanding passed between us, then she released my hand. "You can do this, Ara."

My heart clenched at the thought of ending Ryvin's life. I was back where I'd started, wondering if killing him would change anything. It didn't matter if I felt safer with him than I did my own people, there couldn't be anything between us. Ryvin was a killer. An enemy. I couldn't feel anything for him other than hatred, even if my heart objected.

I had learned early on not to get attached. I was warned that emotions would get me in trouble. That anything I loved was at risk. The only thing I'd allowed myself to form an attachment with was my family. Specifically, my sisters. The ambassador was a passing fancy. Even if I didn't end him myself, he'd be gone by morning. He'd never think of me again. I couldn't feel anything for him.

So why did it hurt so badly when I thought about losing him?

"Save her, Ara," Ophelia whispered. "Save Sophia."

I glanced at my stepmother. The woman I'd spent my life hating. The only thing we had in common was our concern and love for my sisters; her daughters. I knew what I had to do.

"They'll bring lunch in a few minutes," Sophia announced as she walked back into the room. "I asked for extra honey cakes. I'm not sure when I'll get to eat them again."

My throat tightened as I realized my sister was preparing herself for death but maintaining optimism for our sake. I couldn't allow her to go to Konos. If there was a way to prevent it, I had to try.

To save my sister's life, I would sacrifice everything.

CHAPTER 28

I looked up through my lashes, smiling demurely, allowing my cheeks to heat. I knew what it looked like. I knew my nightgown and sheer robe left little to the imagination. Wordlessly, I pressed my index finger to my lips, making a pouty O, before smirking.

Internally, my stomach rolled and my chest tightened in fear. I was lucky the ambassador and his men were still staying in the palace tonight after what had happened today. Though, I supposed after their show of power, nobody would be stupid enough to mess with them.

Still, it was a risk. They could turn me away or harm me for even coming into their wing. Or they could announce my presence, giving away my only chance at defeating Ryvin. Without the element of surprise, I was dead.

My only hope was the rumors swirling about me and the ambassador and our stolen moments together.

Lowering my finger, I bit my lower lip and took a tentative step forward, doing my best to maintain my seductive, flirty persona. I had Cora to thank for the knowledge of how to act. Years of watching her flawless movements and careful seduction had taught me a few things. She was the expert at this, yet I was the one who'd been given the task. All because my father planned for me to end up as payment if his plan failed. I didn't even know if the war at the wall had ended or if the dragons were coming to discuss terms. It all could have been a ploy to convince me to help.

My smile faltered, and I worked quickly to put on my best face. I couldn't think about such things now. I had to focus. Batting my eyelashes, I waited silently for the guards to either send me away or let me pass.

The guard stepped back, a silent demonstration of his compliance. The others nodded or grinned as I passed, some elbowing their companions or lifting their eyebrows knowingly.

They'd all cleaned up since the fight, wearing their black armor and looking just as alert and focused as ever. I wondered if these creatures even needed to sleep. If the ambassador was awake, my plan would fail. I wasn't even sure if he needed sleep, but I'd seen some signs of exhaustion after he'd used his magic. I was hoping that would work to my advantage.

The guards watched me carefully. What must they think of me? The princess who was on her way to seduce the man who'd killed her father? It was all the rumors they'd heard playing out in reality. Confirmation that I was just as debased as they'd been told. Our kingdoms were at odds even without today's attack. Yet, I was here to warm my enemy's bed even as he planned to steal away my sister in the morning.

I knew I looked disloyal. A traitor to my kingdom and to my people. But I'd already crossed that line the moment my father had asked me to entertain the ambassador on the night of his arrival. It wasn't like my reputation could be marred any further. At least not in the eyes of my people.

I could feel their eyes on my nearly naked body as I

padded across the cold marble floor. Bare feet were quieter. And I'd need all the advantages I could get.

The guard at the door moved aside, not making eye contact with me. It was as if he was telling me he'd keep my secret.

I said a silent prayer to the gods before turning the handle, begging them to help my sisters forgive me. Begging them to spare my sisters. To make my sacrifice worth it. If there was one time they'd heed my call, I hoped it was tonight.

The door didn't creak, but I still held my breath as I tiptoed into the familiar room. Dying embers glowed in the large fireplace, giving the space minimal illumination. The sheer white curtains blew in the breeze, offering scant silvery moonlight. It was a cool evening, heavy with the scent of peach blossoms and salt. I breathed in the soothing perfume as I turned toward my target, urging my thundering heart to slow.

Carefully, I freed my dagger from its holder on my inner thigh. The placement unusual, but necessary due to the sheer fabric of my clothing. None of the guards noticed, allowing me to make it this far.

My palms were damp and my chest tight in anticipation as I crept closer to the bed.

Ryvin was asleep, a blanket tangled around his hips, covering only one of his bare legs. He was on his side, facing away from me, his bare skin practically glowing in the faint evening light.

As I approached, I noticed long scars across his back. My brow furrowed, and I paused, taking in the strange markings. I hadn't noticed that before, but I'd never stared at him this long. The marks were faded with age, but I recognized them for what they were. He'd been whipped. Many times, from the looks of it.

How was that possible? I'd watched him take a knife to the chest and walk away. I thought the creatures that lurked beyond our borders were impossible to harm and healed too quickly. It was part of why we couldn't defeat them. What kind of abuse had he sustained to have marks such as that?

A tiny part of me seemed to revel at the sign of weakness. It was visible proof that he wasn't invulnerable. He could be harmed to the point of having scars to show for his wounds. But the sense of elation was short-lived, replaced instead by sympathy and anger. Who could have hurt him in such a way? And why? Who treated someone like that? The urge to comfort him for his long-healed scars was so intense that I nearly set down my weapon.

I shook the thoughts from my head. He was a monster. Someone sent to steal lives away from my people. To steal my sister away from me. He'd killed my father without remorse. He didn't feel sympathy for us, why should I allow myself to feel any for him?

Gripping the dagger harder, I continued forward until I was right next to the bed. Jaw tense, I moved fast, climbing on top of Ryvin, straddling his hips, then leaning forward, dagger in hand.

I pressed it to his neck, ready to end his life.

But I didn't move the weapon. I froze, my heart thundered against my ribs as I stared at his sleeping form. Hand shaking slightly, I hesitated. If I did this there was no going back.

"Do it," his voice was soft, with a rough edge. It caught me off guard, making me tighten my grip on the handle. His eyes were still closed, and he hadn't moved. All his muscles were relaxed. He made no effort to throw me from him.

Yet, I stilled, my breathing coming on faster now. Why did I wait? This was what I came here for and I could do it. I had the advantage, and he wasn't fighting me. He was going to let me kill him.

He grabbed my wrist and held me there, blade still pressed to his throat. "Go ahead. Kill me. The gods know I deserve it."

"Would this even kill you?" My eyes took in the already healed wound in his chest. The injury was a pink scar, not even bleeding. He'd carry the mark, but it healed impossibly fast.

There were scars on his back, but I watched him kill without touch. Sending those shadows to end lives without effort. I didn't know what he was or what lurked below the handsome exterior. I had a feeling there was little I could do to harm him. "If I slit your throat, will you die?"

He opened his eyes, and they shined like molten metal in the dimness of the room. "Only one way to find out, Asteri."

I gritted my teeth, hating myself for not being able to slide the knife across his bare skin. "I don't want to kill you," I admitted. "But you can't have my sister."

"I don't want your sister."

"What do you want?"

He lifted my wrist, gripping under the bandage I'd wrapped around my own injury. Unlike him, the blood from the cut had bled through the bandage and left a dark stain. I was reminded of how fragile I was compared to him.

His eyes darted to the injury, then he returned his gaze to me. Silently, he opened my fingers and I let him take the dagger from me. I didn't take my eyes off him as he tossed it aside, the blade landing on the floor with a clatter.

"I think you know exactly what I want." His hands slid up my thighs, a wicked grin on his lips when he reached my bare ass. I'd not bothered with undergarments. "Naughty girl."

Already slick with need, I struggled with the desires

warring in my mind. Ryvin was my enemy. He killed my father and sacrificed my people. I'd watched him eliminate dozens of men without hesitation. He was trying to take everything from me. But I wasn't sure I could deny the way he made me feel. It was so wrong. I knew it was wrong. But he called to something deep inside me that I couldn't resist. I hated it. I hated him. I hated myself.

But I still wanted him.

"Tell me what you want, my asteri," he said.

"I'm not your star," I hissed through gritted teeth.

He removed his hands, then turned, so he was flat on his back, adjusting me so I was straddling him. The sheets moved, revealing his proud, full length already glistening with need. A shiver ran down my spine. I wanted to taste him, to touch him, to feel him filling me completely.

I leaned forward, causing my pelvis to press against him. He groaned and his cock twitched.

"You are going to be the death of me," he said.

"I wish I was," I bit out.

"You want to retrieve your knife? I won't stop you." His hands roamed my body, sliding across the sheer fabric of my robe. He touched my back and my stomach, inching closer to my aching breasts but denying me the sensation I truly wanted.

"I thought you said you'd make me beg?" I whispered. It had been like this between us since we met. The two of us taking turns wielding power over the other.

"Give me time, Princess. I intend to have you on your knees, begging me to destroy you." He said the words as if it was a challenge. My body responded to the commanding tone, making me feel overheated. It was as if my thin nightgown was a fur coat.

I was so drawn to him that I hadn't realized the feeling

was reciprocated. Even when my father had insisted that Ryvin had feelings for me, I denied it. How was it possible when he'd spent half his time here with other women?

This wasn't just some game between us. This was hunger unlike anything I'd ever felt. I didn't think it was love, it wasn't tugging at my emotions. It was lust. It had to be. I couldn't allow myself to consider any alternative. This was about sex. Heat and desire and need.

I needed him.

The same way I needed the air I breathed.

The same way I needed my heart to beat in my chest.

He was water, and I was dying of thirst.

His hands returned to my legs, then worked their way up, sliding under my flimsy nightgown to my lower back. His touch left a trail of energy in his wake, as if my skin itself was responding to him.

He made me feel alive.

"Tell me what you want," he commanded.

I felt like I was on fire; as if flames were filling my insides and burning me alive.

"Tell me, Asteri," he demanded. "Tell me you don't want me and you can walk away right now."

"I don't want you," the words came out reflexively, but they were lies.

He smirked. "I hate that I find it adorable when you lie to me."

"I hate you," I replied.

"I know you do." His hand caressed my cheek. The touch such a gentle contrast to the vitriol in our words.

"You can't have my sister," I said.

"I told you, I don't want her."

"You didn't tell me what you wanted." I needed him so

badly that everything was starting to ache. It was taking all my willpower to resist.

"You know what I want." His eyes flashed, and he grabbed me, rolling so I ended up under him. Hovering above me, he stared at me. "Say it. Tell me you want me."

"You first," I hissed.

"I want you, Ara."

Shivers danced across my skin at the sound of my name on his lips. I slid my fingers into his dark hair and pulled his face closer to mine. He hesitated, our mouths close enough for our lips to brush against one another. I lifted my face to kiss him, but he pulled back.

"Tell me you want me," he insisted.

I would have told him just about anything in that moment if it ended my suffering. I was certain that if I didn't feel him inside me soon, I would die. "I want you."

The words were barely out before he claimed my mouth with his.

His lips were like fire against mine, burning and deadly. I welcomed the heat. Already, tension coiled low in my belly, begging for release. My legs hooked around his waist, and I could feel his cock at my entrance. I lifted my hips, encouraging him.

"So fucking impatient," he whispered.

"Stop teasing me." My nightgown was a tangle of fabric, bunched and twisted so it wasn't covering anything, but it felt constricting. I tugged at it and Ryvin adjusted so I could reach it better. Finally free of the clothing, I tossed the flimsy fabric aside, leaving me fully exposed in front of him.

He groaned, then took me in, his eyes traveling across every inch of my skin as if seeing me for the first time. "You are incredible."

In the garden, I'd felt a little uneasy, but I could tell his appreciation was genuine. He liked how I looked. It made my cheeks heat.

His large hand caressed each breast before moving to my ass, then back up to my cheek. "You were made to be worshiped."

My breath hitched, and I wanted to think of something snarky to say, but he didn't give me a chance. Lowering his face to mine, he caught my lower lip in his teeth and I moaned, my back arching slightly, my body aching with desire. His mouth moved to my neck, his teeth brushing against the sensitive skin before leaving a trail of kisses to my breasts.

I ran my fingers through his hair, then slid my hands to his shoulders, then down his muscular back. His tongue flicked each nipple, before settling on one at a time to suck and tease.

Panting and needy, I grabbed his ass, trying to pull him inside.

He glanced up at me, a playful smirk on his lips. "Naughty, impatient girl."

I whined, annoyed that he was making me wait. I was desperate. I needed release from the building desire.

"Almost ready to beg for me." He kissed my jaw, my temple, my chin.

"Such a tease," I replied.

He chuckled, the sound vibrating against my cheek while his tongue flicked over my earlobe. "I can wait all night if I have to."

Panting and frustrated, I pulled his face to mine, so we were staring at each other. His smirk faded, replaced by a look so intense it took my breath away. My frustration was replaced by something else. Something I couldn't quite pinpoint. It was hungry yet satisfied; tumultuous yet peaceful.

All these emotions warred within me, a confusing concoction brought on by Ryvin's gaze. He was so handsome, so deadly, so everything...

I was in so much fucking trouble.

"Ara..."

My eyes widened. There was too much power behind my name on his lips. Too much familiarity. I pulled him to me, then pressed my lips to his, distracting both of us and breaking us from that moment that had my pulse racing and my heart ready to explode from my body.

Ryvin broke away from the kiss, that intense gaze returning. It was haunted with longing and desire; full of questions I couldn't answer. He was going to break me with that look. There was only one thing I could do.

Gripping his ass again, I pulled him closer. "Please. I need you inside me." I was begging.

His expression turned feral and one of his hands slid behind my head, pulling my face closer for a ravenous kiss while he thrust into me. I gasped, feeling both relief and pleasure at the fullness of him.

Our bodies moved together, my hips matching his rhythm. Our mouths devoured one another in a clash of lips and teeth and tongues. I wasn't sure where my body ended and his began. We were pure sensation, driving closer with each movement toward release.

He lifted my legs, making my hips hover above the bed, and I sucked in a breath. He was even deeper in this position, each thrust hitting something inside me that made me cry out with pleasure. I grabbed his arms, needing to hold on as he continued, the tension growing to the point I was struggling to breathe. Release came fast and fierce. Screaming, back arching, I dug my fingernails into his arms. My whole body trembled, and I was left gasping as another wave surged through me in the wake of the first.

Ryvin lowered my legs to the bed, and I laid there, boneless and satisfied. He brushed a few strands of stray hair away from my eyes. "I'm not finished with you yet."

"There's more?" I managed between gasps for air.

Suddenly, I was on my stomach and he pulled my hips back so my ass was in the air, my chest on the bed. He grabbed my hips roughly and entered me in one thrust. Fisting the sheets for support, I grunted and gasped as he plunged into me. His movements were fast and deep, and my moans quickly became louder as my climax built. I buried my face in the bedding, letting it muffle my screams as he brought me closer to another orgasm. Soon, I was shaking and gasping as waves of pleasure exploded from my center.

Ryvin leaned over me, then pulled me up so I was on my knees while he was behind me. His movements slowed, and his arms wrapped around my waist protectively. I leaned against him, catching my breath while enjoying the warmth of him.

His fingers moved lazily across my stomach, the two of us just breathing together for a moment. I pulled away from him, then turned to him. "My turn."

"Your turn?"

Gently, I pushed on his chest. He took the cue, sitting down. I pushed again, and he silently complied, laying down on the bed. I climbed on top of him, then guided his cock into me. He groaned, his eyes closing and his head lolling backward. A little thrill flickered in my chest, enjoying the power I held over this dangerous man.

Leaning forward, I braced myself against his shoulders before I started to roll and move my hips. Ryvin locked his eyes on mine, then his hands began to explore my body again before pulling me down to him. My breasts pressed against his chest and his arms held me tight. I continued to move my hips, undulating and grinding, my own breathing growing ragged as tension built.

Our lips met again, but the kiss was different. Slower, familiar, easy. One hand moved to my hips, his fingers softly trailing over my ass and lower back. His other hand was on my face, his thumb brushing my cheek before his fingers twined into my hair, pulling me closer; as if he couldn't get enough of me. The thought made heat flare low in my belly, pushing me over the edge. I moaned into his mouth, my body tensing as another orgasm crashed through me. Our kiss intensified, and his fingers dug into me so hard I knew I'd have bruises in the morning. I was still feeling the vibrations of my own climax when he groaned, finding his own release.

I rested my head on his chest while I caught my breath. Ryvin ran his fingers through my hair, soothing me as his own racing heart slowed to a normal rhythm.

"Tell me, Asteri, do you regret not killing me?" he asked.

I lifted my head so I could look at him. "I haven't decided yet."

CHAPTER 29

The thin nightgown felt too revealing now that I was coming down from chasing the high I got when I was with Ryvin. I hated how much I craved him. After everything I'd seen him do, I should be running from him. Instead, it was as if I couldn't control my impulses. He was able to disarm my walls and break me down without effort.

The sooner I got away from him, the better. Yet, I knew there was likely only one way to get what I wanted. I tied the belt around my sheer robe. "You're still not taking my sister."

"I have to have something to show Athos is trying to atone for what they did. If I return without her, the king will come for all of you," he said. "And not just the royal family, the entire city."

"Why are you doing this? You have the power here. He won't even know what happened," I said.

"He'll know."

"Your men aren't as loyal as you say, then."

"He has other ways of finding information."

"You can't have Sophia," I repeated, wondering how I'd let myself fuck him instead of killing him. There was something so wrong with me. I was twisted and dark, just like

Ryvin had said. I deserved whatever punishment I received. I was the traitor they all thought I was.

None of that mattered now. I had to focus on the reason I was here. "You can't have any of my sisters."

"Ara, we both know you won't kill me." His smile was dangerous; daring.

I hated that he was right. "Then take me. I offered before and the queen was right, I was…" my voice cracked, emotion thick in my throat, "I was my father's favorite." At least I had thought I was, until tonight. How much of that had been an act? A way to appease me until he could throw me away like I never mattered.

"No."

"I know I'm not in line for the throne, but I'll say I'm Sophia. The king has never seen her. I'll be my sister," I said.

"You will not travel to Konos. It's nothing like Athos. You won't survive," he replied.

"Isn't that the point?" I blurted. "I know what I'm asking. But I will gladly give my life for hers."

"I am not taking you in her place," he said.

"Don't you dare pretend there's anything other than sex between us."

He lifted a brow. "We're doing this again? Where you pretend the attraction we feel is nothing more than lust."

"I'm not pretending. I came here to kill you. Just because my body wants to fuck you doesn't mean I have any feelings for you," I spat. "It's stress relief. Breaking through tension. Or maybe it's because you know how to please a woman and I enjoyed it. Or maybe I'm damaged and broken. Whatever it is, it means nothing."

"That's it?" His lips tensed into a tight line.

"That's it. You know there's nothing else between us. I've told you this a hundred times. I hate you. How could I not?

You killed my people. You killed my father. I've seen what you're capable of. I've seen your darkness." I said the words with such determination, I almost believed it myself.

"I could say the same of you, Princess." He moved closer to me, the shadows cast by the dying fire accentuated all the curves of his muscles. "I watched you welcome the anger as you drove your sword into flesh. I saw how you killed an unarmed man without remorse. This darkness you speak of? Perhaps it's my darkness that draws you in. Like calls to like, Asteri."

"I'm nothing like you," I said through gritted teeth. But he'd struck something deep within me. Something I didn't want to release. I shoved it down, unwilling to examine the feelings swirling in the depths. "I did what I had to do and I will continue to do what I must."

I picked up my abandoned dagger, aiming the point at him. He walked forward until the blade was touching his bare chest, right near the already healed wound. I sucked in a breath, but held my ground.

Ryvin smirked as he inched closer, the blade puncturing his skin. A dribble of crimson slid down his magnificent torso.

"This is what you want?" he asked. "To see me dead?"

"I want to protect my sister," I said.

"And nothing more?"

"There can be nothing more." My already broken heart fought against my words, as if something deep inside me was trying to break free. I shoved it down.

"If you insist on playing it this way, I'll go along with it. Just don't expect anything else from me."

"All I need from you is for my sister to be spared," I said, my tone icy even as my heart threatened to shatter. My words should be true. I shouldn't feel anything for him. Why did I feel like I was betraying everyone all at once? Being with him was a betrayal; yet, denying my feelings for him felt almost worse.

What I wanted or what I felt meant nothing. If I stayed behind while Sophia went to the monsters, I'd never forgive myself. At least I could attempt to fight.

"Take me in her place," I ordered.

"You don't know what you're asking," he said.

"I handled you just fine. I think I can handle the king."

"That's what I'm afraid of," he said.

My brow furrowed. "What's that supposed to mean?"

"You're the master seductress," he said. "Just another male for you to tease and torment. And you call me the monster."

"You are a monster."

"Yes, I am."

"When do we leave?" I asked.

He glanced toward the window. The sky was already a deep blue, the color of impending sunrise. "You should pack now. I'll send Vanth for you. He seems to like you for some bizarre reason."

Before I could change my mind or say something that I'd regret, I left.

As I walked to my room, I held back tears. It was what I'd asked for. What I wanted. Why did it feel so wrong?

Iris was asleep in the chair by my window, an oil lamp glowing on the desk. She woke with a start when the door closed behind me. "Your highness. Are you alright? When you didn't return, I feared the worst. I thought perhaps, somehow, Konos won."

"They did," I said bitterly.

"What?" Her tone was breathy, surprised. She truly had no idea what had passed last night.

"They slaughtered nearly all our guards." I wanted to tell her about my father, but how was I to say the words when I'd just come from the bed of his killer? My stomach churned and bile crept up my throat.

Ryvin was right, there was something dark and dangerous within me. I deserved to go to Konos for my crimes. In the dim blue light of early dawn, reality felt heavy. There was no forgiveness for a daughter who betrayed her father's memory. Especially before his body was even cold.

Not that Ryvin had left a body for us to mourn.

I covered my face with my hands, the weight of all that had passed crashing in around me. When I was around Ryvin, I couldn't control myself. I became someone I didn't recognize.

Our tryst had left me feeling like a hollow shell of my former self. I was worried that Konos would break Sophia, but it couldn't claim me; I was already broken.

I deserved whatever punishment they had in mind for me. Perhaps I wouldn't fight them when the time came. I could face my death bravely. Maybe then the gods could forgive me for my crimes. If they even noticed us at all.

"You can talk to me," Iris said, tentatively. "If you want, that is. I won't share. I won't judge."

I turned to look at her. She seemed so genuine, but I'd lost Mila, then my next maid had tried to kill me. Plus, I was leaving anyway. There was no point. "I'm leaving soon. I won't return."

Her brow furrowed. "What happened?"

"My father is dead," I managed. "Lagina will be a good queen. She'll make sure you're cared for."

She shook her head. "I volunteered for this position. Nobody wanted it after Mila passed. I know we're supposed to say she left, but there's rumors... and I don't want to end up like her."

I tensed. My father was responsible for her death. How many others had he claimed? All while telling us how vile Konos was for their fourteen sacrifices every nine years. I was raised in a kingdom of lies. "The murderer was killed. You don't need to fear Mila's fate."

"I have no one. I was scrubbing dishes in the kitchen. I won't go back to that. Take me with you," Iris insisted.

"You don't know what you're asking," I said.

"You're going to Konos, aren't you?"

I nodded. "As a tribute. My life is already over."

"You're a princess."

"I'm the daughter of a dead king. I have no power." I blinked back tears. My father was gone, even if it didn't seem real. Without him, I was simply the half-sister of the queen. I'd have to come to terms with what he'd done and what he'd hidden from me, but he was still my father. The anger and shame of what had passed was mixed with sorrow. I'd loved him. I'd have done anything for him, but he wasn't what he seemed. Nothing was what it seemed.

A gentle knock sounded on the door, and Iris rushed to answer it. Vanth waited at the threshold and I tensed. It was already time?

The shifter stepped into the room and offered a sad smile. His face was covered in scratches and his left eye had purple bruises around it, remnants of the fight mere hours ago.

"You look alright," I managed.

"Thanks to you," he said. "I'd be dead without you."

I swallowed hard. Another reminder of why I should

embrace my fate. I'd done nothing but betray my people since the delegation arrived.

"Do you want to say goodbye to your sisters?" he offered.

I shook my head. It would be too difficult to see them. And I knew there was a risk that Sophia would insist on taking my place.

"I thought not." He looked around. "Do you have any luggage?"

"Do I need any?" I asked, already knowing the tributes were instructed not to bring anything along.

"You won't," he replied.

"What's going to happen when I get there?" I wanted to know how much time I had left, but I couldn't bring myself to say the words.

"I'm not sure," he admitted. "This is the first time I've been involved with a Choosing."

"I'm accompanying her," Iris announced bravely.

"No. Please, stay here," I said again.

"I'm sorry, I was only instructed to bring the princess," Vanth said.

I hugged Iris, grateful for her loyalty, even though I hadn't earned it. I would have liked to get to know her better. "Please tell my sisters I'm sorry and that I love them."

"At least let me dress you for the journey," Iris offered.

I glanced at Vanth. He nodded, then he crossed my room and took a seat in the chair near my desk. "We have a few minutes, if you can change quickly."

Soon, we'd managed to scrub most of the blood splatters from my skin and I'd changed into a saffron yellow peplos. If I was going to spend my last days in the constant cloud cover of Konos, at least I could have the color of the sun with me.

After a rough brush of my hair, Iris quickly plaited it into a simple braid. She clasped a necklace around my neck. A gold snake dangled from the chain. "A reminder. The serpent can blend in and strikes when the time is right."

I touched the metal with my fingertips. It was a good reminder to keep fighting. Even if part of me felt like giving in already.

"It's time, Princess," Vanth said.

"I don't think I'm a princess anymore," I replied.

"You'll always be a princess to me." He offered his elbow.

"Good luck, your highness," Iris said.

I let Vanth lead me away from my room, down the empty halls of the sleepy palace. Just as the sun's first rays reached for the stars themselves, painting the sky with pink and orange.

The sea sparkled like scattered diamonds across the blue expanse. I glanced backward as the carriage lurched forward.

I knew this was the last time I'd see my home. I allowed silent tears to stream down my cheeks until the palace faded from view. Then I wiped my eyes and looked ahead, making a promise to myself that I would never cry again.

To be continued...

KINGDOM OF BLOOD & SALT
THE SERIES

A NOTE FROM THE AUTHOR

Thank you so much for reading Kingdom Of Blood & Salt, *Kingdom Of Blood & Salt, Book 1.*

If you have enjoyed the story, show other readers by leaving a review! Just visit: *Kingdom Of Blood And Salt*
Amazon.com/Kingdom-Blood-Salt-Alexis-Calder-ebook/dp/B0BW4WDY82

Join my *Newsletter* today and get a
FREE Bonus Scene!
https://landing.mailerlite.com/webforms/landing/a4p6k3

NEXT IN SERIES

Court of Vice & Death,
Kingdom Of Blood & Salt, Book 2

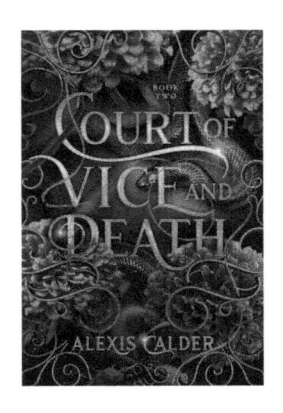

Get yours today!
Amazon.com/dp/B0BXWLM8SG

ABOUT THE AUTHOR

Alexis Calder writes sassy heroines and sexy heroes with a sprinkle of sarcasm. She lives in the Rockies and drinks far too much coffee and just the right amount of wine.

For more awesomeness check out my website
http://www.alexiscalder.com

And don't forget to follow me!

Facebook: https://www.facebook.com/AuthorAlexisCalder
Instagram: https://www.instagram.com/alexxiscalder/
Amazon: https://www.amazon.com/stores/Alexis-Calder/author/B07TP5VCGZ
Bookbub: https://www.bookbub.com/authors/alexis-calder
Goodreads: https://www.goodreads.com/author/show/19382078.Alexis_Calder
Newsletter Signup Link (Free Bonus Scene): https://landing.mailerlite.com/webforms/landing/a4p6k3

Milton Keynes UK
Ingram Content Group UK Ltd.
UKHW041823140224
437823UK00004B/96

9 781960 823014